VALENTINES CUP

By

Robert Wallace

Valentines Cup is a work of fiction. Any resemblance to actual events or persons, living or dead, is entirely coincidental. The roles played in this novel by Adolf Hitler, Field Marshal Erwin Rommel, Admiral Wilhelm Franz Canaris, other members of the Abwehr, the German military intelligence service, the chief executives of German industries and members of British intelligence however, abide by the generally known facts of their real lives, and I have sometimes quoted from their works and letters, et passim. The storyline . . . and all the passages relating to events . . . have no factual basis.

Cover design by www. tradshack.com
Published by www. tradshack.com

ISBN: 978-1-7397822-0-7

This book is in memory of
André Smolinski and Jeremy Warner.
Dear friends taken too soon.
Remembered with love and affection.

'No war can be conducted successfully without early and good intelligence.'

John Churchill,
1st Duke of Marlborough, 1715

20th February 1933
Bavaria, Germany

Six years prior to the British declaration of war on Germany.

TEN MEN'S SHOES CRUNCHED across thin ice and snow. It was morning, well below freezing; each man had clear need of their expensive cashmere overcoats, impeccable suits and hand-stitched brogues. These spectral figures resembled a line of mourners; heads slightly bowed. Each had abandoned chauffeured limousines at the foot of the drive of a sprawling Bavarian country mansion. No one spoke; their breath vaporising in the air, gloved hands clenched. Hazy sunlight filtered through bare trees in the encircling forest. The air was still, save the sound of their footsteps, almost in unison, single file; these men marched with purpose.

Only the last in line, a squat and muscular man, walked contrarily – awkwardly. He looked confident, dangerous; his chin lifted in the chill. Silence still prevailed as they reached the open front door. These ghostly silhouettes all knew one another; all were preoccupied with what lay ahead.

With names such as Gustav, Carl, Wilhelm, Erich ... they were the wealthiest industrialists in Germany and best known for the companies they owned: BASF, Bayer, Agfa, Opel, IG Farben, Krupp, Siemens, Allianz, Telefunken, Hoesch AG and Spengler GmbH. They sat at a large table in an opulent, high-ceilinged, oak-panelled room lit by electric chandeliers. And they waited. A murmur of muffled voices drifted from an anteroom; the doors swung open and President of the Reichstag, Hermann Goering, strolled in, smiling, full of benevolent greetings. The industrialists all knew what he wanted ... money. Lots of it.

Goering walked around the table, dispensing kind words, clasping hands with a self-assured, confident welcome. After a well-timed interval, the new, brown-uniformed Chancellor of Germany strode into the hall. Those who had not met him were curious to see him in the flesh; all they had known was from hearsay or exaggerated media reports. Adolf Hitler was smiling, relaxed, not as they had imagined. Once introductions had been made, the men listened. He spoke clearly and with authority. Changes must be made in Germany, he said. They must put an end to this weak regime, ward off the Communist menace, eliminate trade unions and encourage industry. Prosperity and the work ethic should be encouraged, particularly to the young. Hitler's speech lasted an hour; and, when it finished, Gustav Krupp stood and assured him of their support. He thanked Hitler for clarifying the political situation as he saw it in Germany, and his vision of the future.

Once Hitler left, Goering took to the floor, echoing and enhancing Hitler's ideas. First, they needed money for the 5th of

March elections. The Nazi Party was broke; it needed funding for a successful campaign as Election Day approached. They would all gain when Hitler took complete power. There were nods of approval.

By the end of the gathering, millions of Marks had been either collected or promised. It was a unique moment in German corporate history, unprecedented compromise with the Nazis. This was a business transaction pure and simple, fund-raising. The ten sat like silent cash registers, waiting for the gates of hell to open; another war would make them huge amounts of money.

As the meeting dispersed, Goering approached Erich Spengler, perhaps the most feared man in the hall that day. Spengler, as an engineer, was elite among this assembly of German industrialists. He was certainly one of the wealthiest, with factories throughout greater Germany, the Netherlands and Scandinavia. Shipping, oil, coal, steel, machinery; Spengler had fingers in many pies.

"You were quiet, Herr Spengler. Is everything all right?" said Goering cautiously and respectfully. He glanced at the man's brutal features. An injury in the Great War – 111 Cavalry – had given him a haunted look and his posture was rigid, the result of a fall from a horse in combat.

Spengler closed the notebook in front of him; his sinewy hands caressed the leather surface. He made no eye-contact: "What will it cost?" His words were slow and menacing.

"To do what, Herr Spengler?" Goering innocently put his right palm to his chest as if swearing an oath. But Spengler was not a man to be fooled.

"To re-arm Germany for war. Oh yes, you may need funding for your little rallies and party-political showmanship ..."

Goering made to protest; Spengler stopped him dead. He stood awkwardly, put his notebook in his jacket pocket and continued ...

"... fighters, bombers, U-boats, battleships, tanks ... manpower. You know exactly what I mean," Spengler said with a sigh, "invasions cost money."

"Two million Reichsmark, Herr Spengler," Goering admitted, "that's just what we need today."

Spengler looked Goering in the eye before leaving: "Lucky for you then, we have deep pockets ... the rest of it you'll have to steal."

Goering looked at the retiring figure and swallowed. Spengler knew something. He pictured Adolf Hitler in the next room, listening carefully to every word uttered.

Hooked

Westminster, London, England

PROFESSOR NICHOLAS BRIMBLECOMBE, eminent academic and connoisseur of the finer things in life, was very well connected. As a senior member of British Intelligence, he was the ultimate spymaster. In his capacity as European Chief of Operations he had a network of contacts from Basle to Washington DC, and the sanction of the PM to authorise certain coercive measures when 'deemed necessary.'

But it was his passion for logic, reasoning and subterfuge which had brought him to the attention of Winston Churchill in the summer of 1934. They originally met at a tea party organised by Clementine, Churchill's wife, at Chartwell. Earl Grey and cakes were the last thing on the minds of both men, and they became firm friends and close confidants.

Sometime later over a whisky, Churchill said: "Had much experience in recruitment, Brim?"

"Not really, Winston. But I'm always open to ideas."

*

On a cold January morning a letter arrived on Brim's desk. It was addressed to 'Head of British Intelligence, Whitehall, London, England'. It was postmarked Zermatt, Switzerland and its content stark:

> *"Sir, I have known Alistair Valentine, his mother and brother for many years. His mother and I are distant cousins. Alistair is a multi-lingual athlete: a natural hunter, climber and skier. He would be perfect for British Intelligence. His late father Lt. Col. Stephen Valentine was posthumously awarded the Victoria Cross in 1916 for bravery in France. Alistair inherits his father's loyalty, courage and sense of duty to his country.*
> *Please do not tell Alistair I recommended him; he would never forgive me. He is currently working for Michael Wood, a London wine merchant. He gives talks on wine."*

The letter was handwritten in German and signed by a man called Günter Seiler. Fortunately, Brim was also multi-lingual, though his hunting and climbing skills were somewhat limited.

Brim strolled down Belgrave Road towards Millbank and the Thames. One of his favourite walks in London. He turned up the collar of his greatcoat, strolled over Lambeth Bridge and up to

Waterloo. He had much on his mind. In a few hours' time he would take a taxi to the Coburg Hotel. Somebody would be there who he was very much looking forward to meeting.

*

The young man at the podium certainly knew his subject. And spoke with confidence. He was tallish, just under six foot, with blue-grey eyes and foppish fair hair. He spoke, mostly without notes, about the wines of Bordeaux, and Clarets in particular. Then he moved to red Burgundy; Nuits-St-Georges seemed to be one of his specialities. The audience at the London Wine Society were a mixture of buyers, sommeliers, restaurateurs, and the public. In the winter of 1936, wine was not at the top of most people's shopping list. But there was a small, elite group who were interested. 'Investors, connoisseurs and quaffers,' as Alistair had so elegantly put it to his semi-amused audience.

A man raised his hand to ask a question. He spoke in Parisian-accented French about the wine label Alistair was showing them. A Beaune Premier Cru, 1927. Alistair's boss, Mr. Michael Wood, was at the presentation and looked at him expectantly.

If members of the audience thought Alistair might embarrass himself, they were in for a surprise. Alistair addressed the Parisian – who clearly knew little about wine – of the complexities of 'colour'- 'flavour' – and 'texture' – of wine. Not just taste. He suggested, with charm and self-deprecation, that if the man would like to order a case, he could savour the palette for himself. There was hesitant laughter in the room. Then the man agreed to the purchase and made a show of it, with a plump wallet full of Francs.

Professor Brimblecombe – who clearly did know a little about wine – raised his hand and asked if they could move on to German wines, as advertised in the Society's Winter Programme. Alistair was pleased to acquiesce. He noticed Michael Wood's wife and daughter were also present, busily serving wine 'tasters' to Society members in the bar area. The daughter, Emma, was busily watching him and enjoying his good humour. A subtle hint of irreverence.

"Yes, sir," said Alistair, "but let us first take a quick look at these three Alsace wines out of interest: Tokay Pinot Gris, Gewurztraminer and Pinot Blanc."

Brimblecombe nodded and Alistair spoke with authority about the history of the region, both political and commercial, and this was followed by a tasting. The tasting was informal with various cheeses, grapes, and nuts being served by Emma. Traditional finger food for such times. Alistair, with one eye distracted by Emma, was complimented by a German grower on his extensive knowledge. Alistair replied in fluent German about a car journey he had taken through Alsace and his love of the area. He spoke in detail about soil, climate and the local foods he had relished during the holiday. The German, impressed by Alistair's command of the language, told him he was from Saarbrücken. A friendship was made, and a contact developed for Michael Wood's wine emporium.

The evening was a success. By eleven o'clock forty cases of wines from France and Germany had been sold and Alistair had

"Fear itself, that's a good answer." Brim stood up, flicked at his jacket as if to brush imaginary crumbs away. The invisible-morsel routine was one of the Professor's many traits. "Although not entirely original."

Alistair grinned: "I thought it was too clever to be me!" He laughed at his own joke.

Brim smiled: "Right, a few items to put in your diary. I'd like you to go to the Berlin Olympics. It starts at the beginning of August."

"Which event? Running?"

Brim ignored Alistair's levity: "I want you to meet Manfred Lochar. He's my Nexus contact from Switzerland."

Alistair was now serious and attentive: "Nexus?"

"A highly secret organisation of, let's say, facilitators. Manfred will explain when you meet him at the Olympic village. You'll be given valid papers and identification."

"That's six months off, Brim."

"Quite." Brim pursed his lips as if in thought. "Ever been to Scotland?"

"No."

Brim checked his watch: "You will have by this time tomorrow; perhaps a little bit later." He put his hand into the inside pocket of his blazer and produced railway tickets and what looked like a timetable. "I will see you in a month or so. And good luck. It won't be a holiday."

Brim was known for thrusting people in at the deep end. At the last minute. He handed Alistair a brown envelope. "Fifty pounds; should keep you out of mischief. Although, where you're going, you'll have nothing to spend it on ... Sgian Dubh... bliss!"

Brim chuckled and waddled off like a diminutive, plump penguin, weaving from side to side through the canteen tables. He gave a little wave to the waitress. She blushed.

Alistair Valentine

Sgian Dubh, British Intelligence Commando Training Centre, Scotland

BLOODY HELL, I'M GOING TO DROWN! I thought to myself. I knew I could tolerate danger, but this was something else. Something perilous. And the water was freezing. I dropped further into the darkening abyss. Endless, it seemed, immeasurably deep, my chest tightened. I must push myself further ...

Foul water was starting to seep through my sealed, numb lips and the ancient diving suit did little to disguise the temperature. The loch darkened more as I descended. I just wanted to get this over and knock back a couple of pints with single malt chasers in the bar at Arisaig House. I swam as powerfully as I could, very conscious of my lung capacity ... and time.

The resistance of the water and the awkwardness of my suit impaired both my speed and agility. This underwater world felt alien; myriad eyes of marine life danced and sparkled in curiosity: who was this intruder? I plunged deeper into the icy darkness.

Thirty feet below in the murky water was the object of my mission: a wooden crate nestling in what looked like a field of undulating weed. It resembled a treasure chest. I clasped a padlock key in my right fist with such determination that I was sure I would drop it. This, too, hampered my ability to swim effectively. It was a nightmare. The one-piece diving mask trapped a volume of air around my eye sockets and nose. It had become slightly askew during my descent and some water had leaked in. I blew a cautious sniff of air through my nose to try and push some of the water out. It worked, thank God. And resealed.

It was desperately cold, and I felt my lungs were bursting. I swam deeper, focusing on the crate – twenty feet – ten. I could picture the two men above me – in a fishing boat – stopwatches primed as they watched the seconds ticking.

Five more feet and I was there; my knees scraped the bed of the loch, releasing a cloud of debris and bubbles. The padlock looked old and rusty. I tilted it with my left hand until the keyhole was visible. My bare hands were numb with cold, but I needed the tactility. I felt for the indented aperture of the lock with the pad of my thumb and then inserted the key and rotated the oval shackle.

Thirty seconds with no air and my lungs were bursting. I desperately removed the padlock and opened the lid of the trunk, just enough. A few bubbles of air escaped. The trunk had been sealed and tethered to a rock protrusion with sturdy ropes. A No. 76 Special Incendiary Grenade stared back at me. It was grey and sinister. I thrust it into the diving bag strapped onto the front of my suit, closed the trunk's lid and re-locked the padlock. As I turned the shackle back and re-engaged the mechanism, I dropped the key.

Forty seconds. And then I spotted it, floating just above the loch bed, suspended in the weed like a dead fish. I grabbed it and swam back up towards the boat, desperate for air, willing myself to swim faster and faster. Finally, my palm brushed against the wooden hull, and then a hand was there, hauling me out of the freezing water. I tore off the diving mask, gasping for air, panting frantically.

A burly Scotsman named Captain Sykes looked at me, deadpan: "That wasn't so bad, was it, lad?"

"Alistair Valentine, reporting for duty, sir," I said and collapsed onto the deck, breathless. I didn't notice the grenade had fallen out of my diving bag and was rolling across the wooden planks toward the edge of the deck.

The other soldier, Fairburn, sarcastic to the last: "Lucky it wasn't bloody armed, or we'd all have been toasted."

"Aye, on both sides," said Sykes with a grimace.

"Piss off," I said sharply. Or did I imagine it?

*

They'd told him, of course, that the training would be brutal. And it was. A matter of focused endurance and survival. Besides the 'retrieval test' as it was quaintly known, Alistair would be taught weapons handling, sabotage, radio comms, self defence and climbing. The tools of Intelligence. He couldn't tell a soul, not even his brother Freddie. Not yet.

By the end of the training, his masters in London would receive a missive from Captain William Fairburn:

Valentine (Alistair.) 100%:
outstanding, but dangerous.

Astrid

Baden-Baden, Germany.

THE NARROW ROOM IN THE HOSPITAL at Baden-Baden was stark white, its louvred shutters closed against the brightness of the sun. However, the overlapping slats had been crafted and angled to admit a certain amount of sunlight. Beams projected into the darkened room onto a white sheet covering the still figure lying on a wrought-iron bed.

Astrid Lochar, barely nineteen, clutched the thin sheet tightly up to her neck. The skin covering her knuckles was taut and white. Slowly she opened her eyes and stared up at the high, ornate ceiling. She was aware of two people on chairs at the end of her bed; but couldn't determine who they were or why they were there. It didn't make sense. Nothing made sense.

The figures were silent shadows, illuminated too by strips of sunlight and tiny dust motes which floated in the still, warm air. She blinked and swallowed. Her mouth was too dry to speak; her lips encrusted with dried saliva. Her head throbbed from dehydration. 'Where am I? Why am I here?' she thought.

As soon as she moved, one of the people stood up, then the other. Gently they edged to the head of the bed without a sound. A hand tenderly lifted her head from the pillows. She then heard the gurgle of water being poured. She felt the rim of a tumbler pressed to her mouth.

"Drink, Liebling," the sound of her mother, at once familiar. "You must try and drink."

The tumbler was tipped again, but her uncooperative lips refused to part. Her mother, Ingrid, softly caressed them with the tip of her wetted finger, urging tenderly. Astrid swallowed and licked her lips with her tongue.

"Try now," her mother said again, "please?"

This time she felt the water trickle into her mouth. She swallowed and felt the excess run down her chin and onto her neck. It felt cool.

She knew the taste well, that mineral flavour. Spa water from Baden.

Home. She drank until the tumbler was drained.

"Thank you," she said faintly.

The hand lowered her head gently into the spongy goose down. All of a sudden Astrid felt lightheaded. She closed her eyes; she didn't know for how long. A minute? An hour? When she awoke her mother and father were still there, keeping silent vigil.

"What happened to me?" she asked; she didn't recognise the sound of her own voice; it felt distant and detached. Not her at all.

"You lost a baby, Liebling," said her mother unequivocally.

You lost a baby. Not the baby. A significant qualification of the truth lay in her statement. Of course, because nobody knew about it: it was her secret.

Their secret.

"Where is Oskar?" asked Astrid weakly. Her eyelids flickered with sudden concern.

There was a pause as she waited.

"Don't worry about him now, Astrid," said her father; but the emphasis was definitely on him.

"But I need to know, Papa. Please? I cannot remember."

"He's gone, Astrid. No one knows where." His inadequate words trailed off.

Astrid let out a sharp cry of grief. Where had he gone? What did this mean? Had she lost them both? Oskar and their child? Their secret? Their future? All of their dreams shattered, but why?

"What happened?" she asked grimly. She felt a dismal new world unravelling ahead of her.

"You fell. You were running in the street, chasing after a car," her mother explained, "don't you remember?"

"No."

"We didn't know, Astrid. Why didn't you tell us? We would have understood. We would have supported you, of course." Her father's words were more perplexed than angry.

They had felt bewildered when they had learned their only daughter had been "with child" and they didn't even know. She had betrayed them; at least, not confided in them. Wasn't it the same thing? She hadn't confessed to them because she didn't know how they would react.

Astrid unclenched her right hand and tunnelled it down slowly under the bed sheet. She was wearing a loose-fitting hospital gown, but it had ridden up her otherwise naked body. She cautiously explored. The flat palm of her hand was on her stomach, her fingers stretched out curiously; her skin felt wet and sticky with perspiration. Between her legs some sort of absorbent gauze dressing had been carefully placed. That too felt warm and moist. Her hand immediately shot out from under the sheet; she saw it was caked in tacky blood, the colour of rust.

"Oh God," she called out, shocked. Then she broke down and cried, howling in despair and confusion.

There was nothing in the world Manfred and Ingrid Lochar could do to calm their precious daughter. It broke their hearts. They held each other's hands and gazed down at her pale face.

Oskar Rosenbaum and his family had fled from Germany for fear of persecution. It was their car Astrid had been chasing.

Olympics

Berlin, Germany.

IN SUMMER 1936, BERLIN FELT HOT, HUMID AND AIRLESS. But the city's atmosphere was charged by the energy and excitement surrounding the Olympic Games.

The centrepiece of the 11th Summer Games was the vast Olympiastadion, ordered by Adolf Hitler and built by Werner March. It was constructed as part of the Reichssportfeld, a great sports complex, which included a development of buildings and hotels to house athletes and visitors from all over the world.

Alistair Valentine travelled to the Olympic Village of Elstal, his mind consumed with sadness. It was four days after he and his brother Freddie had nearly come to blows at Waterloo station. It was a stupid misunderstanding concerning their mother, Christina. On the surface he appeared relaxed and carefree; yet he was covertly looking for his Nexus contact.

Manfred Lochar looked through his compact Zeiss binoculars; the blurred image of Alistair came sharply into view.

"What do you think?" He handed the glasses to his daughter,

Astrid, who had discreetly been studying a 10x8-inch photograph.

The black and white print had been taken a month earlier in a studio behind Baker Street, on Brimblecombe's orders. Manfred and Astrid had a secluded vantage point behind a bus stop opposite the entrance to the Olympic Village.

She pressed the glasses to her eyes and looked at the man in question: he was tallish, fair haired and athletic. He moved with graceful economy, observing his surroundings keenly.

"Definitely him," Astrid mused. "He blends in well; he looks like a competitor, a runner or a swimmer."

"Neither, Liebling. Professor Brimblecombe sent him. I am his Nexus contact. Come, we have work to do."

"When do we meet him?" Astrid asked hopefully.

"I meet him later. Back at the stadium ... inside. You can observe, from a safe distance."

"Oh," she sounded disappointed. She took the glasses away from her eyes and without looking at her father continued: "Let's follow him for an hour and see how good he is."

Seconds later, she looked through the glasses again. Valentine had vanished. She scanned left and right. Nothing.

"Yes, very good," she said.

After her miscarriage in Baden-Baden the year before, Astrid could easily have gone to pieces. But hadn't.

Manfred and Ingrid Lochar not only wanted to support their daughter in her physical recovery, but also psychologically, to distract from the trauma. They chose to introduce her to their world; the clandestine realm of espionage – working with the

British and Swiss against the Nazis. An odd remedy, for certain, but one in which she became a natural affiliate.

Like her parents, Astrid hated Hitler. Seeing what the Nazis were doing to Germany reinforced her loathing. She had the attributes of a spy - intelligence, resourcefulness, and loyalty – and used them wisely. The Lochars and their contacts worked with Professor Brimblecombe in London and Helmut Siebenthal in Basle. Nexus was a highly secret organisation, existing below the surface, out of sight of the authorities. And the Nazis. Their funding came from all walks of life: lawyers, doctors, academics, bankers, farmers, landowners, old German families. With old German money.

Once Astrid learned the truth about what happened to Oskar Rosenbaum and his family, her motivation in life became clear. She had a purpose: to avenge the loss of her child and her lover, by joining a network of people whose sole aim was to destroy the cause of that loss.

She would do anything to help Nexus – and, of course, her beloved parents.

On her first meeting with Siebenthal in Basle he said to her: "I am sorry about what happened to you, Astrid, but there it is. But your feelings have a purpose, you see; they act as a guide to what is important in your life.

"Fear will always keep you safe and alert, but revenge is sweet, no matter what people tell you. That is why we take the risk; it is worth it. It has to be. We must be rid of Hitler and his thugs, no matter what."

She agreed without question. Nexus was her destiny and her

saviour. Yet she would never forget the baby so cruelly denied her and the young man she had loved.

She handed the glasses and the photograph back to her father.

"Yes," said Manfred, pinching his nose in his characteristic way. "Brim says Alistair is one of the best he has ever recruited, a natural with an uncanny flair for languages.

"His German is flawless," he continued. "But Brim wants him, what did he say, 'naturalised' and active within six months. So, no English spoken, no English food, no English newspapers or radio. And no contact with anyone in Britain, apart from Brim. Then he will move into an apartment in Berlin with his new persona in place."

Manfred gave her a sideways glance she did not see. And just as well, for he had something further up his sleeve he didn't dare reveal until the time was right.

"I see. Where will he live until then?" Astrid's tone was more than curious. She could read her father like a book.

Manfred was hesitant: "With us, to start with. I am not sure for how long. He'll spend some time in Basle, training. But Brim believes he won't need much preparation: he spent much of his childhood in Switzerland. He knows the traditions, culture and language. Everything one needs for deep cover in a foreign country. And Brim is not known for praise, quite the reverse."

"A British agent. Imagine!" Astrid exclaimed.

"Yes. And he has a younger brother called Frederick, studying at Cambridge. But Brim tells me his ambition is to join the Royal

Air Force."

"To become a pilot?"

"Of course," said Manfred, smiling at his daughter.

"It was the glint of the glasses that gave you away," said Alistair suddenly and in fluent German, "particularly when you panned one hundred and eighty degrees. A simple glint."

Astrid nearly jumped out of her skin; but she could see her father was already holding his 7.65mm Luger under his jacket. He was always ready, always cautious. Alistair nimbly dropped down from a metre-high elevated ridge behind the bus stop and grinned at them both.

"Astrid, this is Alistair Valentine," Manfred said a little sheepishly.

She looked puzzled: "Wait. You've met before?"

"Yesterday," Alistair interjected politely, "your father wasn't going for a walk after all."

Astrid frowned, irritated and a little humiliated. Her father was always one step ahead; field- craft was his trade.

"I wanted to meet him alone the first time, Liebling. A precaution. Habit, I suppose."

"More like instinct. And it can save your life. I'd have done the same," said Alistair. "Let's go to the hotel. You have the camera?"

Astrid smiled a little coyly: "You speak perfect German, Herr Valentine."

His smile was charming: "Well, I've had plenty of practice.'"

Manfred: "Yes. Here is the cine camera, spare rolls of film, oh, and a press pass for the stadium. Security will be strict." Manfred handed the items over in a leather case.

"Perfect, thank you. I'm going to take close-ups of Hitler's entourage. There may be some new faces."

"Ja. And some old ones: Goering, Himmler and Bormann. The opening ceremony is tomorrow. It will be a spectacle, like something out of Ancient Rome. The world will be watching Germany: newspapers and television from all over Europe and beyond."

"And so will I with this. Does it take stills?"

"Yes. Single-frame or cine. There's a switch to select. Herr Siebenthal was very particular. It's the best camera in the world. Swiss-made, of course."

"Excellent."

Manfred raised his bushy eyebrows: "There are two changes since we spoke yesterday."

"Oh?" Alistair flashed his blue-grey eyes at Astrid and smiled.

"I have secured your identity. Stephan Beck. When the time comes you will have a job at Telefunken in Berlin. And a house in Potsdam. Everything will be legitimate. Until then you will need to lie low. Can you go back to Switzerland? Chalet Monte Rosa?"

"Yes, that's what I plan to do. What was the other change?"

"This is important and, of course, highly classified. Nexus has a spy inside Abwehr headquarters, 76/78 Tirpitzufer in the centre of Berlin. Her name is Monika." Manfred's hushed words were met with astonishment.

"God, that's impressive.

"She will be your Berlin contact. Her loyalty to Nexus is unquestioned. And, like Canaris, her father is an admiral. A core member of the Black Orchestra."

“Understood.”

“In time we hope she will be in a position to have access to the schedules of everyone in the Abwehr, including Canaris. Monika will be very important to you and she’ll let you know when the mission is on.”

Alistair nodded. It was a lot to take in: “Tell me, Manfred. Are you able to get these films to London? MI6 will want to know who is in Hitler’s entourage at the games. And get a feel for the atmosphere. Maybe the faces of some of the Nazi supporters.”

Manfred raised his eyebrows and smiled for the first time: “What do you think, Herr Valentine?”

Alistair turned to Astrid and looked her in the eye: “I think Nexus can move mountains. Especially you and Astrid.”

Freddie Valentine

Tiger Moth over England.

"BLOODY HELL, I'M GOING TO CRASH!" shouted Freddie to himself. He'd lost control. The engine was overheating. It misfired. The nose dipped. He jerked the stick back in panic.

"And I'm just doing Squires a favour!"

Flight Lieutenant Alfred 'Freddie' Valentine was alone flying the Tiger Moth biplane. At 27, he had already enjoyed a varied military career. Now it appeared to be in peril.

He had been seconded, no bribed, to fly the de Havilland DH82 from where he had learned to fly, RAF Attlebridge, near Norwich, to a smaller base in Lincolnshire. He should not have flown that day. He was a fighter pilot, flying Spitfires, but had agreed to the jaunt to appease his old instructor.

"Come on, Freddie," Squadron Leader Squires had said: "We'll send the Humber up to collect you. Back in no time and I'll buy you a few pints in the Mess; doddle for an ace like you."

The Tiger Moth was a friend, so Freddie thought. Yet she'd felt odd when he'd gunned the engine. After flying for half an hour, the aircraft became erratic. He was confused. Should he turn back?

"Only doing circuits and bumps, eh Freddie?" he could already hear his former CO's mocking voice. He flew on. The light was bad; dusk; to the west a setting sun bled streaks of red over the horizon. Twice the engine sputtered and twice Freddie recovered airspeed. The biplane, however, remained lumpy – contrary to the Moth's customary agility. He visualised the mechanical components of the single-prop engine toiling furiously. Somewhere, something was not right.

Sweat surged from his hot flesh inside his flight suit; the stench of oil and grease seemed to permeate every pore. Freddie checked gauges and instruments as he had been taught. Squires had been a hard taskmaster; altimeter, airspeed indicator – 80 knots – too fast to land even if he could. Altitude indicator, climb-and-descent indicator, oil pressure and oil temperature gauges.

Too hot, much too hot, but why?

He glanced at the gyro and compass to check direction. Squire's golden rule was to use the instruments, don't look outside for reference. Glare from the sunset was blinding. Nothing was right. It didn't make sense. The engine screamed, making the airframe shake.

"Damn bucket!" he shouted. He wanted to kick something, but there wasn't room.

"Beer Don One," the radio operator bellowed into his headset, "where the hell are you?"

For a moment he couldn't answer.

His goggles were not fooling him; there were plumes of vapour all around him. He pulled the stick backwards. No response. The needle on the faintly lit altimeter span backwards. The flatlands of the Fens should have been visible below him.

"Freddie!" The RO screamed again. The line crackled with static like distant gunfire.

Freddie was too focused, too hell-bent on surviving. He tried to reply but could barely speak: "Mayday," his constricted throat croaked.

He was below cloud, but it was dark. Sea smells: he saw small waves in the Wash as he crossed the coast. Freddie was exhausted. He lifted his oily goggles, removed a glove, rubbed his sore eyes, and squinted at the controls.

Damn, heading west. The engine protested again. He tried to turn the juddering Moth starboard and north, keeping the brighter horizon on his left shoulder. He was at less than a thousand feet now, too low to parachute.

Finally, the aircraft fleetingly responded. He rotated his cramped body and checked the altimeter; five hundred feet, still falling. Then the engine sputtered, misfired and died. The warm evening air dashed against his face; he was gliding to the ground.

Freddie remembered the buffeting, the lifeless propeller, and the wheels smashing into soggy turf. Thank God he was low on fuel; full and the Moth might have exploded. Trapped and seared in a fiery cockpit, he shuddered at the notion.

Wet turf flipped the biplane, which smashed and sank into the ground. As the Moth had rotated and dropped, Freddie's legs burned with pain. The starboard wing flew off and the fuselage disintegrated.

Then nothing; was he dead or alive? He had considered this moment before; how would he feel and what would he see? Slowly, darkness prevailed.

Later, a blurred choir of masked faces with intense shiny eyes looked down on him, but these angels were not singing. He smelt chemicals and heard a hubbub of serious voices. Sounds echoed in his head: the clatter of instruments on stainless-steel trays, the thump of some machine, like a giant piston pumping up and down, the gentle hiss of gas.

He felt a slap on his arm, then the sharp jab of a needle penetrating skin and vein. The warm, soporific benison of morphine rushed into his bloodstream. He slipped into a realm of curious images and nightmarish ghouls. Welcome to hell, Mr. Valentine.

Himmler

The Bavarian Alps, Austria.

HEINRICH HIMMLER WAS A terrible figure. A cold-blooded monster who ruthlessly ordered the extermination of millions of prisoners by every refinement of sadistic torture. He was pitiless; nothing horrified him. With his shaven skull and steel-rimmed glasses, he personified the face of evil.

After an uncomfortable, protracted journey from the East, Himmler made his way towards the Berghof, in Obersalzberg. He was sitting in the back of a chauffeur-driven Mercedes and glanced out at the beautiful Austrian countryside. The Bavarian Alps in the distance looked magnificent, breath-taking to normal people. They made no impression upon Himmler whatsoever; he had other matters on his mind. Matters of the Third Reich. And an appointment with Hitler and the Presidium. His thin face twisted; they were in for a few surprises, he thought to himself.

He closed his eyes, reassured by the presence of the armed motorcycle outriders and thought about the forthcoming few hours. He had Hitler on his side; of that there was no question. Hermann Goering, Commander of the Luftwaffe, would give him air power; Admiral Karl Doenitz, chief of the German Navy, unlimited naval support. Most important of all, perhaps, Erich Spengler, the most influential industrialist in Germany, had given millions for special weapons development. Even Giles Walcott, the Irish Republican, had given him manpower and money, on the promise of a free Ireland.

Only Rear Admiral Wilhelm Canaris – Head of German Intelligence – the Abwehr – stood in his way. But Himmler had plans for him. Within a matter of weeks Germany would wreak havoc over Britain; a reign of terror that had never been witnessed before. And it was he who had orchestrated it.

Britain would surrender and Germany would be victorious in Europe. And there was nothing in the world anyone could do to prevent it. A smile crossed his face. What if the Führer became ill? He wasn't well. What then? Germany would be his for the taking. And he could not wait.

Berghof

June 1943, Obersalzberg, Bavaria, Germany.

WHEN ADOLF HITLER WALKED INTO THE GREAT HALL of the Berghof, it was as if someone had simul-taneously sucked the air out. Members of the conference assembled that day felt fear. It was raw and undeniable.

Hitler was a slight, pale-looking man with short brown hair, parted to one side. He had a sallow complexion and, with his distinct, blunt, ink-smudge moustache, looked almost comical. Until he spoke. His persuasive rhetoric embraced, almost strangled, the listener into belief and acceptance nobody, it seemed, could inhibit.

The Führer's steel-blue eyes held a bewitching, hypnotic quality. He could hold his audience under a spell by the sheer force of his passion and conviction; his ability to alter tone and syntax of speech mesmerised. Hitler was a skilful performer; a man who rehearsed his act to harvest maximum effect.

The hall looked out onto the sun terrace and it was in this room that a very secret meeting was about to take place. Each of the chairs around the table was occupied by a member of Hitler's elite entourage and notes taken, as usual, by Gertraud 'Traudi' Junge, Hitler's private secretary since December 1942. She sat at a separate desk and took detailed minutes of every word uttered, in rapid shorthand.

Hitler wore his customary silver-grey tunic, pressed black trousers and polished knee-length jackboots. He paced around the room, hands clasped behind his back, occasionally smoothing his hair down with the heel of his hand. He spoke firmly and with passion; each member of this particular meeting believed he was addressing them personally, for every word seemed to have an edge.

The Führer picked up a document from the table and spoke without introduction or greeting:

"This document is Führer Memorandum 267," his eyes flashed, "and the operation described herein will change the course of the war and secure victory for Germany. And the German people ..." He paused for effect.

"It will be presented by Reichsführer SS, Heinrich Himmler, unless there are any questions first ..."

He paused once more. Hitler's eyes scanned the apprehensive faces and continued; his voice lowered a theatrical notch:

"Memorandum 267. You will all see there is a copy in front of you. I have sub-headed this operation: DAS SCHLOSS, for reasons that will become apparent. The document is not to be opened or consulted until the Reichsführer has addressed you ..."

Hitler replaced the document carefully on the table and

continued stomping around the hall, boots echoing. Before he sat, he looked at the men around the table, waiting.

"So, no questions. Good."

This was his inner circle – the Presidium – the most powerful men in the Third Reich:

Commander-in-Chief of the German Navy - Karl Doenitz. Joseph Goebbels: Reichsminister for Propaganda for Nazi Germany. Hermann Goering: Commander-in-Chief of the Luftwaffe. Field Marshall Erwin Rommel. Field Marshall Gerd von Rundstedt. Wilhelm Keitel: Field Marshall of the German Army (Wehrmacht) and Hitler's Chief of Staff. Admiral Canaris, head of the Abwehr.

And finally, Himmler. Reichsführer of the entire SS. He cast his eyes around the table before he spoke:

"Many of our spies in England have either been hanged, committed suicide or supposedly turned. But there are two who have been living under cover in West London – since 1930 – as Admiral Canaris of the Abwehr is particularly aware. The Abwehr, as their controllers, have done an outstanding job ..."

Canaris acknowledged the compliment with the slightest of nods and wondered what was coming next. Himmler continued; his glasses glinting in the sunlight from the terrace:

"They remain not only undetected by the enemy but are also active sleeper spies. They run a hotel and are anonymous; their English is impeccable – an asset of the highest order...

their identities, of course, are not revealed in this file ..." He paused.

Himmler permitted himself a smile: "Thanks to the support of my friend and colleague Karl Doenitz, an essential naval component of the operation has been made available: A U-Boat and her crew ..." Only a few of the men were aware of the whole story; and these key members of the Presidium would exclude Canaris. Doenitz acknowledged the shallow compliment with a brief nod.

Field Marshall Gerd von Rundstedt, cleared his throat: "What is 267?"

Himmler's thin lips parted: "A series of aerial attacks by the Luftwaffe on five strategic targets in the south of England and London; originating from the Fifteenth Army Division in Northern France. But with a lethal pay load."

Von Rundstedt: "Pay load?"

"Yes. It will contain a lethal nerve gas called Tabun."

"How will it be deployed?" asked Rommel. There was a hint of concern in his voice.

It was Hermann Goering who replied, but first he repeated the question to emphasise the cleverness of his answer:

"How will it be deployed? The bomb bays of ten Heinkels have been adapted to facilitate and launch ten high-speed ballistic missiles, each with an explosive warhead. The missiles are primed with pressurised Tabun. A gyroscopically stabilised fin will guide these weapons to their target."

Goering went on to say that their astonishing speed was achieved by a mixture of alcohol and liquid oxygen.

"They can fly," Goering continued enthusiastically, "at more than 1,200 km/h, much faster than an ME 262 Schwalbe. Or a

Spitfire. Too fast for British early warning systems and anti-aircraft guns. They may hear them, but they certainly won't see them. Until it is too late."

The Presidium was silent; Goering rarely consulted any notes. He could see the impression he was making by the looks on their faces. Particularly Canaris. He continued:

"The conversion of the aircraft has been carried out undercover by Spengler GmbH and an assigned team of Luftwaffe engineers. Apart from these loyal Germans and this Presidium, nobody else knows of this offensive."

Hitler paced around the Great Hall again, watching every face and every minute reaction.

Himmler continued with the plan: "The five strategic targets will be attacked by groups of Heinkels from concealed airbases at carefully worked out geographical intervals, to create a domino effect. The first four from hangars in Boulogne, two from Calais, two from Dunkirk and the last two from Koksijde."

"And the targets?" asked Rommel grimly. "What are the targets?"

Himmler looked around the room, assessing the mood as Hitler almost imperceptibly nodded:

"The first four crucial aircraft leaving Boulogne will strike at Biggin Hill, to knock out the RAF radar systems and the others at specific command and control centres in the south, to do likewise. To paralyse their defences."

Rommel looked pale: "But the RAF will try and counterattack, will they not?"

"No. These missiles will be deployed suddenly – after a signal

- less than 4 kilometres from the continental coast. At the speed they are travelling, it will be seconds before they reach their target," said Himmler, "that's the importance of striking Biggin Hill first." He pressed the palms of his hands together as if he were praying and lowered his voice:

"Such an attack has never been attempted before. This operation will certainly cause the enemy to sue for peace. DAS SCHLOSS will end the war. We will control Europe."

The Great Hall went quiet and it was Canaris who broke the uncomfortable silence after a break of more than fifteen seconds:

"My Führer, why is the operation so called?"

Hitler waited, strutting around the room. Nobody challenged. Nobody spoke because nobody dared:

"Because Windsor Castle is the prime target ..." He glanced at Karl Doenitz; a split imperceptible second ...

"U-Boat 302 will leave the Bergen flotilla and make for Cromer on the east coast of England. Her crew will discharge cylinders of Tabun – each with a fixed warhead – into the hands of the London sleeper spies ..." Hitler glanced around the hall to make sure the clever plan was understood. It was ...

"They will then transport the weapons to Windsor Castle in a specially converted vehicle. An on-the-ground attack."And so, the crucial lie had been cunningly delivered to mislead certain members of the Presidium. One man in particular.

"Why Windsor?" asked Rommel.

Hitler answered in a matter-of-fact tone: "Windsor Castle is the symbol of the Royal Family. One of their seats of power. We take that first and then their command centres. It is vital, essential, Windsor is the first strike." His blue eyes shone as he scanned the faces around the table.

The Great Hall fell silent as each man absorbed the words. And, of course, nobody challenged. Hitler and Himmler exchanged the very briefest of eye contacts. Himmler said:

"German boots on British soil." Everybody knew the significance of those words, but none dare acknowledge them.

Hitler turned to Traudi Junge, who sat at her desk, her pencil poised above her notebook. She raised her eyes, and he smiled his avuncular smile:

"Did you get all that, my dear?"

Traudi rose to her feet, instinctively: "Yes, my Führer. Thank you, I did." She blushed; but it was not out of embarrassment. It was out of pride: Hitler had taken the trouble to consult her in front of the Presidium. That simple gesture momentarily defused the tension in the room.

"Good." Hitler nodded at her absent-mindedly. It was as if he was checking she had enough money for typewriter ribbon. This tiny detail was not missed by a single member; so typical of Hitler's skill and ability to switch from serious to mundane.

But suddenly his tone changed again; he scanned the faces of every man in the room before he spoke: "Is there any possibility Enigma could have been compromised?"

The silence in the hall was palpable. It was as if nobody dared commit to an answer they might one day regret. It was Goering who finally broke that silence: "No, my Führer. None whatsoever. Enigma is unbreakable. The enemy are blind."

Hitler considered: "Even so, not one word of DAS SCHLOSS

will be communicated in any form. Secrecy is essential to success. Is that understood?"

They all nodded, and Hitler watched them as they rose from their seats. He then gave his traditional, informal Nazi salute and left the hall. Himmler, Goering and Doenitz gathered their papers simultaneously, each aware Hitler had picked up on a detail they had all overlooked. Himmler glanced at Admiral Canaris with an expression that chilled him.

Once again, Canaris mentally questioned the sanity and rationality of Hitler and Himmler. But it was more than that. Because he knew that, in the end, Germany would pay for such madness. His thoughts briefly flicked back to the meeting in Spain with Churchill and Brimblecombe in the mid 1930's. Well, nobody could say they had not been warned. But never, in the furthest realms of his imagination could he have anticipated a U-Boat discharging chemical warfare and an aerial attack on England that would kill millions and annihilate the British Royals and their Guard.

Admiral Canaris picked up the DAS SCHLOSS file in front of him and put it into a leather briefcase. He locked the two clasps and walked out of the Great Hall, his head slightly bowed. Fear crawled up his spine and lodged itself in the back of his throat.

Driver

Obersalzberg, Bavaria, Germany.

LATER, STILL SHOCKED, THE ADMIRAL walked down the steps of the Berghof towards a dozen or more cars lined up at the bottom. With him was Erwin Rommel to whom he had offered a lift to the airport. The two spoke in hushed tones.

Canaris's black Mercedes Benz Abwehr staff car drew alongside; the driver got out and swiftly opened the rear door.

"Where's my normal driver?" growled Canaris, surprised and suspicious. The driver responded in self-deprecating manner, mixing charm and perplexed confusion.

"To be honest, Herr Admiral, I don't know. It was all last minute. I understood from the dispatcher he was rushed to the Krankenhaus in Salzburg. Ruptured appendix or something."

Canaris sighed; he was tired.

"My papers," said Alistair Valentine, presenting documents, "my name is ..."

"Never mind. Why wasn't I told?" Canaris snapped.

"With respect, Herr Admiral, I was told not to interrupt you, since you were here in conference with ..."

"I know who I was in conference with. Get me back to the airport. I need to return to Berlin. So does my colleague." He glanced at Rommel.

Alistair proffered his documents again: "Stephan Beck, Herr Admiral."

"Quickly."

Alistair opened the back doors of the car; Canaris and Rommel climbed inside and made themselves comfortable.

"Where are you from, and what did you say your name was?" asked Canaris again.

"Stephan Beck, Herr Admiral. I live in Potsdam."

"Then you can fly back with us to Tempelhof. I need a driver in Berlin."

"But my family are here in Salzburg for the music festival, Herr Admiral." Alistair sounded genuinely concerned for his 'family', his protest heartfelt, and his German fluent and flawless.

"Do you want the damn job? There are other drivers."

"Ja, Herr Admiral, of course. I shall be delighted to accompany you."

"Drive quickly, we don't have the luxury of time."

"Ja, Herr Admiral. There is a flask of coffee, fresh bread and cheese in the cabinet between the seats."

Just as Canaris wound up the divider screen between the front and back of the car, Alistair heard Rommel mumble a few words. He recognized the Field Marshall immediately.

"Schlafende Spione in London ... I'm surprised they are not all ..."

The screen suddenly sealed the two compartments. Soundproof. Yet it was enough. A few momentous words: Schlafende Spione in London – sleeper spies in London. This could only mean a deep cover spy network, passing themselves off as English. But where exactly in London? More importantly, who? A member of the general public? Or worse. He would have to communicate this intelligence back to his superiors, as soon as he returned to Potsdam. Spying, after all, was exactly what he was doing in Germany. And he knew the incredible risk he and his partner were taking.

If Canaris, Rommel and Stephan Beck had remained in Salzburg until later that day they might have seen a brief report in the local evening newspaper.

Police mystified by body in Hauptstrasse

The corpse of a man believed to be around thirty years old was found today hidden at the river end of Hauptstrasse. He had been stabbed once fatally, there was no sign of a struggle and no clue to his identity as his body was stripped to underclothes. Police are appealing for information and witnesses.

Shadow

8 Prinz-Albrecht Strasse, Berlin, Germany.

STURMBANNFŰHRER OTTO KREBBS, assault unit leader in the SS, stood stock still, his grey overcoat harmonised with overcast sky; a mannequin shadowed by tall trees. He watched and waited. He always watched and waited. The Admiral was due.

Krebbs was the image of Teutonic visual perfection; his face and physique promoted that coveted image of Aryan master race. A natural candidate: indeed, six foot four, physically honed, blond, with clear, Pacific-blue eyes. Yet his look of Nordic perfection was marred. His left cheek sported a livid, ugly scar running from temple to jawline; the work of a fourteen-year-old girl with a dessert fork. She had witnessed him raping her sister; he would never be caught off guard like that again.

A few days before he had watched, camouflaged by undergrowth and dumbfounded, when Canaris's chauffeur was summarily murdered. Krebbs furtively witnessed the slaying; despised it; wished to intervene; but did nothing. Orders.

Himmler had asked him – no, commanded him - to observe. Take no action. No matter what you see; do nothing, he had said. He obeyed; loyalty immovable. The Reichsführer was his master.

The surveyed execution, for that's what it was – a targeted kill - had been rapidly finished by an agile, dark-skinned, sturdy man of medium build. Krebbs noted his age, nearing fifty or so, his mop of unkempt hair, droopy eyelids and bushy eyebrows. His speed of movement impressed; Krebbs was astonished at the killer's pace, precision and sheer accuracy.

This assassin was no novice. Was he southern Italian or Sicilian, thought Krebbs? His swarthy appearance and nonchalant expression said as much. He wore thin leather gloves, was clinically professional and used a stiletto or switchblade. Whichever; one movement, one blow. Immediate death.

The chauffeur died with no inkling of what was happening. His executioner cut away and bagged up all his outer clothes in less than 20 seconds; no one saw him. This corpse, then hurled into the nearby copse, would be anonymous. Krebbs, in civilian clothes, turned, walked up to the main square and merged into the crowd as the discreet executioner, carrying the bloodied clothes, walked in the opposite direction towards the glistening water.

Krebbs needed no notebook, mnemonic, or camera. Every detail was embedded. Himmler would hear it all.

*

Ten days before the Presidium had met at the Berghof, Heinrich Himmler had summoned Krebbs to Sicherheitspolizei –

Security Police - at No 8 Prinz-Albrecht Strasse in Berlin. As Reichsführer of the SS he had command of the building and all its resources of persuasion.

Krebbs had been told to wait by an office door. It was at the far end of a long basement corridor with a high-arched ceiling lit by small lightbulbs, each encased in a wire-mesh cage. It was a stifling hot day. Even below ground the temperature soared. He was most uncomfortable. Krebbs waited two hours outside the door in full uniform; it was close and airless, and he gulped with thirst as he stood to attention. If seen, he knew sitting on a nearby chair would be insubordination.

It was quiet and eerie, save for the occasional muffled scream. He wasn't surprised. He knew what happened in this building. For several moments he sensed light bulbs flickering. Did he detect faint buzzing?

Electricity was used as torture in the SS, he knew that much. It was quick and effective compared with available drugs. Strong men broke down; conspicuously obdurate women, with increasing voltage brutally applied to intimate flesh, would swiftly confess. Communists; anti-Nazi agitators; Jewish hideaways; homosexuals; gypsy families – all, and many more, were exposed. Krebbs swallowed dryly, because he, too, had inflicted immense human cruelty, without a second thought.

"Herr Sturmbannführer." Himmler's voice echoed as he strode along the corridor. Krebbs jolted; he was absorbed in thought, sweating, weak-kneed and light-headed through dehydration. He had failed to hear the Reichsführer's approach. The subordinate was at the point of collapse; but he dare not.

Himmler unlocked the office door: "Komm," he said calmly.

Krebbs mirrored Himmler's steps into the large, dark office. A huge, circular table in the centre overflowed with SS documents and a selection of foreign newspapers, even American. A little light beamed through a barred window high on the cellar wall; small shafts, like miniature searchlights, shone into the room. Himmler poured himself a glass of water from a silver tray on which stood a jug and two glasses. He drained the glass greedily without looking at Krebbs, then placed it gently back down.

"Now. I have selected you for a special task, Sturmbannführer Krebbs." Himmler paused, dabbing his lips with a handkerchief. "What is your opinion of Admiral Canaris?"

Krebbs hesitated, apprehensively, sensing fear: "I can't say I know the Admiral, sir."

"A good answer, Krebbs, because, of course, you don't. But you will."

Krebbs looked confused as Himmler continued: "Soon you will have the most important job in Germany," Himmler's thin, bloodless lips warped into what passed for a smile, "after the Führer, of course. They call you 'the shadow' do they not, your colleagues in the SS? This is your nickname."

Krebbs was confused: "Yes, but I ..."

Himmler cut him off with just enough intonation to suggest a threat: "As from now, all your other duties are suspended indefinitely. From this moment on, you work only for me. Directly. Is that understood?"

"Yes, sir. If you say so."

"I do say so! You speak to no one else. Clear?"

"Yes, sir. May I ask to do what?"

Himmler lowered his voice: "To watch Admiral Canaris ..."

"But sir, he is ..."

"I know who he is, Sturmbannführer. You watch him. Every step he takes, from now on. Cars, trains, even horses. He is partial to a canter around Wannsee at the weekend. He may be meeting someone. I want to know who, where, and when. You take no action, no matter what you see. You observe, you are a shadow."

"Yes, sir."

Himmler chuckled: "You haven't asked why, Sturmbannführer Krebbs? Or asked if the Führer approves of the surveillance of such a high-ranking officer. He is the Head of Intelligence, after all."

"It is not my business to question your instructions, sir. Or your authority. Merely to follow them as a humble servant of the Reich."

"Another good answer, Krebbs. I can see why you have risen through the ranks with such ease. You will do so more in the future. Obeying senior orders without question."

"Sir." Krebbs looked ahead avoiding eye contact.

Himmler poured some water into the second glass: "A drink, Sturmbannführer?"

A flicker of light from the cellar window briefly caught Himmler's steel-rimmed glasses and in that moment Krebbs realised he'd been trapped.

Manipulated.

The instruction to wear full uniform at the height of a humid

Berlin summer, the specific location and the implication of torture, the two-hour wait, the intense dehydration. Then the praise.

Krebbs shook his head; he could feel the sweat running down his spine: "No thank you, sir."

"Good," said Himmler, "this second glass contains finely powdered cyanide, just in case you had questioned my authority. And I would have hated to – lose you – at this late stage." As Krebbs was dismissed and left Himmler's office with a "Heil Hitler" salute, he had no idea if he was joking or not. Himmler watched the closing door and drank the second glassful with that twisted smile. Now he owned Krebbs.

Signal

Potsdam, Berlin, Germany.

BY JUNE 1943, ALISTAIR VALENTINE HAD SPENT more than six years living incognito at Chalet Monte Rosa, Zermatt. He had trained vigorously: climbing, hunting, swimming and skiing when possible. His skills were honed; he had been waiting patiently for the message from Manfred and Nexus; and confirmation from Brim. His transition from the mountains of Switzerland to Berlin at war had to be carefully orchestrated. Monika, as predicted by Manfred at the Olympics, had been a vital element.

Alistair could not have been 'blended' into that metamorphosis without the help of Nexus. Monika, from her office at Abwehr headquarters, had provided the identification papers he needed if he were ever challenged by the Gestapo or the SS. Stephan Beck existed and Alastair had the documents and ID photograph to support it. He had a work permit and history with Telefunken and domestic bills to substantiate any claim he might need: Beck had been married for two years and lived with his wife

Astrid at the house in Potsdam. There were no children and there was no plan to have any.

Monika also had 'sight' of Admiral Canaris's personal diary and his schedule of Kriegsmarine commitments. The June 1943 meeting at Obersalzberg was internally described as a conference. There was no mention of the presence of Hitler, Himmler, the Presidium, and certainly not the planned aerial assault on England. Das Schloss, as a plan, did not exist.

Canaris's genuine chauffeur had been watched by Manfred in Salzburg until the right opportunity arose. Then he was disposed of quickly and discreetly. Alistair slipped into the role of Canaris's chauffeur with meticulous planning so he could arrive at the Berghof at exactly the right time. But, on the day, neither Manfred nor Alistair noticed the tall blond man with the livid scar, camouflaged by undergrowth. Otto Krebbs – assault leader in the SS – would report everything he had seen back to Himmler.

Alistair returned to his house in Potsdam on the S-Bahn, feeling a sense of risk and danger, his two old demons. Astrid knew at once something was not right; the look on his face sometimes betrayed his innermost feelings. He kissed her on the cheek as a nephew might greet his favourite aunt and looked up at the ceiling:

"I have to go to the attic, Astrid. I have overheard something which I am sure is of paramount importance to British Intelligence."

"Do I need to alert my father?" she asked with a worried smile.

"Yes. Siebenthal's normal weather code. Public phone. I'll explain shortly."

Astrid smiled: "Of course."

Alistair went upstairs and released the attic trap door and a set of makeshift wooden steps dropped down. His heart was pounding like thunder and his mouth was dry, a sure sign of tension. The risk he was taking was chilling, because if he was caught, if the message was somehow intercepted and traced, the SS would torture and kill him, and Astrid. For her it would be worse. Yet the knife-edged danger thrilled him. It always did.

It was midnight in the UK, 12th June 1943.

He slipped on his earphones and tuned the radio to the agreed frequency. He tapped out the identification signal that would ensure the recipient knew it was genuine:

J – U – P – I - T - E – R

A few seconds later the radio operator at Biggin Hill responded:

P – R – O – C – E – E – D

He drew a breath and blinked his eyes tightly:

CODE RED ALERT ... RVR ... SCHLAFENDE SPIONE IN LONDON ... END

Now all he could do was wait. After ten seconds he turned off the equipment. The Code Red Alert indicated the level of emergency: red was the highest. The RVR was a Rendezvous Request – to send a courier – to meet him. Alistair was confident the four words of warning would have the desired effect: Sleeper Spies in London. Brim and British Intelligence would be swept into panic. The brevity of his words reflected their supreme urgency.

"It's done," he said as he saw Astrid in the hallway.

"And I have called Baden," she whispered and gave him a coquettish smile. She bit her bottom lip and wondered: was there any way in the world things could work out between them? The pretence of marriage, which was everything but physical, was for her, unbearable. Could he or would he see sense? Or was it the strain on both of them which made him so preoccupied and aloof all the time?

The look on her beautiful features said: 'I know you can't make love to me. But I really need the comfort and I crave some passion.'

Reading her expression, he thought: 'I'm desperately sorry, Astrid; sorry for you, but that is the last thing on my mind.'

Astrid smiled: "I know why we are here, Alistair. And what we have to do. I was thinking while you were out, about how it all started. Do you remember?"

Alistair took her hand. In his own way, he loved her: "Of course I do. Come on, let's have a drink. I think we deserve one, don't you?"

"Yes."

They went to the tiny kitchen and took cold beers from the

pantry. Astrid poured carefully. The beer frothed into the tall glasses her mother had given them as a 'wedding present.' They chinked the glasses and drank the foaming beer.

Alistair's face cracked into his charming smile, the blue-grey eyes regarded her: "What were you thinking about, Astrid? Tell me, I want to hear."

They sat in the tiny lounge; Alistair turned on the radio, the music was soft and unobtrusive. They always spoke German, as a pretence, even alone, at home. Their masquerade was perfect.

"Oh! Before I met you, back in '35. Then the Berlin Olympics. My father Manfred. When I first met you. You were so ..."

He grinned and sipped his beer: "I still am so ..."

Sally

Bayswater, London, England.

SALLY BROOKE LAY NAKED under a single sheet on the bed. The hotel in Bayswater had few luxuries, but staff asked no questions of Freddie and Sally, indeed of any customer. War had changed the moral compass of London. Their plain but clean bedroom was swathed in shafts of morning sunlight, despite flimsy curtains tightly drawn.

Freddie combed his hair and glanced at the scratched mirror on the dressing table. In the reflection, he couldn't take his eyes off Sally. She looked relaxed in bed, appeared carefree, seductive and happy. He was wearing grey suit trousers and a white pressed shirt, cufflinks engraved with the image of a Spitfire. They were a gift from Squadron Leader David Squires, and made from metal salvaged from Freddie's crashed Tiger Moth. Squires had a warped sense of humour.

"Where did I put my tie?" Freddie said, almost to himself.

Sally reached for a cup from a tray on a bedside table. Despite the drabness of the hotel, room service had delivered tea, boiled eggs and toast, the "Honeymoon Breakfast," as the Night Porter had caustically described it. His furtive glance at the third finger on Sally's left hand produced a knowing look which Freddie had chosen to ignore.

"What time is it, Freddie?" Sally asked sleepily. Her freckled and lightly flushed face dissolved into a mischievous smile as she watched him dress. Something is on her mind, he thought to himself. What can it be?

"Oh, eight-ish," He replied, looking around the cramped room. On an old ottoman lay her silk underwear and skirt. And his tie. Oh yes, he remembered with a grin. It had all happened quite quickly yesterday: a torrent of passion.

"Too early." She reached out, looking gorgeous in the early morning light. Her face captivating and sensual, her golden hair dishevelled. The single cotton sheet slipped down her body as she stretched, revealing her firm, pale skin as she clasped the cup handle and sipped her tea. She quickly covered herself and giggled: the shyness of the morning after.

Freddie's eye caught her modesty in the mirror, and it amused him too; they were fully in tune with one another. Theirs was a comforting, relaxed love. He wandered over and kissed her gently on the lips; she nearly spilt her tea.

"Too late to be bashful," he said quietly, "I know every inch of you."

She kissed him back, a quick, cheeky peck. "And I of you, Mr. Valentine. Those bed baths at East Grinstead were an inspiration. You ask Nurse Lucy Fry. She's in love with you too!"

He laughed, picked up his tie and turned back to the mirror, still not taking his eyes off her. The sheet had slipped down again, but she didn't notice this time. Unless she didn't care. There was a companionable silence between them, a closeness.

"What do you do, Freddie?" she asked suddenly. There was an emphasis on the word do. And a mischievous look in her eyes.

"Do?" Freddie appeared to struggle with his tie.

"You're not in the RAF anymore, after your plane crash. And yet you always seem to be busy. Dashing off here and there." Sally was apparently fishing, her eyes sparkled.

"Ministry of Defence," he replied quickly and unconvincingly, "I thought I told you?"

She sipped her tea: "No. You didn't."

"Oh?"

"Do you all carry guns?" she asked him slowly, cautiously, "I unpacked your case yesterday evening, when you were in the bath. Remember?"

Freddie pulled his tie too tight and it looked misshapen.

"Let me do it," she climbed out of bed, slipped on her gown and padded over to him barefoot. He was still facing the mirror. "You'll have to hunker down a wee bit, Freddie. I'm only little."

She came up behind him and unknotted his tangled tie. They eyed each other in the mirror. She re-tied it perfectly and tapped it, as a mother might do to her son before school.

"There. You're a mystery, Mr. Valentine."

He turned and looked her in the eyes. They still shone with coquettish affection. A love, of sorts. He wrapped his arms around her slender body.

"And I shall have to remain one, I'm afraid, Nurse Brooke."

He kissed her again, turned and put his jacket on.

Sally returned to the bed, took off her dressing gown and sat naked, cross-legged on top of it. No sign of modesty now: "Do you have to go?" Her voice – everything about her - was loaded with sexual promise.

"Only for an hour or so. Baker Street."

"221b?" She flicked a strand of golden hair over her shoulder and her smile was at once delicious and tempting.

"Eat your toast," he said, blowing her a kiss, "and don't get dressed."

*

One day Sally would have to reveal that it was she who had recommended Freddie to Brim in the first place. They were second cousins; Brim's father had been a well-known physician in Edinburgh and was related to Sally's mother. At a Christmas Eve family function, two years earlier, Brim had taken Sally to one side: 'Keep an eye out for suitable candidates, Sally. We're always on the look out for good people. Men and women.'

Sally had been startled at the request: 'At a hospital, Brim? Our patients are wounded; some gravely.'

Brim's reply had been decisive: 'Yes, but they will heal. And if they can't fly a Spitfire or operate a tank, there are always certain other roles. British Intelligence need resourceful, loyal people.'

Sally had sipped her single malt: 'I'll give it some thought. There is one fellow, quite a charmer. A wounded Spitfire ace called Freddie Valentine.'

'You have my number.' Brim had said, 'He sounds

interesting.'

Shock

St. James's, London, England.

AND THAT IS EXACTLY what happened. Less than six months after Freddie's Tiger Moth biplane ditched in the Fens, Brim was driven down to the Royal Victoria Hospital, East Grinstead. Their meeting happened by chance. Brim was allegedly meeting another patient and had popped into the 'Guinea Pig' public house for lunch. Over a few drinks at the bar, he and Freddie had got talking, initially about the RAF, his accident, his prosthetic, his life. Freddie told Brim about his upbringing, education and life in Zermatt at Monte Rosa. Alistair was mentioned but Brim deliberately did not want to develop that discussion. Brim was impressed with Freddie's language skills – not quite on a par with his brother – but fluent in German and French. They moved to a quiet booth at the back of the pub and the waitress took their order for sandwiches.

'What will you do,' Brim asked, 'when you get your new leg?'

After a few minutes, the waitress delivered their sandwiches and another round of drinks: bottled beer for Brim and a double scotch and water for Freddie. He was in an effusive mood; pleased to be away from the hospital and keen to talk about matters non-medical.

'Oh, I don't know,' Freddie had mused, 'Squadron Leader Squires at RAF Northolt assured me there were training positions for wounded airmen. Navigation and so on."

'What happened? Shot down by Jerry?'

'No.'

Sally had told Brim the story of course. That fateful day back in September 1941. The Tiger Moth over England. The erratic de Havilland DH82. The crash. But Brimblecombe let Freddie relate his tale of woe anyway. It was cathartic and the double scotch was a rare treat. Just before closing time Brim had said:

'Can't see you teaching, old sport. You are a fighter pilot who was unfortunate. Skills like yours are rare.'

Freddie was a little bemused: 'Well, there are quite a few of us in the same boat.'

Brim handed him a business card which Freddie read with interest: 'Professor Nicholas Brimblecombe, with an address in Whitehall. What do you actually do, Professor?'

Brim had stood and said: 'Give me a ring on that number. And I'll tell you.'

*

It was now eighteen months or so later, a lunchtime in June 1943. Freddie had been trained by the best of British Intelligence. For obvious reasons this did not include Sgian Dubh, the MI Commando Training School in Scotland Alistair had to endure.

But it did include a month at a facility at Beaulieu in Hampshire, one of the Group B finishing schools. Here he was educated in fieldcraft: ciphers and codes, the elements of spying and surveillance, sabotage, weapons handling, lock picking and survival. By the end of the training, Brim received a missive from one of the instructors Captain David McCullum:

'Valentine (Frederick.) 100%:
outstanding and resourceful.'

*

Brim walked into Freddie's makeshift office that day with a self-assurance that implied he owned the place. As the PM's spymaster, he had unrestricted access to all areas of St. James's and Whitehall. Without greeting, he perched himself on the edge of Freddie's cluttered desk, idly picking up a map of occupied Europe.

"You have a brother somewhere in Europe, do you not?" Brim said with a bright smile.

"Alistair, yes," replied Freddie cautiously.

Brim raised his eyebrows: "Tell me about him." He folded the map and put it back on the desk.

"I don't really know much of late to be honest; what with my accident ... and the war, of course."

"Then what do you know?" asked Brim innocently, brushing an imaginary fleck of dust from his pinstripe suit trouser.

"Well, I think he went to Europe in – what – thirty-six, to learn about wine. I gather the Board of Trade paid for half of his mission and his firm paid the rest. The last I heard he was going to Germany, to the Berlin Olympics. Nothing since; I suspect he's been in Switzerland for at least some of the time."

Brim snorted: "Board of Trade, eh? That's very inventive. And that's the last you heard of him – seven years ago?" Brim, of course, knew this.

A flicker of concern crossed Freddie's face, by the choice of the past tense.

Freddie hesitated: "Yes, I'm afraid so. But we were never that close as children, or adults for that matter." He remembered their last meeting at Waterloo station and the acrimony of an alcohol-fuelled misunderstanding.

Brim sensed dangerous territory but proceeded nonetheless: "He married, didn't he? A German girl from Baden? Astrid Lochar?"

Now Freddie was concerned. This was news to him.

He waited a moment: "You seem to know more about my brother than I do."

"Oh, no doubt I do."

Brim stood up from the edge of the desk and walked over to the stone hearth. He opened a battered silver cigarette case, took out a Senior Service and lit it. He looked at Freddie through a haze of smoke.

"Is he – is Alistair all right?" Freddie looked at Brim. Rays of sunlight beamed in through the window and pierced the clouds of tobacco smoke.

"Last we heard, yes."

"And when was that?"

"Oh, seventy-two hours ago, give or take," said Brim dismissively.

Freddie was shocked at this and made to stand up. Brim firmly gestured him to remain where he was. He pursed his lips and shook his head; it was a curiously feminine gesture, at odds with his distinguished, though portly appearance.

"What's this about, Professor?" asked Freddie, his voice slightly raised; bordering on disrespect. He was irked his boss knew more about his family, in particular his brother's marriage, than he did.

Brim picked up on this nuance but chose to ignore it. He knew the facts. He continued.

"Your brother's fluency in German is remarkable," he said with genuine admiration, "and mine is fairly good. So is yours, of course. You were raised with the language and variations of it."

"In Switzerland, yes, and our mother ..."

"Yes, I know, I know," cut in Brim, "I know the story. Your patriotism is unquestioned if that's what you were about to say."

"I wasn't."

"Good. Your upbringing in Switzerland helped Alistair evolve into an exceptional linguist. His German is refined and he both understands and can mimic regional dialects."

"Why are you telling me this? What's this about?" Freddie repeated, almost pleading. Brim took a moment.

"Because, like you, Alistair works for us."

This time, Freddie, despite his disability, was out of his chair, knocking it over clumsily. He steadied himself against the desk, flushed with emotion. "What?" This time he shouted, unable to control his utter disbelief.

Brim merely chuckled and flashed him his most winning smile. It was an expression that had won over diplomats, soldiers and politicians.

"Yes, Freddie. Your brother is a British agent working right under the noses of the bloody Germans. He's Admiral Canaris's chauffeur."

He slapped his hand across his side and looked very satisfied.

Freddie was shocked. He'd been manipulated and outmanoeuvred. Or at least, that's how it felt. How long had Alistair been working for Brim? Since when? How? A myriad of questions about Alistair and his relationship with Brim and the Service crossed his mind.

"Come on. Grab your coat and I'll buy us some lunch. There's still a restaurant in Pall Mall that hasn't been bombed. I'll tell you all about it."

Mission

Dégustation restaurant, Pall Mall, London, England.

BRIM SAID TO FREDDIE: "Have some more of this rather agreeable claret," he poured carefully, gripping the neck of the bottle with a napkin, "not a bad drop, eh?" To find any red Bordeaux in wartime London was a rare luxury; to enjoy opulent, sensuous, 1929 Château Léoville-Barton, astonishing.

They both sat on Irish mahogany side chairs in a dining room beneath Pall Mall, where, rationing and food shortages allowing, French chef Xavier could always conjure up something highly edible. The pompously named Dégustation restaurant was never a disappointment to the few who knew about it.

Today was no exception: a slow-cooked rabbit stew with crisp vegetables and herb-filled dumplings; small portions but far more than most Londoners could get their hands on. It should have been a singular treat, but the many questions Freddie had about Alistair diminished his appetite.

One in particular lingered in Freddie's mind: 'Why was he

really here and what did Brim have in store for him? The facts he had learned in the past hour had shocked him.'

"Yes, thank you," said Freddie, watching Brim's furrowed brow as he poured the wine. He waited.

Suddenly Brim became serious: "Seventy-two hours ago, we received a code red alert, a really crucial one, so it appears now ..." He paused for a moment ...

"At first we thought it was a bunch of Abwehr jesters playing silly buggers. But now we don't think so. They don't have the codes and have got nowhere near cracking these signals."

"How can you be so sure?" asked Freddie.

"Oh, we have a pretty fail-safe way of checking," Brim replied. "You know those missives that appear every day in the PM's war rooms?"

"Yes, I am aware of them. But a code red alert? That's a new one on me."

"This one was from 'Jupiter' – your brother. Sent from Potsdam, a suburb of Berlin. An RVR."

"My God. How?"

"Army signals at Biggin Hill monitor a certain radio frequency at midnight, every night, to listen. It's just one of many radio routes we use," Brim explained.

"Short blasts of coded Morse." he continued. "The crib is changed every week as are all codes and cyphers. Without the crib, the cypher is meaningless."

Freddie frowned: "I find it impossible to imagine Alistair hiding somewhere with a ..."

But Brim cut him off, deadly serious: "He's onto something,

Freddie. Something big. Something so big – significant – he cannot risk a full coded transmission in any more detail or length. The nature of the words he used, he was incredibly careful ... the Abwehr have ears and eyes everywhere. We hadn't heard from Alistair for a long time."

"I see."

"He must have evidence of something vital. But he cannot tell us exactly what, that much is clear."

Freddie sipped some wine, broke off a tiny piece of stilton and popped it into his mouth. The bread was stale, but at least it was crusty. And warm.

"You mean some kind of attack?"

"We're not sure. Britain is well prepared with troops, field guns and artillery for most orthodox attacks. My God! Have you been in Hyde Park recently? It's like a battlefield. And positively hazardous at night. Ask any members of the team."

Freddie nodded.

"Jupiter – Alistair, that is – used several significant words, seconds apart; on the same frequency: 'Schlafende Spione in London.' Any ideas?"

Freddie was immediately alarmed: "Sleeper spies in London I would say was a good enough translation."

Brim lowered his voice: "Exactly. Our best guess is that it's an undercover German unit, obviously based here in London, spies waiting to be activated on command from Berlin. The Abwehr. It would be typical of Canaris's duplicity and cunning".

Freddie considered the concept: "Covert spies living in deep cover in London. Here. They would have to be bloody convincing.

And consistent."Freddie looked over his shoulder at the other diners, sharing Brim's caution, "Who on earth could they be? And where?"

"We don't know. That's just it. No idea at all. Brother and sister; husband and wife. We've got everybody working on it. As you say, credible people who seem part of the furniture ... invisible, if you want to be dramatic. Unseen."

Brim sighed deeply and shook his head. Freddie knew Brim hated the unknown or unknowable.

"But why are they here? To do what?" asked Freddie.

Brim drank a generous mouthful of claret, swilled it around in his mouth and closed his eyes for a few seconds, savouring the flavours. He took out his distinctive silver cigarette case and lit non-tipped Senior Service with his Ronson.

"The list of possibilities is endless," he said through a plume of exhaled smoke. "Sabotage is the obvious motive, to bomb army bases, aircraft factories, ports and military facilities. And do not forget Parliament, Downing Street and countless other government buildings. Even Buckingham Palace. Destroy or damage any of these landmarks and the Nazis will milk it. A dream come true for Goebbels as Reichsminister for Propaganda. He might even be behind the sleeper cell. Your brother took some incredible footage at the '36 Olympics. All Hitler's top brass were there on show. We have it on file, you must see it, Freddie."

Freddie suddenly felt incredibly proud of Alistair; he had no idea he had carried out such an assignment. But all he could manage was: "I see."

"Expanding on that idea of propaganda, I believe someone in

Germany has come up with a plan which Hitler believes will win him the war. And I am convinced new science and technology might be at its core. Alistair, I am also convinced, has somehow learned what these plans are. That is the crucial significance of the code-red alert RVR. He wouldn't go to the trouble – and enormous risk – to alert us without a damn good reason."

"Schlafende Spione in London .... could they be words Alistair accidentally overheard?" Freddie speculated out loud.

"Possibly."

"I mean why not say: I believe there are?"

Brim cut him off: "Too many words, don't you see? The crucial message is four words. And every word is vital. No flab. Anything else would be conjecture. But you are right in your line of thinking; a conversation overheard is a possibility."

"And RVR means what exactly?"

"Rendezvous request. It means Alistair wants to meet a courier to give him something significant and bring it back here. What if it is something he has discovered? To do with this plan I spoke of?" Brim let his words sink in.

Freddie swallowed deeply and eyed Brim: "You mean me, don't you?"

Brim said simply: "The obvious choice. Our contact's brother. The fact you look quite similar might be an advantage. Who knows?"

Freddie almost laughed. In fact, later he would not remember if he had laughed or not. But he remembered his utter incredulity.

"But I'm pensioned off! Wounded. A desk Johnny. My

goodness, you organised it, Professor, you were the one ..."

Brim needed to nip this in the bud: "You're only pensioned off from flying fighters, Freddie ... nothing else ..."

Brim allowed his words to trail off unfinished. The silence gave Freddie time to realise there was plenty he could do, even if not in the cockpit of a Spitfire.

"What exactly do you have in mind?" asked Freddie. He was being manipulated and it was only then that it dawned on him.

"You have Swiss papers, do you not?"

"You know I do."

Brim enthused – but not too much: "We can get you into Basle within twenty-four hours. Less. You could then travel up into Germany and meet Alistair ... Freiburg, Stuttgart, Karlsruhe ... a rendezvous somewhere."

"Germany! Are you stark raving mad?"

"No." Brim patted his mouth with a starched napkin, one of the few concessions to civilised life before the war. Claret and starched napkins; bliss!

Brim looked at Freddie, he had to get commitment: "We can get you the perfect cover as a commercial traveller. Your late mother's family are all in Switzerland and the Valle D'Aosta. You have relatives there, connections, a safe haven if need be."

"What about my leg?"

"A disability might just work to your advantage."

"Oh! You mean if I was captured by the bloody SS?"

"Well, yes, if it came to that."

Freddie's tone was loaded with sarcasm: "And how do I explain to my captors that I sustained my injury through a flying accident?"

Brim smiled. He and his team at British Intelligence had anticipated all these questions when they'd had their emergency meeting in the Situation Room forty-eight hours earlier.

"You don't. You say it was skiing ... what was his name ... Herr Seiler, your mentor? Or a climbing accident on the Eiger or Matterhorn. Frostbite perhaps?"

"You have this all worked out," said Freddie angrily, "don't you? You and your cronies?"

"Yes, me and my cronies. And you're one of them, Freddie. Perhaps the most important crony of all ...

Put it this way, we have contacted an artificial limb manufacturer in Basle – Siebenthal – they are making you a device to fit your personal specification as we speak. A replica of the one you are wearing. All Swiss components and a surface which will appear aged enough to look worn and weathered. Swiss-made clothes, of course ... he is your contact and a good friend to us. You can trust him completely."

"And if I don't agree to do this?" cut in Freddie sharply.

Brim signalled to the waiter for the bill.

"Then your brother's secret will never leave Germany; and if he is caught trying to re-transmit another code red, in more detail, then neither will he."

It was blackmailing, plain and simple; but sometimes such a threat was the only option.

The waiter appeared; Brim placed a banknote onto the proffered silver tray without even looking at the bill. Like everything in the Professor's life, he had already anticipated the amount and calculated a margin for the discreet service. Who knows, he was probably one of Brim's anyway.

"Keep the change," said Brim, his eyes fixed on Freddie.

"Then I have no choice, do I? I am personally and morally bound."

"He's your brother, Alfred, whatever you think of him. The choice is entirely yours. It's just inconvenient – for you – that you are the best, possibly only, person who could pull this assignment off; to solve this damn mystery."

Freddie closed his eyes and sighed. Flattery always worked and Brim was a master of the art.

"And as I said earlier, your patriotism, your loyalty to the Crown has never been questioned. Or your brother's." Brim stood up and brushed some crumbs from his immaculate suit; he gave Freddie a warm smile. He'd got exactly what he wanted.

Freddie would later remember the significance of those words – on a dark foreign train somewhere – and the fact that Brim had never addressed him as "Alfred" before. And probably never would again; what did he mean by whatever you think of him? What did he know about that argument they'd had at Waterloo that night back in thirty-five?

Journey

Chalet Monte Rosa, Zermatt, Switzerland.

"HOW DO YOU INTEND TO CONTACT ALISTAIR?"

Herr Seiler was a big bear of a man, seventy years old, with a mop of thick, unruly, grey hair. His deeply lined face looked like polished brown leather, aged by years of snow and sun. His exposed forearms were thick and muscular, as was the rest of him, from sixty years of farming, of climbing and of skiing.

"Another small one?" asked Herr Seiler.

His grey eyes were fixed on Freddie as he poured yet another shot of schnapps for both of them. He downed it in one and chased it with a foaming Swiss beer. He'd always seemed immune to such brutal alcohol. Perhaps it was all the years of practice? And never a hangover, he often boasted.

Freddie's mother, Christina, had often retorted: 'No, that's because you're never completely sober.'

They were sitting in the spacious ground floor area of Chalet Monte Rosa. The chalet was a rambling old haunt on the outskirts of Zermatt, familiar to many friends and visitors: always welcoming. It had originally been built for farming and, like Seiler himself, solid and practical. A huge wood burner dominated one side of the chalet to keep him and the animals next door warm in winter.

"I have a German telephone number and a list of call times," said Freddie, weary from travelling, "plus this contraption."

Freddie lifted an attaché case from the floor and opened it to reveal a 3MK11 receiver and transmitter known as the B2 radio set. It came with a headset and a heavy auxiliary battery with an uncertain shelf life. It had been issued two days before by FCO/MI6 Signals Intelligence, otherwise called Poundon Hill, a secret facility in the heart of rural Buckinghamshire.

"The damn thing weighs a ton and if I get caught with it ..." Freddie sipped his beer and his mind flashed back:

The journey to Switzerland had been long, tedious and dangerous. A single-engine Westland Lysander had flown him from an airfield in Newmarket over the English Channel to France; low, in darkness and over the Occupied Zone. It was fast and bumpy with occasional tracer fire from enemy anti-aircraft guns barely a thousand feet below them. They had landed near the city of Lyon on a grass airfield illuminated by makeshift lanterns. Here he had been met by members of local French Resistance - a surly bunch of rogues – who clearly didn't want to be there. They escorted him to Chambéry where he spent an uncomfortable night in a barn with only hens for company. On the journey, none of them had asked him any questions. Nobody wanted answers. He was a loner, an inconvenience whose existence meant only one thing – trouble – and risk of exposure to the enemy.

The following morning, stiff and ravenous, he had travelled by train up to Annecy and then Geneva, a safe haven. But even at Aix-les-Bains railway station, he had been questioned by curious uniformed railway officials. Despite his Swiss documents, the simple question they might have asked him was how did he get there? Fortunately, they did not. Given Swiss neutrality and his evident disability, he wasn't considered a threat.

Freddie had given no warning of his imminent arrival at Chalet Monte Rosa; he simply arrived at Zermatt railway station and took a pony and trap up to the chalet. It was early evening, and the sun was setting behind the Matterhorn; a herd of cows were being led by a farm boy through the village, their cowbells jangling noisily. As he approached the village, Freddie saw the Matterhorn for the first time in more than three years. His mind was filled with memories of climbing and skiing with Alistair and Herr Seiler.

The village was busy with visitors; stout-looking fellows in Lederhosen, some carrying coils of rope, crampons and ice axes; it might be summer in the village, but it was winter up in the mountains. Herr Seiler had been standing outside an inn with a group of other local farmers, drinking beer from a metal tankard. If he had been surprised to see Freddie, he showed no sign of it, merely giving him a bear hug when he stepped down from the trap.

"So, don't get caught with it," said Herr Seiler later at the chalet, looking at the Army radio transmitter, "let me carry it."

"What?"

"I mean, I'll come with you to Germany to meet Alistair."

Freddie sank his schnapps and his beer: "God! For one moment then, I thought you were serious."

Seiler re-filled their shot glasses: "I am serious, Freddie, never more so."

Siebenthal

Basle, Switzerland

THEY FOUND HELMUT SIEBENTHAL'S SHOP on Streitgasse in the centre of Basle near the towering Minster. It was a narrow street of half-timbered Saxon-style buildings which seemed to lean in on either side.

It was just approaching eight o'clock in the evening and almost dark. Herr Seiler winked at Freddie when his back was turned; for Siebenthal was the epitome of the mad professor – short and squat – with a balding head and half-moon spectacles.

The shop's shelves held an array of prosthetics – arms, legs, feet, even glass eyes and wigs. He gave them both a wary look as he admitted them and led them through to a back room and a cluttered workshop bathed in bright light. Here there was everything from skis and climbing gear to radio transmitters and miniature cameras. A disassembled shot gun lay on a work bench, shiny with gun oil and spare rounds. There was an assortment of detonators, timers, limpet mines, even a couple of grenades.

"So how is my friend Nicholas – Brim?" asked Siebenthal, his hands plunged into the pockets of his white doctor's-style coat. He eyed them both carefully.

"You know the Professor - Brim?" asked Freddie, mildly alarmed at the use of his nickname.

"Everybody in the Intelligence world knows him," said Siebenthal, knowing he had trampled on hallowed ground. He smiled to show he was not being disrespectful.

"And are you," enquired Herr Seiler warily, "in the Intelligence world?"

"Yes, I most certainly am," said Siebenthal smugly, "And I can observe by the shape of your attaché case that you are carrying a B2 radio set, not just a pair of pyjamas and a toothbrush!"

Freddie looked at Herr Seiler, alarmed.

"Besides," he continued, "I was led to believe that there would only be one of you. Code named Taurus. Why you have these pointless astrological code names is a mystery to me."

"Maybe that's true, but ..."

"I have arranged transport for you from here in Basle up to Eschau on the Canal du Rhône au Rhin. The two bargemen are Nexus. At Eschau you will travel by road to Illkirch-Graffenstaden, in France. A hotel has been booked for you in the name of Jacques Duval."

"By road from Eschau. How will we do that?"

Siebenthal's eyes sparkled: "All will be revealed in time. Do not worry about the details, every aspect has been considered. Even though there are two of you. Now which – "

"Why a barge?" asked Freddie, interrupting.

"A journey by water carries a low risk. We know the German governors let the French Ministry of Transport and local waterway engineers run business as more or less as usual. But you must stick to the plan Nexus has devised. Clear?"

"Clear," said Freddie.

"Good. Now which of you needs the prosthetic?" Siebenthal switched suddenly to perfect English.

Herr Seiler gave Freddie another look, which Siebenthal did not miss.

"This, of course, is my sense of humour," Siebenthal chuckled in a very Germanic way. "I was watching the whole of Ehrlich Strasse from my attic window since seven-thirty. Your appointment was scheduled for eight, so I saw you arrive. I can tell by your – now what is that curious English word? – like a door?"

"Gait?"

"Ah yes, gait ... so, there are two of you? Related?"

Freddie said no and Herr Seiler said yes. These opposing replies might have confused Siebenthal, but if they did, he chose not to comment on them. For this was his way; he moved quickly on:

"So please come and sit down and I will replace the prosthetic you are wearing with a Swiss-made product."

"Here?" said Freddie.

"Yes, sit here."

"No, I mean, the prosthetic was made here?"

"Ja! Of course. By me. Who else? Your measurements, your height and weight were sent by telegram from the Royal Victoria

Hospital. I assume therefore you are a pilot?"

"I was, yes."

"I - I am sorry – you were a pilot – yes. Shot down?"

"No, I crashed a biplane. Lost control. I don't know why or how it happened. But I was rescued, just in time."

"Gott im Himmel!" exclaimed Siebenthal with a gasp.

"An accident plain and simple," said Freddie.

"So now you have a new job?"

"Yes," said Freddie, "so it seems."

There was a moment of awkward silence. Siebenthal re-composed himself: "So now I will fit the new device ... if you would care to remove the, ah, old one please?"

Freddie sat down and did as he was bidden.

"A drink perhaps, before I commence. Tea or some coffee?" asked Siebenthal out of politeness.

"Do you have any wine or beer?" asked Herr Seiler hopefully.

"No!" barked the old man, "What do you think this is – die Kneipe auf dem Marktplatz?"

"Es tut mir Leid" said Herr Seiler humbly, "I'm sorry."

"Entschuldigen Sie, bitte," replied Siebenthal, apologising for the overreaction and getting to work. He reached for the prosthetic and showed it to them proudly. "I hope one of you can ride a motorbike ..." His words trailed off. Next came the instructions, crucial to their mission.

Update

58 St. James's Street, London, England.

WINSTON CHURCHILL FROWNED; it was an expression of exasperation they all recognised:

"The point is clear. We still don't know what this bloody code red RVR is all about." Churchill's deep, croaky voice echoed in the sparsely furnished room at MI5 headquarters. "We got it a week ago," he growled, "and we still appear to know nothing. What the devil is going on?"

The office at 58 St. James's Street in the heart of London was the hub of MI5, a warren full of spies tasked with counterintelligence. Sitting in the office of Director-General Brigadier Sir Cyril Downing were the Prime Minister and Professor Nicholas Brimblecombe, there to assuage the PM's rising anger and look after MI6 interests.

This meeting was a first. Churchill had never appeared at one before. It was late evening, dark save for a desk lamp, the air thick with ubiquitous tobacco smoke.

"What news from Basle, Brim?" asked Churchill. He was

smoking a Cuban cigar and nursed a tumbler of whisky, his expression grim.

The professor responded with a measured tone. "We know the younger Valentine made contact with Helmut Siebenthal and has departed from Basle on a canal barge, as planned."

"Yet you look concerned," said Downing with clipped diction.

Brim tapped and lit another Senior Service: "Freddie was with a man called Seiler."

"A threat?" asked Churchill, mildly alarmed.

"More an inconvenience."

"Who is he?" asked Downing.

"Family friend from Switzerland; he owns the chalet the brothers grew up in," said Brim. "Seiler is surrogate father to both the brothers."

"Does this matter to us?" fired Churchill abruptly.

Brim: "No, it doesn't," he was emphatic. "We didn't brief you because we didn't know he would tag along ... I've been deliberately ambiguous about which brother carries out which task. Freddie's prosthetic contains a hidden compartment, ideal for a courier ..." Brim paused to see he was clearly understood ...

"Alistair will have to hang on to the belief he may be returning to England shortly. That's the position."

"So, you're juggling, eh? Exactly how long since you got the Jupiter code red?" asked Downing.

"A week, just on."

"And they still haven't met?" enquired Churchill. "So, we don't know what the code red is, why he wants a rendezvous, who these sleeper spies are and if they really exist?"

"No, Prime Minister, we don't," admitted Brim.

"This is intolerable, Brim," said Downing pompously, "quite intolerable."

"I know, but whatever it is, Jupiter can't risk sending another signal. He believes Jerry will intercept it and kill him."

"So we know nothing, in point of fact," said Churchill finishing his drink, "we're in the dark. How good is Jupiter's cover? Will it bear scrutiny?"

"Stephan Beck exists on paper," Brim explained. "Nexus furnished Alistair with a credible identity and relevant paperwork. Stephan is 'married' to Astrid Lochar - now Beck - from Baden. They live in Potsdam. His brief was to gather intelligence, nothing more. How he does it is his concern. So yes, his cover will bear scrutiny."

"Does this wife – Astrid – know Alistair is a British spy?" asked Churchill.

"Yes, Prime Minister, she has to know," Brim continued. "Siebenthal and her father, Manfred Lochar, run Nexus from the shop in Basle."

Downing offered the decanter of whisky to his assembled guests; all declined.

"Thank you, but no," said Churchill rising to his feet. "I have to go to the American Embassy. Please keep me posted. I want to hear everything about this threat - whatever it is – the moment you know. Understood?"

"Of course, sir," said Brim.

"And I don't want the Americans getting wind of this. Nothing must get in the way of our other plans, unless of course, it concerns our other plans. This is absolutely top secret."

They nodded assent and were on their feet as the PM left the room.

Downing looked across at Brim: "I hope you know what you're doing, Brim."

"What do you mean?" Brim's voice was raised.

"That your man is not crying wolf."

"I have no way of knowing. We have procedures and they must be followed. If one of my agents sends a signal like that, I must respond."

"Was sending his, ah, shall we say incapacitated brother over there a bright idea?"

Brim stubbed out his cigarette and downed his drink: "There was no other option."

"How so?" asked Downing. There was an undertone of sarcasm in the question.

"If Alistair has somehow infiltrated himself into the Reich – which I believe he has – he can't suddenly disappear, can he? But if Freddie can replace him – even for twenty-four hours – it might buy Alistair enough time to get back here and report. Possibly with some concrete evidence of an enemy plan."

Brim puffed out his cheeks and considered the risky plan in his mind and then continued: "No. It depends entirely upon which way I decide to play it. In other words, which brother does what."

"Are they that similar in appearance, to fool people they have already met?"

"Similar, yes. But vastly different characters," said Brim. He rose from his chair, "Freddie's impersonation of his brother is my least favourite option, I have to say."

"So, Alistair doesn't know he might not come back – in spite of everything?" Downing's tone was scornful.

"Alistair doesn't know a lot of things; particularly not that. He wouldn't have gone there in the first place," Brim said firmly.

"You're a ruthless bastard, Professor" said Cyril Downing.

"So are you, Brigadier, you have to be. We all have to be. The Nazis are too. That's what makes it interesting. In the balance of power, it's who has the greatest resolve and ingenuity that will determine the outcome of this mission ... and the war. Good evening."

Brim picked up his hat and coat and left the room. He wondered what Ann his housekeeper was up to tonight. She had been most entertaining the last night he'd spent with her.

And she definitely knew there was a war on.

Canal

Canal du Rhône au Rhin, France.

HELMUT SIEBENTHAL WAS A METICULOUS planner. He had rented Freddie and Herr Seiler a working canal barge. It came with a crew of two – Nexus agents – and a motorbike and side car. From Basle the barge would join the Canal du Rhône au Rhin and travel north in the direction of Strasbourg.

After Mulhouse, where they took on supplies of food and wine, they chugged their way north through Neuf-Brisach – past the medieval fortress and up to Markolsheim - though still in France, they were a stone's throw from the German border. Before they had left Basle, Siebenthal had instructed the crew to moor up just after nightfall. No one was certain if German troops continually watched the border area. However, they knew to be aware of sporadic foot patrols.

A barge travelling at night might look suspicious. It was fairly light and visibility on both sides of the canal was good. Siebenthal's men took watch – in three-hour shifts – throughout the first night as a precaution. They were too near Germany to take unnecessary risks.

The following day, the canal barge made its way further north again, up to Erstein, with its fabulous mountain scenery. Freddie and Herr Seiler sat at the stern and reminisced. For a few moments, Freddie almost forgot why he was there. He sat back and closed his eyes, listening to the rustle of trees overhanging the canal. Herr Seiler was familiar company and spoke in animated terms about their times together in Zermatt. That night, after a half bottle of the "Bon Père" eau-de-vie and too many beers, he put his arm around Freddie and looked him in the eye.

"Your dear mother and I were more than just friends you know, Freddie," he confessed, his words slurred and his eyes glassy.

"I believe I knew that, Herr Seiler."

"You did? I am shocked."

"I often wondered why you put Alistair and me up in that attic room at Monte Rosa, away from the rest of the household."

Herr Seiler wiped a tear from his eye: "I miss her so desperately. I've never told anyone else this before."

Freddie had never seen him display such emotion and wondered if he was in good health. He seemed a little frailer than he remembered, he'd lost weight and was often coughing. And he was drinking more than he ever used to. If that were possible.

"We miss her too. I would never discuss such a matter with Alistair, it would cause an argument."

"He is not as ... sensitive ... as you, but he took it badly. You know."

"Yes, I believe he did."

Freddie thought of the drunken row at Waterloo station all those years ago. He bit his lip; he should never have said those words he did about their mother, Christina. Would Alistair ever really forgive him? Would the war and the mission they now both shared dull his memory?

*

At Eschau the barge crew unloaded and assembled the motorbike and side car Siebenthal had given them in Basle. He had briefed Freddie and Herr Seiler with the salient details:

'I hope one of you can ride a motorbike ... this NSU HK101 Kettenrad is a half-track machine. The solid front wheel has increased strength for weight, both off-road and on-road. The bike is registered to Manfred, with German number plates. All valid. His address in Baden and all the documents are under the seat. Be careful with the bike, it's his pride and joy.'

Herr Seiler clung onto the handlebars and they sped away from Eschau in a cloud of dust and exhaust. Freddie sat in the sidecar with a battered European Michelin and the B2 radio set in the footwell. They soon found the road to Illkirch-Graffenstaden and the Hotel Dollenberg more or less in the centre of it. It was more a guest house than a hotel, but comfortable and clean. Herr Seiler insisted on parking the motorbike a few streets away. He was always cautious, always thinking two steps ahead.

After a delicious dinner of duck cooked with a piquant orange sauce and potatoes, Herr Seiler and Freddie sat in the small sitting room, each nursing a cognac. At midnight Freddie sent his first radio signal and had a swift reply. It instructed him to telephone a number in Baden-Baden, and he would be told where and how to meet his next contact.

The cypher had been carefully worded by Brim's contacts at Poundon. The words and numbers of the cypher would be meaningless to the uninitiated. What they represented, however, was crucial. Freddie could risk such a signal as he was continually moving.

Freddie would later realise that it was the telephone number of Astrid Lochar's parents in Baden-Baden, the owners of the motorbike. Manfred and Ingrid Lochar, together with Helmut Siebenthal, were key members of Nexus. He would also realise how complex Brim's network of contacts was. He walked along the narrow corridor of the old hotel and tapped on Herr Seiler's door to tell him he'd sent the signal and received his instructions. No response. Freddie turned to walk away but stopped.

Something irked him. He turned, opened the creaky door. He expected the old man to be asleep or, at least, sitting in bed reading. Yet his senses immediately told him something was wrong.

He crept alongside the bed and shook Herr Seiler to wake him. Freddie and Alistair had roused him from his alcoholic slumbers hundreds of times at Monte Rosa. But this time his beloved guide and mentor failed to stir. Freddie quickly listened to his chest, felt for a pulse, checked for breathing. Nothing. He was dead, his body already cold to the touch.

Freddie caressed Herr Seiler's clean-shaven face with his fingertips, gently closed the dead man's staring eyes and sank to his knees, overwhelmed by grief. He suffered an amalgam of emotions he'd never experienced before. Not even when his mother died had he felt so overcome. He knew why. Herr Seiler had been the most vital element of his childhood and the man who had taught him to be just that – a man.

He cried unashamedly, then slowly recovered his senses. Reality struck. What must he do? He thoroughly checked the man's body; no evidence of violence. His mind cleared and Freddie wondered what must have taken that big old bear. He wasn't medically trained but assumed it must have been heart related. Or lungs. He had certainly developed a hacking cough the last few days.

Why had he been so stupid not to see it all sooner? Why had he let him drive a bloody motorcycle? What on earth was he thinking? It was his fault; he was too wound up worrying about himself and his mission. He was gripped by guilt. He should have saved him. He could have saved him.

Herr Seiler was the father who had really raised him. And Alistair. He covered the body with a blanket and took hold of his gnarled old hand. He kissed it affectionately. It smelt of his favourite eau de cologne and cigars. But it was stiff and cold. His features grey, their contours fast changing into a mask of death he would never forget.

"Oh my God," he said out loud.

"Oh ... my ... God."

A series of images appeared in his mind, dancing like

shadows.

Herr Seiler, Alistair and he, three thousand metres up the mountainside above Zermatt at Trockener Steg. They had climbed for hours, their long wooden skis and poles strapped to their backs, stopping only occasionally to sip water from their flasks. How old were they? Twelve and fourteen, maybe.

They came to a snow track about two metres wide. "Here," Herr Seiler said suddenly, "here we will ski down. I know this track. It is steep and icy, but I know we can do it."

He strapped on his skis and was away, pounding through the snow and singing at the top of his voice. Operatic and Italian.

Alistair was next, head down and determined.

In a short time, they looked like two black ants waiting for him at the bottom of this narrow cut – a firebreak through the tall, snow-clad pines. There wasn't a soul around. It was deathly cold.

Freddie clipped on his metal and leather bindings but turned fast to hear something behind him. The sound of a rustle, then urgent panting.

Four mountain wolves appeared from the trees, the white fur around their snarling mouths stained with fresh blood. One moved towards him, breathing hot clouds in the freezing air, a sinew of bloody gristle dangling from bared teeth.

He could hear Herr Seiler shout: "Komm! Schnell! Freddie," but it was distant, meaningless.

The pack moved forward; their hungry eyes fixed on him. He had to move. But his frozen hand stuck to his binding. He panicked. He quickly pulled it away, stripping skin from his fingers and palm. He shrieked in pain. The wolves, smelling fresh blood, edged nearer. Freddie froze, this time with fear.

Then a gunshot. Herr Seiler always carried a gun.

The wolves scattered, but not far. And not for long. Live food was nearby. They panted and waited; they had all day.

"Komm!" Herr Seiler roared out again from the bottom of the track.

Freddie struggled with his binding; and, knowing it wasn't clipped properly, started to descend anyway, just to get away. The ski soon detached, leaving Freddie struggling on the other. He managed to stay upright for a remarkable ten seconds, then lost balance and rolled down the track until a large snowdrift broke his fall.

"Neat descent, Freddie," Alistair quipped, his blue eyes sparking and challenging. Then he skied away without a second thought for his younger brother.

Herr Seiler unclipped his skis and climbed up the track to collect Freddie's skis. He returned, took out a hip flask and had a hefty gulp.

"Drink some," he said firmly.

"No. I'll walk down," Freddie said childishly and turned away.

Herr Seiler grabbed hold of his Loden jacket and pulled him close: "No! You will have a sip, put on your skis and ski down with me."

"But I can't," Freddie found himself admitting, "I'm frightened."

Herr Seiler slapped him on the back: "Ha! And you should be. Those bastards would have torn you apart. I had the same sort of encounter when I was your age. Now drink some schnapps."

Freddie took a cautious sip and almost gagged. Herr Seiler convulsed into fits of laughter: "Now don't tell your mother I gave you that, she will kill me!"

Freddie smiled into the face of the wily man: "Fear is a terrible thing, Freddie. Your brother does not possess it. But I can tell you, if you don't ski down right now, you will never ski again. Or climb. Do you understand me? This is important."

Slowly, Freddie put the skis back on. Herr Seiler went slightly ahead, held out his pole and towed Freddie down until they were nearly in sight of his brother. Then he let go. Freddie continued as if nothing had happened.

For twenty minutes Freddie sat in the Hotel Dollenberg bedroom transported into the past. He looked at Herr Seiler's lifeless body, tears still rolled. He would never forget. Never.

He made decisions. Was the old man communicating with him, telling him what needed to be done? Could Freddie hear his voice, warm, encouraging and cajoling? Even in death, Herr Seiler had the power to guide.

He went through Herr Seiler's pockets, salvaging his wallet, his keys, his Swiss ID, a small diary and a leather document wallet, the size of a paperback. He had never seen it before.He opened it carefully and respectfully.

Inside were several black and white photographs: faded images of them all outside Chalet Monte Rosa. There were old tickets: train, theatre, zoo. A bunch of high denomination Swiss bank notes. Finally, he removed a carefully folded letter written on heavy paper resembling vellum. He knew at once it was from his mother. He put it to his nose and lips and recognised the familiar maternal scent from his childhood. He felt apprehensive when he opened it:

Priory Farm, Wicken, Cambridgeshire. January 14th, 1917

Dear Seiler,
I hope this letter finds you well and wish you a Happy New Year. Sadly, for me, it is not.
I cannot endure this place any longer. I miss Stephen so deeply and his few relatives dislike me. They stupidly still think I am a German spy because of my accent and appearance. Local people are even worse; they are hostile and cross the street to avoid me. Neither the postman nor milkman will speak to me. I try to explain I am Swiss, but no one listens.
When Stephen was here last summer life was wonderful, but as soon as he returned to France a black cloud descended. Then he was killed. In spite of his VC, the townspeople hate me.
I am lonely and the boys are demanding, particularly Alistair; and I have no help whatsoever. The local school is being awkward and the War Office unhelpful, despite Stephen's "valour". I need your help. We need your help.

I want to return to Zermatt with Alistair and Frederick. I have some family money from my late father. Stephen's Will stipulates the boys should attend Gresham's School in Norfolk. Sadly, his relatives control that education money and insist his wishes are upheld. That, of course, will be in a few years' time. Maybe I will again be welcome in England and, who knows, the boys might get dual Swiss/British citizenship if they are schooled in England?

However, it is right now I need you.

I pray you will again allow us to come and stay with you at Chalet Monte Rosa. I have enough money for travelling and will, of course, cover all your extra costs.

I know you will not let us down."

God Bless, Christina.

Freddie was horrified. He had been so wrong about his mother, incorrect about crucial family details. He had argued with Alistair at Waterloo station for nothing; always believing their mother had 'shipped them off to Gresham's School' to get rid of them. This letter proved it just was not so.

He gathered all of Herr Seiler's personal effects and stood up. One last glance and he softly closed the door. How could he leave him? But he knew he must. His mind made up; he would leave a vast sum of cash – a mixture of currencies - at reception with a brief letter.

Sirs,

My uncle unexpectedly died peacefully in his sleep last night. I am desperately sad at his passing; even more so because I simply cannot stay and deal with his affairs and funeral.

I know this is an imposition, but can you please let the authorities know of his demise? Could you also arrange for his death to be certified and his body taken to a local funeral home and, if possible, cremated?

The enclosed money will readily cover all expenses and pay for your inconvenience. This letter should also provide evidence of your power of attorney. Thank you so very much."

Jacques Duval, room 8.

Freddie returned to his bedroom and was unable to sleep. Images of the past were all he could think of and they unfolded in front of his eyes like a bad dream.

Station

Illkirch-Graffenstaden Station, France.

BEFORE DAWN THE FOLLOWING MORNING, Freddie discreetly left his letter and money in an envelope at reception. He crept silently out of the hotel and walked away as quickly as he could to the railway station. The further he went, the more his leg felt stiff and awkward. He found a public telephone and got through to the Baden number via the operator. A woman answered, she was guarded, cautious.

"Ja?"

"Good morning," Freddie said, equally guarded.

"Where are you?" The woman asked quickly.

"Illkirch-Graffenstaden. At the station."

"Stay where you are."

"Understood. Waiting room."

"A man will meet you there later today."

"How will I know him? How will I find him?"

"Don't worry," the voice said cautiously, "he will find you."

Click, the line went dead.

Freddie waited for the hollow echo, the tell-tale sign of a tapped line. There wasn't one. Freddie felt lonely. Solitude seldom bothered him; today it did. Even when he was recuperating at East Grinstead, there were always people around: other patients, visitors, doctors, nurses. And Sally Brooke, of course. Now he was isolated in a foreign country.

Worse still, his fate was held in the hands of other people; he had no plan or structure. He was merely responding. His only means of communication was the cumbersome radio set and the occasional public telephone.

Freddie knew he was being manipulated by others – who did have a plan – but he was not privy to it. He hated that.

He had had no choice but to leave Herr Seiler's body in the room. Luckily, they'd had the foresight to leave the motorbike and sidecar several streets away and Freddie had taken Manfred Lochar's registration documents with them. The bike would have to stay where it was.

And where was he ...?

Sitting in a stiflingly hot railway station, tired, hungry and wary. He felt his chin hit his chest with a jolt and was asleep in seconds ...

A soldier shook his shoulder aggressively:

"Papers?"

Two SS officers in black uniforms eyed him with distaste; both wore Swastika armbands and carried Lugers in leather holsters. Behind them a black Mercedes Benz idled.

Freddie reached inside his jacket pocket:

"Easy!" shouted Obergruppenführer one: 'On your feet! Undo your jacket! ... slowly so I can see!"

Freddie's eyes flickered ...

Later, someone shook his shoulder gently.

"Herr Valentine? Freddie? I am Manfred Lochar. You spoke to a woman earlier this morning. This was, in fact, my wife Ingrid in Baden."

Freddie blinked: "Yes, so I did. God. I was in a deep sleep. Where am I?" He looked up at the other man, confused, disorientated.

"Illkirch railway station."

"Of course, yes, sorry."

Manfred said: "You are certainly Alistair's brother. No mistake."

Freddie said nothing. The nightmare had been intense. So real. But the reality was now, playing in front of him. He came to his senses.

"These are your things?" asked Manfred, "I will put them in the truck. Now we must leave ..." He paused ... "I thought there were two of you?"

"There were," said Freddie, "I'll explain on the way."

"Alright," Manfred replied doubtfully.

Freddie stood and stretched. He felt wretched. They walked out of the station and over to a black Opel truck. The sides of it bore gold letters:

NSU – LOCHAR.
REPARATUREN UND SERVICE
BADEN-BADEN

Freddie looked at Manfred with a puzzled expression.

"I came here to recover you and the bike. A breakdown. I had to make my journey appear legitimate if we were stopped and questioned at the border. You are my nephew, Richard; I have your identity papers."

"I see."

Manfred looked around the car park with sudden realisation, as if a thought had just occurred:

"Where is the Kettenrad and sidecar Helmut Siebenthal supplied you with? My bike."

Freddie gave Manfred a weary and condensed story of the fate of Herr Seiler and the whereabouts of his precious bike: "We could go and collect it, if you want. Herr Seiler parked it a few streets away from our hotel, last night. There is no reason why it shouldn't still be there."

Manfred looked a little anxious: "Alright. Which street?"

"I don't know, he didn't say. But we can soon find it. I have your registration documents in my case, fear not."

Manfred pondered the predicament; this didn't fit in with his pre-conceived plan: "I would feel happier if we had the bike, yes. It is the reason I came to Illkirch after all. You and the bike."

Manfred opened the back of the truck and loaded Freddie's two pieces of luggage.

"Careful!" said Freddie, "with the attaché case."

“Ah yes. The attaché case, of course.” Manfred pinched his nose and raised his bushy eyebrows with a knowing look Freddie missed. The two men got in.

“By the way, where is the – ah – body of Herr Seiler?” asked Manfred, firing up the engine. He pulled out of the station car park and glanced at Freddie, waiting for an answer.

“It’s a complicated story, Herr Lochar,” said Freddie gloomily. “Do you mind if I explain more fully when we’re out of Illkirch? I’m tired and quite frankly upset.”

“Of course, I understand.” said Manfred.

But from the look on his face, it was clear he didn’t: he was just being polite.

Admiral Canaris

Unter den Linden, Berlin, Germany.

ALISTAIR BLINKED HIS EYES tightly for a split second, a sure sign of tension. It was June 1943. He was chauffeuring Admiral Canaris from Tempelhof Airport into somewhere in the centre of Berlin. He didn't know where yet. But he knew he was being tested. Felt it, rather. Canaris's real chauffeur lay dead somewhere in Salzburg – Police mystified by body in Hauptstrasse – the newspaper none of them had seen. Alistair knew it was Manfred; it was all part of the plan: a discreet kill.

Out of a cloudless blue sky, sunshine seared Berlin's streets. Alistair guided the Mercedes Benz W136 sedan out of Tempelhof and into Berlin. Both front wings of the gleaming staff car sported Swastika and Reich eagle pennants. The ensigns fluttered as the vehicle glided into traffic.

The airport was busy: rows of aircraft lined the grass runway beyond: Focke-Wulf 189s, Heinkels, ME 109s. A throng of black uniforms and red armbands exchanged Nazi salutes. Among them were pilots of the Luftwaffe and civilians. All busy, all going somewhere vital to the Reich.

"Take me to Alexanderplatz," said Canaris softly. "I need to stop on the way; first a flower shop on Behrenstrasse; second, my sister's apartment on Unter den Linden. I will give you warning." He settled back in his seat and closed his eyes.

Alistair was relieved to be away from the scurrying Nazis at the airport. Such hives of activity were to be avoided; one mistake could cost his life. Chauffeuring the eminent Canaris was chilling enough. They drove in silence, but the thick glass dividing screen was wound down. Alistair could hear Canaris humming a tune he could not identify. It didn't sound like German music, more like Italian opera.

Alistair spotted Canaris's leather briefcase in the rear-view mirror, lying on the seat beside him. What state secrets lay inside? Directives from Hitler no doubt; he wanted to see. He reminded himself exactly what he had overheard Rommel say in Salzburg:

"Schlafende Spione in London ... sleeper spies in London ... I'm surprised they are not all ..."

What? Dead? Captured? Turned? What did he mean? And where was these sleeper spies? Where were they based? What was their purpose? Could it be somebody in Government? The War Office? His mind whirled with possibilities.

He re-ran those few moments at the bottom of the Berghof steps; so many of the High Command with limousines at the ready. He would commit the faces to memory: Himmler, Goering, Goebbels, Speer, Admiral Doenitz plus Generals, Rommel, Jodl and Keitel. He recognised them all. Many of them had been at the

Berlin Olympics in '36. He had captured them on the cine film Manfred had sent back to Brim in London. His mind flashed back to that moment in the Olympic village:

> *'What do you think, Herr Valentine?*
> *I think Nexus can move mountains. Especially you and Astrid.'*

Back to the present: what was Hitler's meeting at the Berghof about? Alistair speculated as he drove. The backlash after defeat at Stalingrad? Eisenhower? But what else? Whatever it was, those sleeper spies must be part of the jigsaw. He must find out what. He spied the briefcase again. Instinctively he felt inside his jacket pocket for the Minox Riga subminiature camera, a token from Brim at their last meeting. Intuition told him this was serious. But why? What irked him? He needed evidence. He had to see those papers. But how? His thoughts switched to Astrid in Potsdam, his radio transmitter stowed in the attic, the risk he was taking. The risk they were both taking. They had lived under enormous pressure for a long time.

"Pull over there, Stephan," said Canaris, interrupting Alistair's thoughts, "Schweitzer, the flower shop. Wait outside."

Canaris got out of the car and dismissed Alistair's offer to assist. Before he stepped onto the pavement, he wound up the glass divider screen. Alistair feigned not to notice. The admiral emerged from the shop with a gargantuan bouquet that nearly engulfed him. As soon as his car door was shut, he gestured for Alistair to drive on. Valentine moved the big car into the traffic with skill, headed for Unter den Linden and arrived there promptly.

"Number, Herr Admiral?"

"Over there by those two trees."

This time Alistair got out of the car. He swiftly opened the rear door. Canaris faced a dilemma. He couldn't quite manage the bouquet and the briefcase.

"Let me help, Herr Admiral," Alistair said attentively.

"You take the flowers."

"Yes, sir."

The Gothic-style house was magnificent, like many residences and offices on the tree-lined avenue. Canaris opened the unlocked front door and closed it firmly behind them. Inside, a wide, sweeping staircase rose from the marble-tiled hallway up to a galleried landing. Canaris led, Alistair followed. As they arrived at the top, a pair of large wood-panelled doors swung open. An elegant woman stepped out onto the landing. She must have heard the front door close. She looked Mediterranean, with high cheekbones, full lips and brown eyes. Around her flowed a low-cut, close-fitting, silk gown. She was strikingly beautiful.

"You're early, Wilhelm," she purred, in perfect German. Her eyes sparkled.

"Actually, yes."

"Then we'll have time for a cocktail before La Bohème."

Ah, Puccini thought Alistair. That was what the admiral had been humming. Canaris carefully put down his briefcase, took the flowers from Alistair and presented them.

"A gift," he said unnecessarily.

As she leaned forward to accept them, Alistair caught a glimpse of her breasts, full and suntanned. A hint of a smile crossed her face as she straightened up. A woman who knew just how beautiful she was.

"Do you still wish to go to Alexanderplatz this evening, Herr Admiral?"

Canaris looked at the woman: "No, I think not. There isn't time. It can wait."

"Shall I wait in the car, Herr Admiral?"

"Please," Canaris replied, glancing at his Rolex. "A staff car is taking us to the Opera."

"Yes, Herr Admiral."

"But I shall need to return home to Wannsee later tonight. I may be some time."

"At you command, Herr Admiral."

Alistair saluted politely and turned away with a private smile. Whoever she was, she wasn't his sister. He went downstairs, through the main house door and settled into the Mercedes, wondering how he would kill the next four or five hours. It was a long opera, nearly three hours, and there would no doubt be dinner afterwards at a discreet restaurant reserved for the Nazi elite.

Across Unter den Linden, outside a bakery, the man with a livid scar on his cheek watched proceedings carefully. Krebbs took no notes or photographs but would report everything he had seen to Himmler. And he looked forward to killing that chauffeur, whoever he was.

*

The following morning Alistair drove Canaris to the Reich Chancellery on Wilhelmstrasse in Berlin-Mitte. The admiral looked tired and preoccupied. Valentine pulled the car into the courtyard and waited once again for his master to return. This time the admiral left the briefcase in the back of the car, but he wound up the dividing screen from the rear and carefully locked the back doors. There was no access; it was sealed.

Alistair whisked out his miniature camera, quickly focused, set the 'F' stops and fired off two shots of the briefcase from outside the car. The light was poor and reflected on the glass. It would have to do. Canaris was gone twelve minutes. He returned in a fluster:

"Take me to Abwehr headquarters."

"Yes, of course, Herr Admiral."

Once again Canaris settled in the back as Alistair drove off.

"I will be an hour, perhaps less," he said when they arrived at the Tirpitzufer HQ. "Wait."

Canaris got out. Once again Alistair was left alone with the briefcase on the back seat. The dividing screen was closed as before. Alistair took out a pencil and a pocket diary and sketched an outline of the briefcase, from where he was sitting. It was fairly standard, with two lockable clasps on either side of a folding flap, rather like a student's satchel. Four hours later, Canaris emerged from the Abwehr building. Alistair got out and jumped to attention.

"I have a lift with a colleague," said Canaris, again flustered, "I need to speak with him further, so we'll return to Wannsee together in his car. This Mercedes will be brought over to my house in Wansee early tomorrow morning."

"Yes, Herr Admiral. Have a pleasant evening, sir."

"You can catch the S-Bahn to Potsdam," the admiral said wearily. "That is where you said you lived, isn't it?"

"Ja, Herr Admiral," Alistair said formally.

"Potsdamer Platz is only a few stops. I will see you in the morning at Wansee. You will know which house is mine because this car will be in the driveway. Eight o'clock sharp, understood?"

Alistair lowered his head: "Ja, Herr Admiral. Understood. Good evening, sir."

*

Across the road, concealed in a doorway, Otto Krebbs made more notes: times and addresses. He smiled and watched Alistair walk away.

Luck

Jägerstrasse, Berlin, Germany.

SOMETIMES LUCK INTERVENES, sometimes it doesn't. Alistair felt tired from driving the big old Mercedes around Berlin. And the constant waiting for Canaris. It was approaching six when he found the shop on Jägerstrasse, near the leafy Dutch quarter. He showed the elderly man behind the counter the drawing of Canaris's briefcase and explained what he wanted.

"So, it must have two lockable clasps?" asked the old man examining the drawing, "with keys?"

"My uncle insists," said Alistair innocently, "for the shop wages."

"Ah yes, of course." He turned and walked to a packed stockroom; the store smelled of leather and old wood. Finally, the owner returned, he shook his head in regret:

"No. I have similar, but not really the same."

Alistair shook his head: "I am in trouble then."

"You could try Herr Weber on Luisenplatz," he looked at his watch, "but I fear he may be closed by now. It's nearly six."

"Oh dear, I need it tonight. I promised him ..." said Alistair, manifestly disappointed.

The old man puckered his lips and scratched his unshaven chin: "Must it be this colour?" the old man asked and looked at the shading on the torn-out page.

"No. That was just to show where the flap and where the clasps were."

"I have an old pigskin briefcase, but it has been used."

"Show me, please."

An agitated, red-faced woman – perhaps his wife - appeared from the stockroom. She stormed around the counter to the door, flicked the sign to GESCHLOSSEN and pulled down the blind loudly. The old man re-appeared with a pigskin briefcase identical to Canaris's.

"Like this?"

"Perfect! How much?"

"But it's mine!" The old man's eyes twinkled, an unspoken message therein. This was Berlin; everything was for sale.

Alistair took out a roll of notes and peeled off two ten-Reichsmark notes, much more than it could be worth, even when new. He held out the money. The woman, momentarily bemused, darted around, snapped the money out of his hand and returned to the stockroom. The old man shrugged, outwitted, and definitely outmanoeuvred. Alistair checked the briefcase was empty.

"Keys?"

The old man handed them over.

"Thank you," said Alistair, "I am no longer in trouble."

Chance

Unter den Linden, Berlin, Germany.

CHANCE WAS ON ALISTAIR'S SIDE. Next morning, he took the S-Bahn from Potsdam to Wannsee. He walked in clear, shimmering sunlight from the station to Canaris's house, carrying the bogus briefcase inside a suitcase. It was too cumbersome to be concealed in his uniform. The magnificent houses overlooked the lake and public gardens. He spotted the Mercedes outside in the driveway of one of the biggest. The garage door was open, revealing a pre-war sports convertible. Canaris was in the front garden with pruning shears. He glanced at his watch:

"You're early," he said, eyeing the suitcase, "are you going away?"

"Good morning, Herr Admiral. No, sir. The hinge is broken, and my wife asked me to get it fixed."

"I see. She's back from Salzburg; the music festival?" Canaris eyed him carefully.

"Um ... no. She asked me weeks ago. She's still there."

"Lucky she has a spare then."

"Indeed, Herr Admiral. It is."

"I am sure you will find a leather goods store somewhere, Stephan," Canaris eyed him suspiciously. "to repair it."

Alistair's heart sank. Was he being followed? No, surely not. Then he reminded himself he was trying to outfox Germany's chief fox.

"I thought I might clean the car," said Alistair, trying to steer Canaris off track.

Canaris looked at his watch: "Very well. But we leave at nine sharp." He handed Alistair the car keys. "Put your suitcase in the boot. There are some cloths in a box, but it really doesn't need much doing."

Alistair opened the boot of the Mercedes and placed his suitcase inside. Was he being watched? The remark about his wife and the Salzburg music festival unsettled him. It demonstrated that Canaris listened. He was not a man to be fooled, or a man to be taken for a fool. Alistair would have to be careful. Diligent. On his guard. Always.

He busied himself with a cloth. It was mainly surface dust; the paintwork underneath was glistening. He cleaned around the massive headlights and chrome grille, paying attention to the Mercedes badge and bumpers. With a damp sponge he had discovered in a bucket in the garage, he cleaned the huge windscreen. He looked over his shoulder.

Casually he went to the open boot, undid the clasps of his suitcase, and removed the bogus briefcase. He opened the rear passenger door and quickly stowed it out of sight, taking out the floor mat simultaneously to shake off the dust and blades of grass. All the time he watched the house for any sign of movement. He cleaned around the door frame and buffed the windows, trying hard to look convincing. A clock chimed nine from within the grand house. Then, all of sudden, Canaris was there – out of nowhere – eyeing him carefully. He was wearing his Kriegsmarine uniform and carrying his cap and precious briefcase.

"Let's go, Stephan." Canaris climbed in.

"At your command, Herr Admiral." He closed the boot firmly then looked around. Had he noticed something or someone out of the corner of his eye? A shadow? A movement? And then it had vanished. They drove back into Berlin.

"Do you know where you're going?" Canaris asked. Was there something in his tone? Had he seen something at Wannsee?

"I assumed Unter den Linden, Herr Admiral, as you said last evening."

"Correct," he said simply.

How tempted Alistair was to say: to your sister's apartment? The Mediterranean-looking lady with the suntanned breasts and summer dress.

"Do you remember the address, Stephan?"

"I remember the building, Herr Admiral, I didn't notice the number."

"A tactful answer, Stephan, you are clearly a resourceful man …"

"Thank you, Herr Admiral. This is a wonderful car, by the way." He desperately needed to change the subject.

"I hate it," said Canaris surprisingly, "it's ostentatious and bourgeois. Do you know Mussolini has an Alfa Romeo? An Alfa Romeo!" He let out a deep sigh of disapproval.

They arrived outside the magnificent old house on Unter den Linden, and almost at once the front door opened. The exotic-looking lady stepped out, wearing yet another figure- hugging dress. She had evidently been crying and her hair was in disarray, but that did not detract from her natural beauty. She remained in the doorway, clutching a handkerchief; she had obviously been waiting at the window. Alistair got out of the driver's door and opened the rear door for Canaris.

The admiral walked swiftly over to the woman; they exchanged a few words. She looked at him, her eyes imploring. He hugged her briefly, but paternally. Alistair leaned into the rear footwell and grabbed the bogus briefcase, exchanged it with the genuine one, and took the Admiral's uniform cap. He closed the door and walked towards the couple, but stopped respectfully a few metres away from them. He waited. They were engrossed in animated conversation. She was clearly upset about something; tears streamed down her face.

Canaris turned, saw Alistair holding his cap, the briefcase and nodded in acknowledgement of his courtesy. After a few moments, he took his possessions from him with an appreciative nod.

"Wait with the car, please. I may be some time."

"Ja, Herr Admiral."

The couple went inside the house and closed the front door. Alistair turned, opened the rear door of the Mercedes and retrieved Canaris's briefcase. His heart thumped. How long did he have? An hour? Or minutes? Here were Canaris's Nazi documents from the Berghof. Whatever they were. He felt for the miniature camera in his pocket and got into the driver's seat. He would have to photograph the documents here. Now. In broad daylight. There was no other choice. He could not just suddenly disappear and go somewhere.

His body tensed with anticipation. The briefcase was on his lap, the camera now in his hand. He twisted the two clasps simultaneously, expecting resistance. There was none. It was unlocked. Why? Alistair lifted the flap and peered inside. There were no documents, it was stuffed with old newspapers. My God! Canaris had swapped them back.

But when? How?

He didn't see Canaris until the driver's side window smashed. The admiral's Luger pointed at his head through the broken glass.

"Get out," he commanded loudly. Alistair closed the flap of the briefcase, opened the car door and reluctantly got out as instructed.

"I just received a call from my Adjutant. My chauffeur was murdered in Salzburg, a few days ago. Stabbed. Walk slowly to the front door and go inside ... run and I'll kill you."

Alistair had no choice: "Herr Admiral ..."

"Silence!" barked Canaris. "Up the stairs. Move!"

They climbed the stairs, Alistair in front, hands in the air, Canaris behind, his weapon trained on Alistair's spine: "Now, inside."

Alistair stepped into a palatial lounge, adorned with long, silk drapes and Catalonian landscapes. Canaris's briefcase was on the table, its contents spilled out: Nazi documents, diagrams, maps, photographs, and a file marked DAS SCHLOSS.

"Who are you?" snapped Canaris.

The woman joined them. Alistair couldn't read her expression; he just saw her tear-stained cheeks.

"Stephan Beck."

"The truth or I shoot. You killed my chauffeur in Salzburg. Why?"

Alistair took a breath and looked at the woman.

Canaris continued: "The SS can be here within minutes. Or maybe I should I just kill you now? This is your last chance." He raised the Luger, "Who are you?" He cocked the gun, pointing it at Alistair's head.

"Valentine. My name is Valentine," said Alistair flatly. "I didn't kill your chauffeur."

"You are English?"

"Swiss, raised in Zermatt."

"And England? I detect it in your accent, though your German is excellent, for a Swiss. Not that it matters; you're a spy and you will be shot as a spy."

"I know. I've always known." said Alistair almost dismissively, steeling himself for the inevitable.

Canaris waited, as if making a judgment.

"No, Valentine. You do not know. You know nothing at all." Canaris eased his tone. "You should tell me, before I set those SS hounds on you."

Alistair was shocked. He should be dead. What the hell did

Canaris mean – you know nothing at all – why was he even bothering to talk him? Was he just playing a game?

"I'm not sure I can tell you anything," said Alistair.

"Oh, you can," the admiral smiled, "for example, who is the spy in London leaking classified information to the KGB?"

"What?" Alistair rocked back on his heels; he'd clearly been away from England for too long.

Canaris laughed: "I see I have touched a nerve. Yes, Mr. Valentine. Someone has disrupted all my attempts at a rapprochement between Germany and Britain. That man is a traitor to your country. He has destroyed any chance for peace in Europe."

"I have no idea," said Alistair genuinely. The words 'peace in Europe' echoed in his mind. He suddenly realised Canaris might be telling the truth. Was the old fox a secret rebel?

"But you are a spy," said Canaris, "and yet you say you know nothing about this turncoat. Impossible."

"No, I'm telling the truth. I am afraid you will have to kill me if you don't believe me," said Alistair.

"Kill you? Why, I will, of course. But not yet." The admiral still had menace in his voice.

Somehow Alistair didn't believe him. Yet he was mystified. He could sense the wily Prussian's voice and manner slowly shifting from violent threat to a calmer, almost indulgent tone. Was this a trick, thought Alistair? Canaris was a master of bemusement; that much he knew for certain. Yet there was a hint of genial warmth in his voice and a kindlier glint in his eye.

"You are here because you want something, Valentine."

Canaris moved closer to Alistair: "You're a brave man. Brave but stupid."

Then Canaris did the strangest thing: he strolled to the glass table and put the gun down.

"A Swiss spy then, eh Valentine? Not a Swiss name. The Swiss are barely involved in this misguided war. You wheedled your way into my confidence because you were ... what, looking for these?" Canaris pointed at the documents and the file, in particular.

Alistair nodded, caught. To run would be crazy. He had no options whatsoever. Where would he go? And who the hell was this traitor in British Intelligence?

"I was after something, but I didn't know what," said Alistair.

"You didn't know what?" Canaris sounded amazed.

Alistair nodded: "No."

Canaris laughed and seemed to be considering his words: "Let me see now. You are a spy. So, who do you work for? I wonder. Brimblecombe's lot? Menzies? Downing? Dalton? You look surprised, we know them all. Every line on their unknowing faces."

Alistair should have been surprised, but he wasn't. He was speechless.

Canaris sat in an armchair and made a steeple of his hands. Raising his eyebrows, he looked directly at Alistair. Over the next few minutes, he gradually opened up with an honesty that shocked him. Was this really the head of the German secret service exposing cards in his hand to an unknown opponent? Dumbfounded, Alistair listened. He knew he should have been dead five minutes before. Was he being instinctively toyed with like a cat with a mouse, only to die anyway?

Canaris explained in detail why he had both liked and followed Hitler's rise in the 1930s. "Like so many true Germans, I was convinced we were let down at Versailles. Hitler seemed to have the answers. Yet he has overstretched himself and revealed his true persona ... and put the future of Germany at risk ..." Canaris swallowed deeply, before continuing:

"Hitler is a madman, Valentine, a madman. My days are numbered ... largely due to the spy in your government and his KGB masters."

Alistair looked at the concerned face, bemused. He had never been more uncertain about anything in his life.

"I've been betrayed. That maniac Himmler wants me dead. I doubt I'll see the end of the year, let alone the war."

Canaris looked away before continuing softly, almost casually: "And the SS ape who follows you will probably kill you – and me - if I'm not careful. Be on your guard. Himmler's monkeys believe everything they are told. They are dangerous and what is more, they are not real Germans. They have no conscience whatsoever." Canaris walked over to the window, stared at the lime trees and paused. What had he heard? Alistair knew he had just returned from the dead. What twist of fate, of sheer luck had intervened to save him? As if reading his mind, the Admiral turned to him, his expression grave.

Blueprints

Unter den Linden, Berlin, Germany.

"HAVE YOU EVER HEARD of the Schwarze Kapelle - The Black Orchestra?" Canaris asked, using both languages.

"No," replied Alistair, "I haven't." Bizarrely, he was very slowly beginning to relax. The adrenalin subsided. He felt he was out of imminent danger.

"To be honest, I'm not surprised. It's what the Gestapo call us: Black Orchestra. An inappropriate name. The communists they call the Red Orchestra. I have become ... how would you say ... involved? We are a group trying to overthrow Hitler and replace him with a sane government – preferably without getting caught.

"You said overthrow, Herr Admiral?" Alistair enquired.

"Yes. I warned the British in the thirties about Hitler's plan to invade Poland. I was ignored. They did not see, no, could not grasp, the threat he posed." He paused: "I tried again in 1940 to warn about his ambition to invade the Low Countries and occupy France. Again, I was ignored.

"But why were you ignored? I don't understand." asked

Alistair, more annoyed than intrigued.

"I don't know. Perhaps Chamberlain was a fool."

"Wait a minute though," Alistair found himself saying; defending a man he really knew nothing about. "Maybe they were all foolish."

He huffed: "I was still ignored," Canaris said, still obviously piqued that he had not been taken seriously. "Do you know how many assassination attempts there have been against Hitler – at least the ones we know about?" Alistair shook his head, bewildered: "No."

"Four I know of; three that have been made public, only because they happened in public."

"May I sit down please, Herr Admiral? This is all quite a revelation; you know, for a humble Swiss spy."

Canaris flashed a brief smile, sensing Alistair's humour: "Yes." He gestured to a chair and Alistair made himself comfortable.

The Mediterranean lady coughed judiciously and moved towards them from the kitchen. She had witnessed their disagreement but could now see the admiral was calm; the danger passed. And she looked relieved.

"Sorry, this is Maria Franco from Barcelona. She is staying here in exile. Political problems in Spain. " She acknowledged the introduction and turned back to the kitchen, with a sway of shapely hips.

"Franco?" Alistair sounded surprised.

"Yes, she is related; a once-removed cousin of General Franco." They had switched to English again. Canaris seemed just as much at ease with either language.

Canaris sat forward, his brow furrowed: "The German Army is trying to defend a line stretching from Leningrad to the Black Sea. Along the Mediterranean we defend 3,000 kilometres of coastline; in the west, 6,000 kilometres of territory from the Netherlands to the southern tip of the Bay of Biscay."

Maria returned from the kitchen with a tray of cups and saucers and a jug of hot coffee. It smelled good and strong.

"Come and join us, my dear," Canaris said in perfect Spanish.

"It's madness," Canaris continued in German, "millions of German soldiers, hundreds of thousands of crack Waffen-SS Troops, Ten Panzer divisions, Fallschirmjaeger – the Paratroop Divisions, the Luftwaffe being shot out of the sky by the RAF ... Hitler will destroy Germany and bankrupt her economy for generations to come."

Again, Alistair shook his head in disbelief.

"And all because that lousy little corporal believes Germany was cheated by the Allies because of the terms and conditions of the Treaty of Versailles."

"Was Germany cheated?"

"I don't know," said Canaris exasperated, "I used to think so. We had to make reparations, apologies. Now I'm not so certain. Ask the Kaiser!"

"It's a little late for that, Admiral."

"I fear it's a little late for everything. Help yourself to coffee. There's no milk, cream, or even sugar."

"Black is fine." Alistair sighed quietly, relieved to be alive. He shot a glance at Canaris as if to seek permission to pick up one of the items spilling out from Canaris's precious briefcase. It was a black and white photograph of Windsor Castle. "May I?"

Canaris nodded as Alistair picked up the photograph.

"What's this is all about, Herr Admiral? Can you explain, please?"

Canaris drank some coffee and sat back. Maria watched him carefully; Alistair was not sure how much of the conversation she followed.

"The original plan was to abduct the daughters of the British Crown – the two Princesses - from their very own protectors. An idea was to pollute the water supply at Windsor Castle with a powerful sedative to paralyse the Royal Guard and the Secret Service ...

They would have been abducted using an aircraft hidden nearby. A propaganda coup for Goebbels. The idea seemed audacious, but plausible ...

Canaris paused to let the words sink in: "I had agreed to this original plan. Largely to appease Hitler and Himmler. To get them off my back."

Alistair was amazed and waited for more.

"With Himmler's backing, it has now escalated into something monstrous. I want you to be clear why I'm telling you this. I want it stopped. Not just because the plan is barbaric, but because of who is behind it: Heinrich Himmler. I want Churchill and the Allies to know exactly what is planned."

"And what is planned, Herr Admiral?"

Canaris thought back to the Berghof and Himmler's address to the Presidium: "A series of aerial attacks by the Luftwaffe on five strategic targets in the south of England. But with a lethal payload."

Alistair was alarmed: "Payload?" This was an expression he was unfamiliar with.

"Yes. A lethal nerve gas called Tabun."

"How?"

Canaris drew breath as he explained the unimaginable: "The bomb bays of ten Heinkels have apparently been adapted to facilitate and launch ten high-speed ballistic missiles, each with an explosive warhead. They will be primed with pressurised Tabun. A gyroscopically stabilised fin will guide these weapons to their target."

"Like the vengeance weapons? V1 and V2?"

Canaris, a trace of a smile: "Yes, except these won't miss. I understand they cannot miss."

Alistair shook his head, imagining the worst.

Canaris continued: "These missiles will travel at more than 1,200km/h. Faster than anything you – or we – have ever had. The man behind this is Erich Spengler. Remember that name. He is as bad as Himmler. If that's possible."

"Spengler, yes, I will."

Canaris went on to reveal all he had been told at the Berghof: the targets, the launch sites and the intended catastrophic result. Alistair could feel his heart thumping, his breath short; he was speechless. He had to get this information to Brim and the others.

"It is chemical warfare combined with rocket technology. These scientists believe they can put a man on the moon within twenty years."

Alistair forced a smile: "Unimaginable."

Canaris picked up the photograph of Windsor Castle: "Operation Das Schloss must be stopped. You must stop it. But there is something else."

"Go on."

He paused as Maria poured some more coffee for the three of them.

"A U-Boat – 302 - will leave Bergen and sail to Cromer on the east coast of England. Her crew will discharge cylinders of Tabun into the hands of London sleeper spies. They will transport the cargo down to the grounds of Windsor. I'm not sure how exactly. Some sort of reinforced vehicle."

Alistair innocently sipped his coffee: "Schlafende Spione in London?"

Canaris's brain computed the four words and recollected them: "You overheard a fragment of a conversation at the Berghof and you took your chances. Is that it, Mr. Valentine?" Canaris looked impressed.

"I thought I might have been wrong."

"You weren't. But I am sure, the ground assault on Windsor will trigger the aerial assault; one cannot happen without the other. Distraction is the key."

"How?"

"We were not told. But it is imperative for you to get a message to England as soon as possible to alert them that an attack is imminent. But it will have to be very brief and coded for security. German Intelligence know a lot more than you realise and scan all radio frequencies for just this kind of subterfuge. Can you send that message?"

Alistair pictured his radio transmitter in Potsdam: "Yes. I can."

"But more than that," said Canaris, "you have to somehow get this evidence back to Churchill and British Security Services. These are the original Reich documents – the blueprints. Once they see these first-hand – on German paper – genuine Abwehr documents too, from me, they will know it's authentic. You understand this? They must believe you have met me, and that I surrendered them."

"I'll find a way." Alistair stood and turned to Maria. "It's been a pleasure, señorita," he said with his most charming smile, "thank you for the coffee."

"It's certainly been enlightening," she said in perfect English, quashing all his theories about language. And positively everything he knew about women.

Admiral Canaris packed all the documents – the blueprints – back into his leather briefcase and handed it to Alistair: "Good luck, Mr. Valentine. I have a feeling you'll need it."

*

Across Unter den Linden, Otto Krebbs sat in a battered Mercedes, hunched down, out of sight. He had to decide: remain watching Canaris as he had been instructed by Himmler or pursue the bogus chauffeur. But what if something happened here and he missed it? What would he tell Himmler? Every instinct in his highly trained body told him to pursue ... but he must follow orders. He valued his life too highly.

*

As Alistair left Canaris's house, he paused, pulled up his collar and glanced across the road. Canaris was correct; he was being followed. He noticed the blond hair and the livid facial scar. A big man trying to hide. But he'd remember that face.

*

Alistair returned to their house in Potsdam on the S-Bahn. Astrid knew at once something was not right; the look on his face always betrayed his innermost feelings. He told her everything about Canaris, the planned aerial attack and the U-Boat.

"What should I tell my father, Alistair?"

He considered the question carefully and how to reply: "Right, use Siebenthal's Nexus weather code, from a public telephone as before. The Morse here is too risky ..." he paused ... "Tell him I have evidence from 'Raleigh' – that's the agreed code for Canaris. Storm warning high, that sort of thing. You know how to word it, Astrid."

"Yes."

He gave her his winning smile. Now all he could do was wait. A few crucial words of intelligence which might, or might not, alter the course of the war. Astrid came over and rubbed his shoulder.

Baden

Illkirch to Baden. France and Germany.

FREDDIE AND MANFRED WERE in the Opel truck driving from Illkirch-Graffenstaden railway station to Baden-Baden. The motor bike and sidecar were safely stowed in the back, tied down with rope. It had taken them less than ten minutes to find it and Manfred couldn't relax until they had. He was a perfectionist. Freddie felt tired and ill at ease. Not only the ordeal with Herr Seiler – and that was bad enough – but finding the letter from his mother. Their mother. It changed the dynamic between him and Alistair.

"You were saying, Freddie. About your friend, Herr Seiler." prompted Manfred after a while and seeing his passenger was finding it hard to stay awake.

"Yes, sorry. When I returned to his room, he was dead – cold, rigid, gone." Freddie's eyes watered at the memory of the previous night, the memory so fresh.

"My God. To die like that, so quickly." said Manfred Lochar, glancing at his passenger and seeing his grief.

"I know. He was a tough old bear. He smoked, drank, loved his food. He lived life to the full. But I didn't expect him to die; not yet."

"Maybe his battery ran out," said the German spy." He died through living too much. Not a bad epitaph. And you had no choice but to leave him there."

Freddie described how he'd left a carefully written note of explanation and lots of money in the hope Herr Seiler's demise wouldn't ruffle too many feathers.

"Let's hope," said Manfred, "with no identification the authorities in France have no way of tracing you. A sad end though, for you and him."

"Yes." He didn't want to talk about Herr Seiler but felt Manfred did.

Freddie looked out at the striking countryside, lost in thought. Amid miles of forest and rolling green hills, Freddie reflected on how this part of Germany was so unaffected by the ravages of war; the opposite of the northern cities flattened by Allied bombing. Here, there were few buildings – save for sporadic farms and barns stacked with logs for winter.

"So, Herr Seiler was the man who taught you and your brother to ski and climb, yes?" persisted Manfred. "And drink like men. Alistair has mentioned this mysterious man many times, of course."

"Mysterious?" asked Freddie.

"Ach, yes, Alistair was never completely sure about him, you know, after your father was killed. He thought maybe your mother and he were ..."

"I don't know what you mean," Freddie blurted out too quickly. Oh, but he remembered that night on the barge all right. Herr Seiler's admission of his relationship with his mother. The burden of guilt he must have carried. And for no reason. He would never really know the truth. It bothered him.

Freddie warily peered across at Manfred. He was a big-built man, with droopy eyelids and bushy eyebrows. His dark skin gave him an Italian or Sicilian look, his nonchalant expression likewise. Yet beneath his swarthy veneer, Freddie sensed a solicitous man of many parts. Not a man to cross.

An eerily long silence pervaded before Manfred spoke. Perhaps he felt he should speak, considering how direct his comments on the sainted Herr Seiler and the brothers' heroic father had been. After your father was killed in combat, was what he should have said - after all, he was killed by Germans.

"Astrid telephoned to let us know she and Alistair are coming to Baden. Hopefully tomorrow."

"Excellent news."

"How much do you know about what Alistair does?" Manfred asked cautiously.

"I know he works for British Intelligence, of course. Brim briefed me about Admiral Canaris. That Alistair may have something – evidence – of vital importance. Hence the code red RVR." Freddie's mind flashed back to the meeting with Brim in June and their subsequent lunch at the Dégustation restaurant in Pall Mall. It seemed like a lifetime ago. In fact, it was only a matter of months.

"How much do you know about Nexus?" Manfred asked him

quietly, as if they might be overheard.

"Not much really. I think Brim expected you to fill me in."

"I see."

Manfred was forced to slow down because of a group of cyclists. He seemed to be composing his answer; how much to disclose: "Helmut Siebenthal and, yes, and an elite group of people, control Nexus. Our principal aim is quietly to defeat Nazism ..." He paused, irritated at the hold up the cyclists were causing him. Finally, he resumed:

"We come from all walks of life. Old German and Swiss money. Traditionalists, if you like: lawyers, doctors, bankers, academics. Cultured professionals. Even musicians. A conductor, no names, of course. Before the war we smuggled people out of Germany. Our methods are ingenious; no, very ingenious. Against tyranny you need to be inventive."

"And Astrid is involved with Nexus?" Freddie asked carefully. He only knew part of the story, after all.

"Of course. She is my daughter and Alistair's wife. That is to say, they are married on paper, as a cover." Manfred filled Freddie in on all the details about their house in Potsdam, the faux job at Telefunken and how Nexus had infiltrated him into the Abwehr as Canaris's chauffeur. He omitted to tell him who killed the old one and Freddie didn't ask.

Freddie listened in awe; he was thrilled at the prospect of seeing Alistair, but worried about how he would report Herr Seiler's death.

*

Baden-Baden lies amid the undulating foothills of the Black Forest on the River Oos. The town looked prosperous with its three-storey houses, villas and tree-lined avenues. They drove into it around Mount Merkur, lush with grass and trees.

Manfred pointed up: "There is a funicular railway – Merkurbergbahn – up to the top. This is a spa town, built originally by the Romans. We are rich, at the moment." He shrugged his familiar shrug.

Schwartzmattstrasse was a wide avenue of substantial houses – Alpine-chalet style – with wooden shutters and sloped roofs.

Today, however, it was 30C, the air hot and dry. They pulled into number 27, up a little ramp and straight into the open garage. Freddie noticed the well-equipped workshop and shelves of spares: an assortment of mudguards, brake leads, clutch assemblies, even a spare fuel tank.

Manfred pinched his nose and tapped the side of the truck: "I'll unload her later."

They walked outside into the sunshine. The front garden was in full bloom with trimmed grass and pristine borders. Someone had been busy.

"Ach, meine Frau!" he announced, as the front door of the villa opened.

Ingrid was the epitome of the German Hausfrau; she came to greet them, wearing a typical Bavarian pinafore:

She put her hand to her mouth: "Mein Gott! So like Alistair!"

Ingrid almost curtsied, then seemed to change her mind and

thrust out her hand and smiled broadly.

Ingrid was in her early fifties, Freddie assumed by sheer mathematics, but looked ten years younger. She wore her blond hair plaited, had blue eyes and a faultless complexion. Her figure, while somewhat full, didn't diminish her allure; a look of flirtatious mischief thinly concealed in her welcoming smile.

"You must be hungry," she said with distinctive south-German inflection, "I am sorry if I was brief on the telephone. You can't be too careful."

"Understood."

She pecked Manfred once, dutifully, on the cheek and led them into the house. It was cool and well furnished; she raised her arms as if to share their good fortune: "Please come in, make yourself at home."

Freddie nodded his approval: "Thank you, very homely."

She returned a warm smile: "I have prepared Sauerbraten mit Salzkartoffeln. Manfred will open some cold Riesling to celebrate, yes?"

"To celebrate what?" Freddie questioned with a raised eyebrow.

"Astrid coming home and your safe arrival, of course." She looked Freddie up and down, as if to check he was actually there; that he had arrived. This was no apparition.

Reunion

27 Schwartzmattstrasse, Baden-Baden, Germany

ALISTAIR AND ASTRID reached the house next morning, a very hot day in August. Manfred and Ingrid were overjoyed to see them. They made an unashamed fuss of their precious daughter. Freddie heard his brother's voice from his room upstairs; the Lochar family could clearly keep a secret, he thought, as he realised, they had not said a word to Alistair about his arrival. Freddie found the element of surprise exciting and touching.

Alistair and Freddie had last met seven years before in a smoky buffet at Waterloo station. Freddie, well-oiled, had affronted his brother by accusing their mother of not caring enough and shipping them off to boarding school. Now he knew what had enraged Alistair. He had the evidence in his pocket.

Freddie knew he had wronged his brother. He had borne the burden of guilt since discovering their mother's letter and now he had to tell Alistair – somehow – the terrible news about Herr

Seiler.

Freddie gingerly stepped unannounced from the bottom step of the stairs down into the hallway. His arrival heralded a storm of emotion. The look on Alistair's face was incredulous and thrilled.

"My God, Freddie! What the hell are you doing here?" he cried out, "Manfred!" Alistair bellowed, "What's going on?"

Alistair ran to Freddie, clasped his hand and looked him in the eyes: "Freddie, it's so good to see you."

Freddie was delighted to see him and felt the warmth of his brother's greeting. He knew he meant it. He was relieved. Despite upheavals and years apart, their affection had endured.

"Good grief, you've taken a risk," Alistair fired first. "What on earth brought you here?"

"Brim," said Freddie, "I'm your RVR man."

"Christ, you; my RVR; in Baden; phenomenal! Talk about scraping the barrel," chuckled Alistair. "You are a flyer, not a spook; how come you're one of Brim's people?"

Astrid and her father strode across the hallway to join the brothers. For Manfred, it was no surprise; Astrid appeared stunned.

"This is Freddie," Alistair said, still flabbergasted.

Astrid took his hand: "I've heard so much about you, Freddie," she said graciously. Alistair studied his brother as an art expert might scrutinise a likely fake, his head cocked to one side.

"What happened to your leg?" asked Alistair.

"Crashed a Tiger Moth. Not my fault; the kite was kibosh.

Doing a favour for the CO."

"God! I'm – I'm sorry, Freddie. But at least you are still active, eh? Active and serviceable. Unlike the bloody Moth, clearly." He proffered a half smile.

But Freddie was serious: "It was damn stupid. I can't fly; and that's the end of it. Physically debilitated. Flying Spits was my life."

An awkward silence passed until Alistair said: "So, Brim recruited you? From the RAF? Why?"

Was there a slight caustic edge to his question? Was he saying Freddie shouldn't be there; he wasn't up to it? Why? His injury? His intellect? His mobility? Nobody could be sure what Alistair meant. but everyone sensed his acerbic tone, Freddie most acutely. He puffed out his cheeks indignantly.

"A passing resemblance to you, Alistair, I would imagine. However, my immediate mission is as your RVR. And here I am."

Alistair seemed to read the mood: "Good. That's good. I think I can smell food and we are starving, aren't we, Astrid?"

"Yes. It's been a long journey, Stephan," said Astrid meekly, trying to inject a little humour into the air. The tension was palpable.

Manfred frowned and pinched his nose, the way he did:

"Alistair, before we eat, Freddie needs to speak to you privately." Manfred's tone was firm, but diplomatic, knowing the sensitive subject.

Alistair looked wary: "What?" he laughed, "I thought we were celebrating?"

"We are. But go into my study." Alistair and Freddie walked

into a large sun-filled conservatory lined with potted plants.

"This isn't about Brim or British Intelligence, is it?" Any trace of amusement in Alistair's tone had vanished.

"No."

"Well, come on then; you're getting me worried."

Once they were in the study, Freddie produced Herr Seiler's precious wallet from his pocket:

"It's about this."

Freddie opened the wallet, took out their mother's letter and handed it to his brother, "But before you read it, I owe you the humblest of apologies for that night at Waterloo. Please forgive me." Freddie sounded how he felt, desperate and sad.

"Well, I was pretty shabby too. Alcohol and I are a dangerous combination, you know that, Freddie. But you can get me a beer from Ingrid all the same," he took the document, sat down and started to read. Freddie went to the kitchen.

"Is everything all right?" asked Ingrid.

"We'll see, Ingrid, won't we? Alistair needs a beer. In fact, we both do."

"In the larder. Help yourself."

"Thanks. We won't be a minute."

When Freddie returned, he found Alistair white as a sheet with a look of rage. He had seen that look before and it scared him. A childhood memory. Something in the recesses of his mind.

"How did he die?"

"What?" said Freddie, flummoxed.

"If you have this, Herr Seiler must be dead."

Freddie sank onto the settee beside his brother.

"How?" Alistair repeated loudly.

"I'm not entirely sure, Alistair. Heart, I think. I wasn't with him ... at the exact moment. We were in a hotel, on the way here."

"Why the hell was Herr Seiler with you on a mission for British Intelligence?"

"He insisted on coming with me, Alistair. He knew what I was doing, and he wanted to see you. I think he knew he was dying."

"Herr Seiler was an old man, Freddie." Alistair's tone was loaded with sarcasm.

"I know. I know."

This wasn't what Freddie had foreseen. What about the letter? What about the content? What about his apology?

Freddie handed him a cold beer, which he opened and gulped half of thirstily.

"What a welcome," said Alistair bitterly.

"Please don't, Alistair, I want to say sorry ... to ..."

Alistair stood up theatrically: "And just how am I supposed to be? How? Herr Seiler is dead, and this is how I find out. Through a letter from our long-dead mother, written in 1917." He was agitated and loud.

Astrid, Ingrid and Manfred walked in, looking wary and concerned in equal measure.

"We heard shouting," said Manfred, rather unnecessarily.

"Herr Seiler is dead."

"Yes," said Manfred diplomatically, "we had no way of telling you. We are sorry. All of us. Of course, we didn't know him, but we feel for you both."

Alistair let out a solitary sob: "His body ..."

Manfred knew he must seize his chance: "Freddie had no choice, Alistair - except to leave a note at the hotel and a lot of money to pay for the formalities. If he had stayed, he would have blown his cover, together with all we have worked for. The authorities might still chase him, but Freddie made the right decision. Of that I am sure. And I have given it much consideration, given the gravity of the situation."

"But why was Herr Seiler there?" Alistair repeated.

Freddie said. "He was coughing, and his breathing was terrible," he paused. "He wanted us to travel together and he needed me to find that letter, to put the record straight. So we could find some sort of a resolution."

"Do you really believe that, Freddie? From your heart?"

"Yes, I honestly do."

Silence. Silence for well over a minute. Then Alistair held out his hand:

"Sorry, Freddie, I overreacted. It's the shock. Seeing you. Brim. The RVR. Not what I expected. Or anticipated."

Freddie shook his brother's hand firmly, the way Herr Seiler taught them after a childhood quarrel.

"Thank you," said Freddie. The moment had passed. And that door was now locked: Herr Seiler, the letter, their mother. A closed chapter. Until the next time.

*

Later, they all sat at a big, round pine table in the kitchen. Alistair and Freddie were amicable, the ice was very slowly thawing. Open French doors led to a sun terrace and large, well-kept garden. German cheese, potato salad, various pickles and thick black bread filled every inch of the table. Nearly all was consumed with gusto, along with cold steins of beer.

Manfred, Ingrid and Astrid swiftly tidied away the remnants of the meal, leaving the table clear.

Alistair produced Admiral Canaris's distinct briefcase which had sat on the table at the Berghof. In the presence of Hitler, Himmler, Karl Doenitz, Goebbels, and Goering. The Presidium.

It was like a piece of provenance at a macabre auction and the contents were spread out:

'The blueprints,' as Canaris had described them:

DAS SCHLOSS: photographs of Windsor Castle, Ordnance Survey maps of Berkshire and official Reich documents. There were also copious notes of times, radio frequencies and tide tables of the east coast of England.

"Feast your eyes on that lot." Alistair said with pride. Astrid watched him with an undisguised admiration, but was there something else?

Alistair explained the precise details of that day at the Berghof, Obersalzburg. How, in the car, just as Canaris wound up the divider screen between the front and back, he had heard Rommel mumble those precious few words:

> *'Schlafende Spione in London ... I'm surprised they are not all ...'*

"The code red. I see," whispered Freddie, "now it all makes sense."

Alistair went onto explain about swapping the briefcases. Canaris catching him on Unter den Linden. The confrontation. Schwarze Kapelle. The planned aerial attack on Britain, U-Boat 302, Cromer. The on-the-ground planned attack on Windsor Castle. They were all spellbound at the significance of this moment. Freddie in particular:

"What you have achieved in obtaining this intelligence is outstanding, Alistair. The risk both of you took in Potsdam ... courageous."

"Thank you, Freddie," said Alistair with genuine affection. "But you know, I couldn't have achieved it without Astrid ..."

Astrid demurred with a smile.

"And Manfred and Siebenthal. Nexus did the real work."

They all knew that wasn't quite true. But Manfred pinched his nose and raised his bushy eyebrows anyway. Astrid watched Freddie with interest. Was it the striking resemblance to her husband or something more? She understood much about the disparity between the siblings but there was more than that. Freddie radiated compassion and warmth, seemingly out of reach at first; Alistair did not. He could be cold and distant.

Manfred acknowledged the praise with a glance at both Alistair and his daughter: "We can discuss the next part of the plan later."

*

Astrid wore a thin, cotton blouse and pleated skirt. Her hair was piled up on top with loose ringlets either side of her face. She wore no makeup or jewellery, not even a wedding band.

Freddie could see she was a youthful version of Ingrid except her hair was more auburn than blond. Her skin, kissed by the sun, had a cluster of freckles around her nose and cheeks, and her eyes constantly sparkled. She sported an athletic and taut figure. This, Alistair had constantly failed to notice during their time together at the house in Potsdam.

Freddie, however, did not.

Union

27 Schwartzmattstrasse, Baden-Baden, Germany.

A FEW DAYS LATER, after dinner, Alistair chose to turn in early, as did the Lochars just minutes later. This left Astrid and Freddie relaxing with a large carafe of chilled Riesling and a packet of cigarettes.

They sat together on the terrace; the warm air was resonant with the sound of crickets. Despite the cloudless and moonlit night, Ingrid had lit candles. This gave the veranda a tavern-like air.

"Why is there anger between you and Alistair?" asked Astrid. She lit a cigarette, leaned forward on the table, resting her chin on her fist, and studied him with child-like curiosity, "Why don't you get on?"

"We used to back in the old days," he said defensively, "until one night, we had a fearful row about our mother. I, I was wrong. I misconstrued something. It will be alright."

"I hope so, Freddie, for both of you." She brushed the back of his hand making him flinch. She smiled coquettishly. "I really do."

"So do I. It's been a long time since we last met – almost seven years – and there has been no continuity. The worst thing was having to tell him about Herr Seiler. I feel so guilty."

"I understand. But he's still your brother." She touched his hand again and gave it the tiniest of strokes.

He stared at his hand, astonished at this casual intimacy: "He'll always be my brother, but he blames me for leaving Herr Seiler and I can see why. Although I think he knows now it was not intentional."

"He does, I am sure," Astrid said in a conciliatory tone. She drew deeply on her cigarette, exhaling slowly. "Alistair can be moody you know, and his mind is always elsewhere. Defying and battling the Nazis puts a huge strain on us both. We are living a lie."

Her candour startled him: "I can understand that, of course. But, as I said, what you both achieved was astounding."

"It had to be done. Orders from Nexus," she said a little flippantly. "I am sure everything will work out. It can't go on for ever, the way we have been living." She looked away, her mind racing, overflowing with trepidations she wanted to air. Freddie felt awkward.

"I know I couldn't have done it," he coughed and nervously cleared his throat. This was Freddie's terribly English way of changing the subject. He hated talking about intimate matters and was uncomfortable with anything linked to other people's relationships, let alone his brother's marriage.

Astrid poured them both more wine and took a generous sip. Freddie had lost count of the number of glasses she had downed. It seemed to have no outward effect. She was happy, talkative and her frankness surprising. She flicked the butt of her cigarette out onto the garden. It fell smouldering among the flowers, wisps of blue smoke rising into the air.

"Your father won't like that."

Freddie stood up, stepped towards the offending object, stooped down and stubbed it out. When he straightened up, he turned, and she was right in front of him.

"Kiss me," she said.

"What? Don't be ridicu ..." But it was too late.

Astrid took Freddie's head in her hands and kissed him passionately on the mouth. She pressed herself against him. It was so sudden and electrifying that he couldn't stop himself. He hadn't touched a woman in many months, since his last night with Sally.

Astrid gripped him tightly. She was so beautiful. He responded.

Her golden hair.

Her laugh.

And now, a pang of guilt.

He tried to pull back, but Astrid held him tightly. She unbuttoned the front of her blouse and looked him in the eye, panting with excitement.

"I need you, Freddie."

She drew back, lifted her skirt, and removed her silk underwear. The scent of her was overwhelming, the intimacy exquisite ...

"Astrid..." he could feel reality ebbing away.

Freddie was completely shocked, so much so, he could hardly speak:

"But I ..." His protestation was feeble; and she silenced it with her lips. She led him from the villa, further down the garden, under the branches of a tall fir: "Lie down here," she said softly.

Freddie struggled down awkwardly and lay on the warm grass. In seconds, she was on top of him, deftly unbuttoning his trousers.

She lifted her dress, straddled him, and sank down on top of him until he was inside her. It felt exquisite; warm, engulfing, and sensual. Astrid threw her head back, her breasts and hips moving rhythmically.

When it happened, he felt a wave of relief and comfort. Astrid lent forward and kissed him, still with passion, just a little diminished. He could feel the rapid beat of her heart. Finally, she lifted herself and lay quietly beside him. He felt content, the unique pleasure of physical contact and love. He had never experienced such sheer ecstasy in his life. Not with Sally; not with anyone.

Nothing was said for several minutes; then he took her hand and stared up at the stars:

"Why?"

Her breath was still fast, it was a whisper: "Because ... I need a child, Freddie." Was she stifling a cry? "... and you must be the father, don't you see?"

Need. It was a curious choice of word. He would replay this

exchange over in his mind many times. And so, would she.

Astrid wanted desperately to tell him what had happened back in the summer of 1935. When she lost her baby. When her world fell apart. When she lay in that hospital bed, heartbroken. And she would when the time was right. Freddie was the one for her and she had known it from the first moment she had set eyes on him.

Freddie caressed her hand and gently whispered: "Oh dear, what have we done?"

Plan

27 Schwartzmattstrasse, Baden-Baden, Germany.

NEXT MORNING, THE SUN BLAZED. It was warm, an exquisite day. By 7.30 the Lochars were scurrying around the kitchen preparing breakfast. French doors, latched wide open, led to the terrace and gardens.

Manfred meticulously laid the table outside; buffing cutlery and checking the plates were pristine. Ingrid, dressed in a bright pinafore, sliced potatoes and cracked eggs. There was no sign of the others.

Astrid appeared first wearing a thin cotton dressing gown and precious little else. Even with no makeup she was a picture of naïve beauty.

Manfred kissed his daughter on the cheek: "I hope you are dressing for breakfast, my Liebchen?"

"Yes! I just need coffee to wake me up. You know how I am first thing, papa!"

Freddie came in next. He saw Astrid sipping a mug of coffee.

Light shone through her gown and he could clearly see the outline of her curves. My God, he thought. Was it a dream?

"Good morning, Freddie," she said innocently. She caught her father's eye. "I'll go up and change."

Not on my account thought Freddie. He wondered for a moment if Manfred caught the unspoken nuance.

Alistair arrived next. "Sleep well, Freddie?"

"Like a log, must be the fresh air!" he tried to sound jovial.

Ingrid was busy: the smell of breakfast infused the air, sizzling and mouth-watering: Bauernfrühstück!

Manfred pinched his nose and raised his eyebrows: "The plan," he said flatly.

"Yes," said Alistair, perking up, "I've been looking forward to a parachute jump back onto English soil. There are things I miss, although I can't imagine what."

"A parachute jump ... no, we don't think so." Manfred sounded firm; a decision made. Brim, Siebenthal and other Nexus members had decided this last week.

"Breakfast," said Ingrid. Astrid appeared at the foot of the stairs in a long, cotton dress, looking radiant.

"Come, Astrid. No work at mealtimes," announced Ingrid, "even the work of Nexus must wait. There is plenty of time, is there not, Manfred?" She flashed a smile which told everyone, in this matter, she was in charge. Nobody disagreed with Ingrid.

"The hand that rocks the cradle rules the world, eh Ingrid," Manfred said jovially, quoting in perfect English. Nobody noticed Astrid mouth the word cradle.

"I thought with Freddie here, we could swap roles. He would stay and I could go back to England with the evidence for Brim," said Alistair sounding less than convincing. He looked at Freddie with enquiring eyes: "Isn't that right, Freddie? What did Brim say? He must have briefed you?"

"My brief was to get here, that's all." Freddie sounded apologetic. "I assumed further details would be arranged locally, here."

Manfred pinched his nose, looked at Freddie, and then spoke as if he wasn't in the room: "No, we have made a decision. Alistair cannot risk travelling with these documents. If he were caught here in Germany, it would ruin the whole operation. If he were arrested and tortured, Canaris would be exposed as a traitor and compromised."

"If I confessed," Alistair said indignantly.

"Oh, Alistair, please. We know you are brave. But the chemicals used by the SS and Gestapo defeat even the most resilient. No, it's too risky."

Alistair huffed, unconvinced. Manfred ignored him and sifted through DAS SCHLOSS. Manfred's sense of urgency was palpable. Alistair tried again:

"But that's why I have Stephan Beck's identification and Abwehr documents, to travel freely."

"Yes, excellent for movement inside Germany, Alistair. As Canaris's chauffeur. Not on the run with stolen Nazi documents." Manfred looked at Alistair. This was an order, not to be debated. "No. Freddie must exit through a safe haven." Manfred was firm.

Freddie was alarmed. The words: Chemicals, SS, and Gestapo frightened him. What if he were arrested and tortured. He'd last about half a minute, he thought dubiously. He sighed deeply to show his concern.

"Where?" asked Freddie, "and how?"

"Spain," said Manfred. "Spain is ostensibly neutral, and we have a network there. Who will stop a war-wounded British soldier?"

"It's too far," said Alistair bluntly, "to travel north is surely more logical."

"Where?" shouted Manfred. He was at the end of his tether now and everyone could see it. Except Alistair. "The only neutral countries are Sweden, Switzerland, Spain and Portugal. This is not up for debate, Alistair. Do you understand?"

Alistair looked at Freddie and there was a hint of a smile around his mouth. Freddie knew that expression from Zermatt. Being chastised by Herr Seiler for some misdemeanour. Freddie was touched he shared that unspoken moment with him. They were brothers again, despite everything.

"Yes, Manfred. Sorry if I was insubordinate."

"Apology accepted, Alistair. I too was disrespectful ..." He looked at the others, the tension now vanished ...

"We know everything north of here is controlled by the Third Reich." Manfred's voice was now calm. The room fell silent, the three men were studying the table of maps, working out the logistics. "And the options are few."

"Alright, but how?" ventured Freddie.

Manfred stood up and wandered over to a large French-style

armoire and opened the door. Inside was a British Army Officer's uniform.

"Inside your prosthetic limb, Freddie, Siebenthal has crafted a compartment to conceal these documents. This inner skin does not show – and will not show – if inspected. But it won't be examined. Because you won't be searched."

"I see," said Freddie. "Route?"

Manfred closed the armoire door: "Rangsdorf Airport to La Coruña, in the north of Spain, on a Lufthansa flight. A Lysander will take you from Biarritz back to London."

"When?" asked Freddie, with immediate concern.

"Tomorrow," replied Manfred.

"I see," said Freddie. Ironically, he could think of only one thing. It wasn't the journey, or the threat posed by the sleeper spies in London. It was Astrid; he was overwhelmed by her. He longed for her again and stared out into the garden, the memory of the lawn, their moment of unbridled passion. He was suddenly immersed in a daydream. All he could think of was what she had said about need.

"Freddie! Did you hear that? Major Alfred Valentine, your papers are flawless."

"Yes, Manfred, I understand. Don't worry."

Commander

Admiralty Citadel, London, England

THREE DAYS BEFORE FREDDIE'S passionate encounter with Astrid in Baden, London was in the middle of a heatwave.

Commander Ian Lancaster Fleming, in Savile Row suit, starched white shirt and polka-dot bow tie, strolled down St. Martin's Lane ignoring the stifling temperature. He knew he was heading underground where the air would be cooler.

Fleming was renowned among the Intelligence community for his aquiline good looks and elegant demeanour. After a brief spell in the City, he had taken the role of Personal Assistant to the Director of Naval Intelligence, with the rank of Commander – signing his memoranda with the codename 17F.

Today he strode into Trafalgar Square with a jaunty step, looking stylish and confident. He stopped and took in the view, so drab, he thought, even London's most famous streets dominated by heaps of abandoned rubble, blacked-out windows, piled sandbags and anti-aircraft guns. A group of tired and sweltering servicemen wandered out of Northumberland Avenue, heavy packs weighing them down. Fleming had been carrying his hat and, despite the heat, put it back on as he approached his destination. He expunged everything from his mind apart from the duty at hand.

The Admiralty Citadel is a squat fortress north-west of Horse Guards Parade on the southern side of the Square near the top of Whitehall. It was built in 1940/41 as a bomb-proof operations centre for the Admiralty with foundations thirty feet deep and a concrete roof twenty feet thick - a bastion linked by inter-connecting tunnels to other government buildings above and below Whitehall. The Submarine Tracking Room, an underground fortress below the main fortification, lay down a series of winding staircases and was guarded, round the clock, by two Royal Marines.

Fleming received salutes as he approached the vaulted door.

Inside was a hive of activity. He instantly sensed the mood heighten, the bustle more frenetic than normal. The white brick walls had been painted a dull-cream colour and were covered with naval maps and charts, blurry monochrome photographs of U-Boats and warships. This was the engine room for war at sea. And there was a flap on.

Thirty or so uniformed officers and Wrens – typists and cryptographers - worked at desks around the edge of the chamber; their space illuminated by angled desk lamps. The insistent metallic clatter of typewriters and clicking bakelite Morse-code tappers resonated loudly.

Most women staff had seemingly abandoned the latest

wartime hairstyle to wear clumsy, ill-fitting headsets. Rows of men sporting short-back-and-sides inevitably had it easier.

Above all, it was evident most were addicted to tobacco; every wastepaper bin was nearly full of a mishmash of redundant paperwork and empty packets of Craven 'A'.

The North Atlantic Plotting Table dominated the centre of the room, mapping the expanse of ocean from Baltic to New England. Colour-coded pins signified every warship, freighter, frigate and submarine; each carefully advanced, reversed or re-routed as news arrived. Correct positioning and exact measurement were vital.

Precious Allied convoys were a priority for every member of staff in this hidden bunker. Upon these boats, mainly US Liberty ships, the logistics and balance of the war hinged. Keeping them all protected and clear of German U-boats was paramount.

Aerial reconnaissance photographs of the U-Boat pens at St. Nazaire and the Kriegsmarine 11th U-Boat flotilla at Bergen, although inevitably out of date, gave operators a measure of German strength, which, they knew, was considerable. Allied losses were inevitable. The team in the tracking room hated that fact above all else.

A large, black and white photograph of Grand Admiral Karl Doenitz, supreme commander of the Kriegsmarine, looked down on them. Some bright spark had added the words: "KNOW THINE ENEMY" in bright red pencil. Numerous pin pricks in his picture also evidenced it doubled as a dartboard during quieter shifts.

"Good morning, Tom," said Fleming, softly, "any news?"

Thomas Trout, a tousle-haired civilian volunteer with freckled complexion, was a good man and the ultimate enthusiast. His passion was ships, German ships. He had read just about every book ever written about German naval tactics and history, mostly in German. He could instantly, and often excitedly, recall known details of the careers of every Kapitän of the U-Bootwaffe. Above all, he had the uncanny instinct to predict and anticipate U-Boat movements. Trout's knowledge and skills were unsurpassed: "He can smell U-Boats in his sleep," was Fleming's wisecrack.

Trout had lectured officer candidates at the Royal Naval College at Dartmouth before the war and was granted the rank of temporary Commander early in 1940.

Given his knowledge, Trout was soon whisked to London, given a small, central-London flat and put in charge of tracking all enemy submarines at the Citadel. Part of his team's role was to monitor intercepts of routine communications between U-Boats and their command HQ's in Germany and Holland.

Something had caught his attention less than an hour before: "Yes. A Wren at Cromer Y-Service Station intercepted what she believes is a communication between a U-Boat and a wireless on-shore."

"Triangulation?"

"Yes. Amsterdam."

"OS grid?"

"TG219422."

Fleming studied a map of the North Sea: "Which one?"

"U-302, the one that's been hanging around the North Sea ... certainly Holland and down to Zeebrugge."

Fleming sighed: "Umm. So, U-Boat 302 is patrolling, either waiting for a 'go' signal or looking for a put-down point. No wonder you're all so busy. What's the weather like up there?"

Trout chuckled: "Choppy. I wouldn't fancy collecting a group of German spies in those waters."

"Or disembarking them. Does the Professor know?"

"No. I thought I'd consult you first."

Fleming gave him a laconic look: "Good man, Tom. Alert Brim, the War Rooms, all branches of Military Intelligence and Cyril Downing. I'll get over there right away, see what's cooking. Well done."

He was about to leave when a young Wren came bounding over, bubbling with excitement.

"Sir! Sir! Another signal from U-302 ten minutes ago!"

"Go on then."

"Well, Vera said it was definitely land-to-sea – and the 'fist' is definitely the same."

Fleming and Trout knew every person sending Morse-code had significant 'tells' to make their individual 'fist' unique – these were often linked to the inter-character and inter-word gaps in the message – much in the same way people space their language when speaking. Skilled Morse listeners could readily spot different senders.

"What was the message?" asked Fleming.

"Tea pot whistlers playing ... 3008 – continuous."

"In German?"

"Decrypted by Bletchley, yes."

"What can it mean?" said Trout.

"My best guess – a date – 30th August," said Fleming, glancing at his Rolex, "and that's in five days. Whatever happens, it's happening soon."

U-Boat

The North Sea.

SLEEK GERMAN U-BOATS were military kings of the Atlantic for much of the war but inside they reeked. Crews had an unpleasant life, constantly on high alert. A patrol could take anywhere between three weeks to six months, depending on mission objectives. During this time, men could not bathe fully, shave or even change clothes. Freshwater was limited and strictly rationed for drinking.

There was no privacy, and all space was filled; some even slept in the torpedo loading bay. Crews resorted to hot bunking, where as soon as one person had crawled out, the next would crawl in. Using the toilet and eating were difficult. Fresh food spoiled fast from exposure to diesel fumes and damp; crew then only ate canned goods.

U-302 (a type V11C) was submerged roughly 12 metres - periscope depth - below the surface of the North Sea, ten miles off the coast of Cromer in the east of England. By 4.30am that day the crew had been at sea for exactly twenty days. They had skimmed the coast of Holland from Den Helder down to Schouwen. At Zeebrugge they took on diesel, food and water. Kapitän Klaus Neidhart stared through the periscope, drinking foul-tasting, cold, black coffee. His eyes burned with grit from gazing out at the equally cold, black sea. His head throbbed; he was tired, dehydrated and longed for fresh air. The submarine stank of sweat, urine, rotting potatoes and the bodily stench of 43 men, and two women (45 was the usual crew number for a V11 series boat). But this crew had been cramped together for too long without surfacing. Worse, four of those on board, including the two women, were "passengers" who took up more space than regular crew.

Above all, so close to England, everyone feared depth charges or torpedoes. Neidhart knew his boat was probably being tracked, even as he stared out through the Zeiss lens at nothing but the North Sea swell.

His First Officer, Ernst Hilger, came to the bridge and cleared his throat: "I don't like the look of those cylinders."

"You've been saying that since we left Germany, number one. What's the matter?"

Hilger was sweating profusely and looked pale: "The spies are talking in English – I think they are English!"

"Nonsense. They are German, trained to sound English. They haven't spoken a word of German for months."

"They keep themselves to themselves, Herr Kapitän."

"That's the point. They try to avoid hearing German; everything must be in English - orders from Doenitz and ultimately the Führer. This is the most important sea voyage of the year!"

He wiped his forehead with an oil-stained rag: "When is the rendezvous, Herr Kapitän? The crew are restless."

Neidhart turned unhurriedly from the periscope and faced his second-in-command: "What is really the matter, Ernst? The cylinders, eh? Crew morale? What is it?" He tried to placate his colleague, using his first name, not generally accepted behaviour at sea.

"We are so near the coastline, and so shallow," said Hilger. "Corvettes are bound to be in the area, and there will be aerial surveillance. We are ... what is it the British say ... 'ducks sitting'?"

"That's why I'm glued to this damn thing every minute of the day. Not because I enjoy it. I have my orders and you have yours. Understand? The drop-off is in a few days. We surface and send away our passengers and their mysterious cargo. It will be dark and any chance of being seen will be minimal, all right?"

Both men knew, when the time came, they would need to be at least two miles off the coast. Their passengers would row ashore in their inflated boats before dawn, assuming the tide was right. The location had been very carefully chosen because their operatives in London would have to travel up to meet them. That was all the detail they knew.

"Why are they to dress as RAF pilots, and why do they need two women?" he persisted. "Spies caught in enemy garb are shot, and those two women are little more than teenagers. It's not natural."

"Sorry, those answers are classified well above my rank. Now go back and rally the crew. Tell them it will all be over soon. Tell them they are doing it for the Fatherland."

He forced a smile: "Ja, Herr Kapitän."

Neidhart returned to his periscope and wondered if he had chosen the right words.

It might be all over soon for everyone if one of those cylinders explodes, he thought. He had an unwholesome feeling about them. He was petrified but dare not show it.

Neidhart had been chosen specifically by Admiral Doenitz. And more specifically by Heinrich Himmler, but he would never know that. His fate was sealed.

Conference

St. James's Street, London, England.

THE THICK, ARMOUR-PLATED DOOR was firmly shut. Four men sat uneasily on straight-backed chairs around the polished walnut table. They had gathered in the opulent, sound-proofed office of Brigadier Sir Cyril Downing on the top floor of 58 St. James's Street, wartime home of MI5. For several moments, silence reigned as each man glanced at each other, sizing them up for the debate to come. Brimblecombe sat beside the Prime Minister, opposite Downing and Commander Ian Fleming. The professor-turned-spy was restless; he knew flak was about to fly.

Why had he brought Fleming? He knew his knowledge in Naval Intelligence (NID) might be vital to the meeting. Fleming's star was in the ascendant and Brim had been watching him brighten the espionage cosmos.

Fleming's former boss was the gifted Rear-Admiral John Godfrey. They didn't like each other but, for operations, that mattered little. Together they had orchestrated Operation Golden Eye - the Allied plan to monitor Spain after a possible alliance between Francisco Franco and the Axis powers. Fleming had been a key player in other operations too and he needed no introduction to this meeting.

Downing began: "Professor, may I firstly thank you for wiring us all yesterday? I understand Major Freddie Valentine landed last night at La Coruña in Spain and is en route to Biarritz as we speak."

"Correct, Director," said Brim.

"Any reason for the change of plan?" asked Downing.

"No change of plan," said Brim. "It was always my thinking Freddie should be the return courier too. More importantly, if Alistair was captured and interrogated, he might expose Canaris. And that's a risk we cannot take."

"Can you get him back after this crisis – if we ever find out what the devil it is?" asked the Prime Minister.

"For now, the SOE in France couldn't extract him and neither could we, even if we wanted to," Brim replied. "He is essentially a German with German papers. Even if we could arrange new identity, he would struggle to get home. He is still of most value to us in Germany."

"I see," said Downing. "Where is he?"

"In Baden, staying with his wife and her parents, the Lochars."

"Ah! Siebenthal's network," said Downing, "Nexus?"

"Indeed ... Alistair's matrimonial sojourn," said Brim. "He is waiting for orders from my office. He will be furious he wasn't selected as courier, but we have to play our cards right on this one. Manfred Lochar is in complete agreement."

Churchill lowered his glasses and peered directly at Brim: "What about C? You must keep Menzies up to speed."

"Of course," Brim replied, meeting his gaze. "I shall brief him as soon as he gets back from Scotland this evening. He's been inspecting the latest batch of MI6 gofers."

"Good," said Downing. "Now, what do you make of this signal from U-302 intercepted at Cromer?"

Fleming, dressed in uniform, with his naval commander's three gold stripes on the cuff, looked vaguely amused. He sat cross-legged in his chair, seemingly relaxed. He took out a cigarette from a black gunmetal case, inserted it into his ivory holder and lit it with a battered Ronson lighter. He exhaled as he replied, the Balkan and Turkish aroma sweet:

"I think this U-Boat's movements are too erratic for normal surveillance or attack duties. It's there to off-load, probably a crew of specialists. Guessing further, it might be linked to Jupiter's message.

The Kriegsmarine wouldn't patrol in the North Sea so openly and so close to the coast without a damn good reason. They are waiting for a signal. Maybe it relates to tides, weather, Home Guard, police presence and so on."

"Brim?" asked Downing, looking across at the PM.

"I agree with Fleming. I'm sure there is a dormant enemy force in place here, because that's what Jupiter warned us about. He was quite specific – Schlafende Spione in London - remember?"

"So, even if the U-boat and the undercover spies are linked, we are no further forward?" said Churchill in his typical gruff tone when agitated.

"With respect, Prime Minister, I believe we are," said Fleming. "Since the alert from Jupiter, Freddie Valentine has collected a package and it's on its way here. Huge progress, I would say."

"Within the structure of a prosthetic limb, Prime Minister," said Brim in jocular tone, reminding them all this was his idea. His conjecture had paid off. He pursed his lips and glanced at the PM.

"Yes, yes, I know," said Churchill irritably.

He rose awkwardly from his chair and brushed ash from his trousers: "I have to return to the War Rooms. I'm not sure I've learned much. We still don't understand the nature of the threat." He put his coat on before continuing:

"What about Manfred Lochar? Can't he tell us the secret? He must know what the danger is if the brothers have been with him."

Fleming was quick to respond: "There is no secure, secret line out of Germany, Prime Minister; never has been." He paused. "The SIGSALY phone scrambling between the Allies for high-level messages could never be applied here; you may recall the equipment is huge and heavy – as big as an average room – and Jupiter won't risk another code red. We just have to be patient ...

He sent us his message of dire warning – a code red – and that's it." Fleming looked at Brim who nodded gently in full agreement.

Churchill grunted and nodded; the other three men rose as

the great man left. The thick, armour-plated door clunked shut once again.

Downing, Fleming and Brimblecombe sat for a moment in silence, collecting their thoughts, in the wake of Churchill's huffy departure.

"What do we do?" said Downing, now sitting behind his cluttered desk. "What I mean is, what would you do, if you were this sleeper spy? Or spies? ..." He looked at the others ...

"Imagine you have to offload a 'crew of specialists', as Ian put it, what would you need?"

"Transport? A safe house? Equipment?" said Fleming.

"Anonymity?" put in Brim.

"Yes, all of those. Let's go one step forward. Say the crew of specialists from the U-Boat are three, maybe four people – plus equipment – and your sleeper spies are two or three, that's six or more people."

"They'd need a lorry or small bus to move," suggested Brim.

"Yes, they're unlikely to risk trains, and a carful would be conspicuous, packed with passengers of a certain age and physical appearance. They are unlikely to be in uniform. Who might have an unobtrusive bus?"

"School? College? Hospital? Hotel?" said Fleming. "Maybe our sleeper spies run a guest house or hotel?"

Brim again: "Possibly, yes. A privately owned bus would give them cover – and get a higher level of petrol rationing. It wouldn't appear much out of the ordinary in most parts of Britain."

"You could be close," said Fleming.

"Contact Sanders at the Yard," said Brim. "Let's keep watch on the roads from London to Cromer. And I mean all, but discreetly. Also get them to check on possible transport locally along the east coast; for all we know, they may already be there."

"Yes," said Downing, "and until Freddie gets back, it's about all we can do. God, I hate this damn war."

"Whisky and soda; and a cheese sandwich?" asked Brim. "We deserve one. That's unless you can think of anything more exciting, Commander."

Fleming sighed: "Before the war, Scott's in Coventry Street was my favourite. Maurice's chef-d'oeuvre was fresh, dressed Devon crab washed down with a pint of black velvet. I even had my preferred niche: a corner table for two on the first floor. You could admire the working girls of Piccadilly, a regular procession of entertainment. And simply imagine the frou-frou of stockings and summer dresses."

"Black velvet made with champagne, not cider?" Brim speculated.

"Oh, Bollinger, of course. Followed by Welsh rarebit; a decent savoury before coffee."

Brim salivated at the thought: "Do you know such a place, Ian?"

"I most certainly do, Brim. Although I can't guarantee Devon crab, I'm sure we can find some champagne."

Downing smiled: "Shall I call for a cab, Ian? Or can we walk from here?"

Return

RAF Northolt, West London, England.

LANDING THE WESTLAND LYSANDER at Northolt was a challenging task for Pilot Officer Ken Morgan. The small black plane juddered furiously as he dipped its port wing for final approach through pulsing sheets of rain.

"August downpours. Bloody typical," he thought cynically. The runway was new to him and a radical change from his home base at Newmarket.

Repeating volleys of anti-aircraft fire had burst within inches of the Lysander over La Rochelle; searing bright blasts followed by escorting clouds of noxious smoke. He didn't know flak had pierced 40 holes into the flimsy fuselage. Strictly speaking, the plane was no longer airworthy. As for the German .88s, one direct hit would have vaporised plane, pilot and passenger.

Yet these diminutive aircraft were loved by their hardy flyers. They were tough and manoeuvrable. Skilled pilots like Morgan could land safely in a field at 60mph in the dark and take off in 36 yards. To navigate, pilots used dead reckoning from a fixed point – this time from Biarritz.

"Better tighten your seatbelt again, Wing Commander," Morgan had said to Freddie through the in-flight headset. "First the damn flak, now we're in for a rough landing."

It had been 1am when Freddie had trudged through darkness and a thunderstorm. He'd been escorted to a remote field in south-western France, had no clue exactly where he was, but strangely felt safe. Hot bread, jam, strong coffee and local Armagnac shared with his newest contacts before midnight in an old cellar invigorated him after an already lengthy journey. In the few hours since his arrival he'd concluded that his escorts were among the bravest people he'd ever met. This SOE team, combined with French Resistance, had been conspicuously nervous and secretive - yet practical, reasonable, and as hospitable as limited resources allowed. The flight from Rangsdorf Airport to La Coruña in the north of Spain had been long, but straightforward. His paperwork was faultless and his answers well-prepared; he was cleared to leave Rangsdorf with little probing or concern.

Morgan had plotted a course north-east, up the Côte d 'Argent, hugging the coast to La Rochelle. His plan was to swing in towards the direction of Niort and then up to Cholet, Rennes and out over the coast at St. Malo.

Unluckily, Morgan had overshot La Rochelle. He found himself – according to his chart – flying over La Roche-sur-Yon, in the airspace above Nantes and St. Nazaire. This was home to

U-Boat pens and heavily protected by anti-aircraft batteries. Search light beams scanned the night sky, quickly followed by tracer fire from German guns more than a mile below them. The old bucket shook as Morgan dodged bullets as best he could.

"Sorry about this, Wing Commander," Morgan had said through his headset, "we're in for a bumpy ride."

Dozens of rounds had ripped into the fuselage and exposed undercarriage: "Please God don't hit the fuel tank," Freddie had prayed inwardly. He'd closed his eyes and focused.

Astrid.

Saying goodbye had been sad, because he couldn't say goodbye; certainly not in private as he wanted. The Lochars were also sorry he was leaving, but, of course, knew he had to. Manfred had taken him to one side and re-assured him: "Every detail of your journey has been planned and anticipated. You will be alright. Good luck from all of us in Nexus, Freddie. You are a brave man. The RAF would be even more proud of you. What a pity you can't tell them."

Saying goodbye to Alistair had been equally tricky because of what had happened. There was an air about him as he left. He had wished Freddie good luck and mysteriously said: "See you soon, Freddie. I am sure. Don't worry; all will be revealed."

This parting shot troubled Freddie during his flight to La Coruña and his rail journey to Biarritz. What did he mean: all will be revealed?

Finally, the little aircraft cleared the enemy bombardment and tracked west and up the French coast trying to gain height and rise above the next gathering storm. As they headed out over the Channel, the first hint of dawn appeared below the heavy cloud on the horizon in the east.

"We'll make it now." said Morgan. "We are out of trouble. London will be quieter; you have my assurance of that."

Freddie felt impatient. He wanted to get back. He wanted answers.

The noise was deafening as they touched down in pounding rain. Almost as soon as they landed, they taxied into the massive open aircraft hangar and the huge metal doors were immediately slid shut by a troop of RAF mechanics. The plane dripped with rain; it glistened as the huge arc lights flickered and turned on to full power. Morgan switched off the engine and the single propeller came to rest.

"Someone's taken a ruddy pounding!" a voice called out. "Bugger! Look at the number of bullet holes in her."

As soon as it was deemed safe by the on-duty officer, ground staff went through the well-rehearsed routine of unstrapping the pilot first, undoing his headgear and assisting him to the ground. With the canopy off, two more crew helped Freddie get out of the cockpit and down to the concrete floor.

He felt dizzy. Was it the heat from the engine or the suddenness of no longer moving? He looked around the huge hangar – other aircraft – mechanics dashing around. He had no idea of the exact time and felt disorientated.

Brim was there at once. He thrust his hand out in greeting: "Welcome home, old sport! How the devil are you?"

Freddie's immediate impression was that – in a short time – Brim had visibly aged. Despite his corpulent stature, he looked almost under-nourished and pale. He sniffled with either a summer cold or hay fever, attempted a smile, but could not miss the sight of the Lysander riddled with bullet holes.

"How was the journey?" he asked gravely.

"Better than mine in Squires's Tiger Moth," he couldn't resist saying. He undid his flight suit; he was hot and felt trapped inside it.

PO Morgan saluted the two men and walked away without a word; SOE pilots were used to discretion; in and out of occupied France at a moment's notice. Did he even have any idea what this was all about? Or who Brim was?

Freddie took Brim to one side and launched into a flurry of nervous and excited words:

"The news is not good, Brim. Himmler is behind this. The Nazis plan an aerial nerve gas attack on the south of England; Biggin Hill, all Command Centres. Ten Heinkels armed with new, high-speed ballistic missiles primed with a lethal gas called Tabun."

"Good God."

"There's more," said Freddie; he was breathless. "They plan a ground attack with cylinders of Tabun at Windsor Castle."

Brim was too stunned to speak as Freddie continued:

"The sleeper spies Alistair warned you all about – at the start of all this – are real. But there's a U-Boat involved in the equation too. She's sailing from Bergen to Cromer."

Brim pursed his lips and considered: "How did you uncover

all this naval intelligence, Freddie?"

"Alistair did. From Canaris."

Brim turned paler than before: "Canaris? Dear God. When? When will this happen?"

"Soon," said Freddie, "soon is all we know."

Suddenly Brim's mood darkened, he spoke, almost to himself: "The land to sea signal ... my God ... tea pot whistlers playing ... 3008 ... continuous."

"Sorry?" asked Freddie. He hurled his flight suit to a passing member of the ground staff.

Brim explained, realising: "A Wren at the Cromer Y-Service Station intercepted what she believed to be a communication between a U-Boat and an on-shore wireless – that was the message."

"Well, that fits in with precisely what Canaris told Alistair," said Freddie, recollecting the detail:

"U-Boat 302 will land a crew of spies or commandos, at Cromer, to meet the sleeper spies and deliver cylinders of Tabun. From there on by road to Windsor."

Brim: "U-302 eh? Good old Alistair."

"The spies are crucial to this, but I ..."

Brim cut him off: "We must get back to London. I take it you have some evidence. Canaris is a cunning old fox ..."

"Yes. I'm standing on it."

Brim gave a rare smile: "Good. I knew you could do it – both of you."

"There's one more thing though," said Freddie.

"Go on," said Brim; what could possibly be worse?

"The Admiral told Alistair the KGB have a spy in the SIS, leaking secrets to the Kremlin. And he had disrupted his attempts at rapprochement. His exact words, more or less."

"Christ, are you sure? Come on, we haven't a moment to lose."

Brim turned rapidly and whirled out of the hangar, coat tails flapping. Freddie watched him with undisguised amusement despite the situation.

Clarissa

Barneville-Carteret, Normandy, France

CAPTAIN RICHARD LAMBERT WAS A versatile, resourceful man. He had been trained in the manner of a commando. Unlike most other members of the Kriegsmarine of his rank he was paid four times his naval salary. The source of his wealth came from a number of different origins and was paid into a Swiss bank account.

The man who sponsored and advocated Lambert was Erich Spengler of Spengler GmBh, Der Jagdhund as he was known, had been present, with other German industrialists, at the fund-raising conference in Bavaria in 1933. Spengler, Doenitz, and Himmler had spent two years scouring the ranks of the Kriegsmarine and Luftwaffe to find the right man to captain the FV Clarissa for a special mission. Secrecy was paramount and Lambert was generously rewarded for his loyalty. Not even his family knew the truth.

Richard Lambert's name was both English and German, which made obtaining documents and identity papers convenient and practical. Why had they chosen him? Part of the reason, Spengler had told him, was because his father had been a senior diplomat in London during the Weimar Republic and Richard had studied at Eton College for five years. No Englishman would ever suspect Lambert was German. He was articulate, physically strong and his loyalty to the Reich was unquestioned.

Today Captain Lambert sat on the quayside at Barneville-Carteret, a pretty coastal town in Normandy. He had travelled from Germany with his associate Dieter Scheiderbauer more than a year previously, planning and training for what had to be done. Scheiderbauer was the helmsman and navigator, a German national who spoke only in his native tongue. They would have to be careful if challenged, but his navigation skills were faultless as was his carefully studied knowledge of tides. He would spend all of his time in the wheelhouse. The rest of the Clarissa's 'crew' were French fisherman recruited from villages on the Normandy coast.

The Clarissa looked British; she was a British-built Brixham trawler that had run aground during the 'Little Boats' evacuation of Dunkirk. She had been refloated by the German navy, completely re-equipped and harboured in Nazi-occupied Jersey. She carried the requisite white letters GY212 (a genuine Grimsby registration) on her bow.

Lambert and his crew's first challenge would be to cross the Channel without incident. They had done it before and got away with it, despite vastly decreased numbers of British trawlers – most of which were also serving the Royal Navy – and vastly increased numbers of British warships with eagle-eyed crews on constant alert.

To that end, Clarissa had made several excursions into British waters in the past year. Lambert and Scheiderbauer knew their way around British minefields and had even fished among other British trawlers in the western Channel, right through the Irish Sea, almost up to Fleetwood, the town which had become the main centre for the UK fishing fleet. The North Sea and Grimsby were deemed too dangerous; many east coast boats had been docked for the duration of the war; this made Clarissa's Grimsby registration all the more authentic. Lambert would exchange conversation via radio and cheery shouts, pretending to be part of Fleetwood's fleet.

Few English fishermen would doubt a British-built ship, in British livery, under British flag, fishing with apparent skill, with a captain who jauntily waved and chatted like a native. To add credence to Clarissa's routine, she often left harbour before dawn and didn't tie up again until after dark. In these grey dawns or dusky evenings there were often still many trawlers at sea, too many to spot one less when Clarissa headed for a patch of sea mist and onward to Jersey.

Lambert had twice been stopped by Royal Navy Corvettes. Both times, after a friendly chat and a look at the ship's impeccable papers, she was waved on her way. Clarissa's hull was wooden but with steel reinforcement, with an enclosed windowed wheelhouse. Her appearance was sturdy, some seventy feet long and eighteen feet wide with two masts, large sails and a powerful British-made, diesel engine. Clarissa's greatest asset was simply that she looked like other British trawlers and hence, never aroused suspicion.

The boat's radio was tuned to the British Coastguard channel. On deck were two potent winches powered by a hefty generator. Below, the fishermen's quarters were small but comfortable – made somewhat more cramped by the space given over to a specially built and reinforced loading bay. She sported a Reichsmarine flag on her bow. Once beyond Jersey and out of German-patrolled waters, this would be rapidly switched to a Red Ensign. Lambert, although Clarissa's captain, was also wireless operator and made all transmissions in both English and French.

Today Lambert and the three French fishermen, dressed in lightweight polo necks and weatherproof trousers – despite the warmth - were unloading wooden crates from a lorry. On its side were the words:

DIDIER ET FILS
MATÉRIEL AGRICOLE
RENNES

The crates, each three metres long and a half metre wide, looked extremely heavy. Lambert thought they resembled sinister black coffins, but considered it unwise to air such thoughts. Once unloaded from the lorry onto the quayside, they were winched aboard into the custom-built loading bay. The few local people who walked along the quayside took little notice of the Clarissa's crew of fisherman or her cargo. They had seen it all before, and familiarity was what Erich Spengler and his fellow Nazis were banking on.

Debriefing

10 Downing Street, London, England

"THE KING SAYS NO. And quite frankly, I can see his point," said Winston Churchill. He chewed on his Romeo Y Julieta and gazed out of the window. It was a late summer's afternoon, and he was attired in black-tie evening dress, ready for a night out on the town. Or so it appeared.

The long, narrow room at the back of 10 Downing Street overlooked a secluded garden. The Prime Minister exhaled imaginary smoke from the expired cigar with a sigh of disappointment. He sat back in a leather armchair, ignoring the botanical view he had previously cherished.

Cyril Downing, Ian Fleming, and Professor Brimblecombe waited for an explanation of the Royal verdict. Churchill had just returned from the Palace. He seldom used Number 10 and felt uncomfortable there since most of the furniture and paintings had been removed for safe keeping during the Blitz. The wartime house had a deserted air about it, with few staff and sparse comforts. But this room had always been a place of comfort. He balanced a Spode cup and saucer on his lap.

"But why?" asked Cyril Downing.

Churchill placed his champed cigar in an ashtray and finished his tea. He put both items unsteadily onto a small mahogany table and composed his answer:

"The Princesses were moved from Buckingham Palace to Windsor Castle because it was deemed safer, was His Majesty's view. The castle's roof has, as we know, been reinforced to protect against Luftwaffe air raids." Churchill's voice was not as reassuring as it might have been.

"The King also made the point that Windsor has half an army of soldiers and secret service on duty round the clock. It is a fortress. The Queen agreed, by the way, with this point of view. Where else would the Family go without drawing too much attention? His Majesty is right."

Silence followed as the other three in the room absorbed Churchill's words. It was Brim who spoke first:

"The Princesses are more secure in Windsor, I suppose," Brim agreed. "They have an excellent tutor on site; she's one of ours. '*Armed and dangerous*' as Hugh Dalton put it."

Churchill raised an eyebrow: "Yes, Brim, I know."

Brim internally huffed. How did he know? He turned his attention to Ian Fleming: "Any news on the North Sea U-Boat, Fleming?"

Fleming took his time; he didn't like being the bearer of bad news. That is, news that was not positive: "Sadly not. Nothing. We've sent upward of two hundred men to Cromer to scout every inch of coastline ..."

He paused to see what effect his news was having ...

"With the Home Guard, Army and Police, it must be closer to four hundred on the lookout. Beaches, fields, farms, roads and all the local villages are being scoured as we speak. People are glad to get involved, help the war effort. No one should slip through, least of all the enemy."

"And your man at Scotland Yard?" put in Downing. "Odd vehicles? Buses? Lorries?"

"No, again nothing abnormal; and they've stopped plenty, just to make sure. Nil on the radio, either. Cromer Y-Station is listening, as are Biggin Hill and Bletchley. The Admiralty, likewise," continued Fleming.

"I see," said the Prime Minister; it wasn't the news he wanted to hear. He had much to consider. He was all too aware that the Nazis were forging ahead with rocket technology. Science was at its heart. But how far ahead? He wasn't certain.

To quash part of that threat, he'd that morning authorised a 600-bomber raid on a remote island on the Baltic coast. Aerial pictures, taken two years before and recently interpreted by chance at RAF Medmenham, showed they were developing advanced rocket technology nobody among the Allies understood.

The Prime Minister returned his thoughts to the matters concerning the people in the room that day.

"Then we have no choice with the U-Boat, do we?" said Downing cautiously, "We'll send a couple of Corvettes and blow it out of the water. It's all we can do, assuming the Commander's timeline is right ...

Tomorrow is the 30th. We can't just sit on our hands and wait for them to act."

Downing understood the likely weight of public opprobrium if news leaked out of a German U-Boat being allowed to roam freely near the Norfolk coast. The loss of HMS Royal Oak to a sneak U-Boat attack in Scapa Flow at the start of the war still haunted everyone in the room.

Churchill rose and wandered to the window took take a closer look at the garden: "What about your courier, Brim?"

"Freddie Valentine, Prime Minister." Brim reminded him.

"Yes, Valentine. He's done an extraordinary job bringing these papers back to London."

"Indeed, Prime Minister. And direct from Admiral Canaris personally," said Brim proudly. Freddie and Alistair were his agents, and this mission was his idea. All of it. And nobody in the room would be allowed to forget it, not even the PM.

"Quite so," said Fleming.

Churchill turned, his eyes twinkling: "Any chance they could be fake? Admiral Canaris is a cunning old fox. I wouldn't put anything past him."

"No, definitely not," assured Brim.

"But how do you know?" the PM persisted provocatively.

"Because we have controlled every step of the mission, from Siebenthal in Basle to Manfred Lochar in Baden; and I have mentored the agents myself," said Brim, acutely aware he was beginning to sound pompous.

"I see."

"Moreover, how would Canaris have known Alistair was going

to come knocking on his door, so to speak? He didn't announce himself on Unter den Linden. He was caught. By Admiral Canaris."

"That's true, of course," said Churchill, "and very valid."

"The senior curator at the British Museum – Professor Simon Pettifer – verified them microscopically," Brim said defensively. "Das Schloss is genuine, unfortunately. It's authenticity is unquestioned: papers, photographs, maps. The file came from Hitler's meeting at the Berghof. I would stake my life on it. So would Pettifer and his assistant, Miss Smallbone."

"Just a consideration," said Churchill, returning to his armchair, "given the inactivity at Cromer ... and despite your best efforts."

"Of course, Prime Minister," said Brim, inwardly calming himself.

"And where is Mr. Valentine now?" the PM asked in a more reasonable tone.

"At the Baker Street safe house, Prime Minister," said Brim, still just a little vexed at the implied accusation. "He is tired. It was a long and necessarily convoluted journey. His injury doesn't help."

"Yes, yes, of course."

Fleming looked at Downing and Brim, as if for approval and cleared his throat.

"Arrangements with the Admiralty, Prime Minister; there's a Corvette less than fifty miles off the coast of Cromer. She's blacked out and can stay well out of sight of the U-Boat's periscope."

"Very well," said Churchill sombrely, "telephone from the drawing room. The line is secure. You have my authority and the agreement of everyone in this room." Churchill looked around; all nodded in accord.

"But do not attack her until any passengers are off the U-Boat and heading to shore," Churchill continued. "Catch them, and we can learn much. Kill them and we can't."

"Yes, Prime Minister, I fully understand," said Fleming, looking at Downing and Brim again to show their unanimous assent.

"Good. Then I will bid you all good evening. Mrs. Churchill and I have a dinner arranged with Eisenhower at the American Embassy. That's why I'm attired in this damn evening dress and the jacket is too small. It's shrunk."

They all rose as the Prime Minister left the room.

"After you, Director," said Brim to Cyril Downing with a smile. He thought he had handled the confrontation with Churchill rather well.

He would double check, all the same. Seeds of doubt had been planted by the PM, who was rather good at doing just that. Moreover, as Brim knew, although veiled, it was a direct order and one he could not avoid.

Baker Street

London, England

"ANY CHANCE THEY COULD BE FAKE?"

Churchill's growled question echoed in Professor Brimblecombe's mind. It irritated him, as, of course, it was intended to. He paid the cabbie, adding a fair tip, and stepped onto the uneven pavement two streets short of his first destination. He mused at this precaution. As an academic, he wasn't used to such subterfuge. These days he had changed. Maybe the Valentine influence was rubbing off on him.

Fierce heat pervaded the fringes of Regent's Park; scorching sun unusual for London, even in summer. Brim, who was dressed in a beautifully tailored charcoal-grey suit looked most elegant. He might have been on his way to a society wedding, rather than matters concerning the Service. He walked briskly, ignoring the muggy heat. He glanced at his pocket watch and simultaneously heard the chimes of St. Mary's Church clock. He was prompt, as always.

Brim left Park Road at the edge of Regent's Park and headed

down Baker Street. By 6.15pm precisely, the appointed time, he'd arrived at Norma Smallbone's house in Blandford Street. She worked with Professor Pettifer at the British Museum. Brim knew she carried out much of the detailed work to establish provenance of historic items and documents. This research was her life. He checked his tie once more and rang the bell.

*

"Ah yes, the Canaris Papers," Norma Smallbone said as she responded to the doorbell, "I have an office on the first floor. Come on up ...

Here we are ... without doubt, they are authentic. Who is questioning my verdict?"

She was small, precise and spoke with Home Counties clipped inflection. Her starched blouse and tweed skirt somewhat aged her seemingly youthful figure. Looking at Brim through pince-nez, she wrinkled her nose and smiled sweetly.

"Churchill," said Brim plainly. "You recall I needed you to sign the Official Secrets Act before I gave you the Papers? He was why."

"Well," she said in an amused tone, "If one is going to be questioned, it might as well be by Winnie himself." She chuckled.

"So?" asked Brim, not put off by her use of the word Winnie. It was simple. Everything he dealt with was checked and checked again.

"Cup of tea?" she asked.

"Thank you, but no. So?"

"The cardboard file with the red and black swastika motif and stamped DAS SCHLOSS is standard Third Reich stationery from a mill in Dresden. We have other examples – on file – as it were." She chuckled again at her little joke, "I compared them under my microscope at the Royal College of Art. I have a tiny office there...

The fibres are the same." She poured herself a glass of tap water from a little hand basin in the corner. "Yes, the drawings and diagrams are on paper made in Heidelberg ... have you ever visited Heidelberg, Professor? Quite charming."

"No. And I have no desire to, Miss Smallbone."

"Norma, please. The black and white photographs are light-sensitive emulsion and silver halide, certainly of German origin; Agfa-Gevaert the company. Agfa photo GmbH the brand."

"Understood," said Brim. He didn't really. He couldn't care less. What he wanted was the truth. She persisted.

"The paper is Brovira. Given the quality of the photographs, I would say the camera was a Zeiss Ikon Box Tengor, 6 x 9 54/2, probably made in 1936."

"Yes, but is ..."

Miss Smallbone continued: "I would venture to suggest; venture mind you, that an exposure of F11 was used and clearly in sunlight."

"Clearly, yes." He tried to sound enthusiastic. It sounded haughty and sarcastic, but it wasn't meant to. He was rather taken with Miss Smallbone.

"Are you mocking my expertise, Professor?" She raised her eyebrow questioningly.

"Certainly not."

"Good. The photographer knew what he was doing and

probably used a tripod. Now, given time, we could identify all those streets depicted, but there is no question as to the location of that Schloss, is there, Professor?"

"No, quite so," he said guardedly." "There is no question as to authenticity then?"

"None."

Brim pursed his lips the way he did and smiled, not a common occurrence: "That's good. Thank you."

She came over and stood a little closer to him: "Are you sure you wouldn't like some tea? Earl Grey? Mummy knows the importer on East India Dock Road. They were engaged once, you know," she whispered, "imagine!"

"Quite sure."

"Is there anything else?" she licked her upper lip; their proximity was closer now.

"No. I don't think so. You've been most – ah – thorough."

"I like to be thorough; it is the essence of my work." She took a breath. "Well, if there's anything else, ring me here or at the Museum. Simon's office. I do some work for your friend Matheson at Scotland Yard." She handed him a business card.

"I don't have any friends at Scotland Yard," said Brim with an awkward smile, "I'm merely an academic."

"Ah yes, an academic. Please convey my good wishes to Mr. Churchill and assure him of my certainty in this matter."

"I will, of course. Good evening, Miss Smallbone."

"Norma," she said softly as he turned to walk away.

Brim did not notice Norma peering out of her window,

watching the well-dressed figure cross Baker Street. Nor could he have read her mind: What a charming man and so courteous. Oh goodness me, could he possibly be a secret agent? How exciting!

Safe House

Baker Street, London, England.

THE BAKER STREET IRREGULARS were originally a group of fictional characters featured in several of Arthur Conan Doyle's Sherlock Holmes adventures. In wartime the name had re-emerged for the Special Operations Executive (SOE) when it took offices in Baker Street. The organisation's given role was espionage, irregular warfare (sabotage and raiding operations) and special reconnaissance. These characters were far from fictional.

Brim had worked closely with Hugh Dalton to set up SOE, in the early war years. He knew this area of London well and it was in the Baker Street safe house near SOE headquarters at number 64 that Freddie was temporarily billeted.

The professor clumped up the narrow wooden staircase, the noise of his footfalls a simple courtesy to warn Freddie of his arrival and let himself into the two-bedroomed flat. It had a basic kitchenette, sitting room and bathroom; it was a far remove from Norma Smallbone's delightful town house, only a short distance away.

The evening light was fading. Freddie sat at a small, rickety table looking out of the window through a gap in the curtains. All looked drab and dull; a tray of uneaten food cluttered the floor beside him - no doubt delivered by one of the SOE team as a favour, thought Brim. Threadbare carpet and peeling paintwork completed the cheerless picture; these gloomy digs were for suspects and informers, not heroes like Freddie. But Downing and Fleming believed he needed protection and this lacklustre flat was available at short notice.

"Good evening, Freddie," said Brim, mustering joviality. "Do you mind my joining you?"

Freddie looked up blankly and managed half a smile. He looked tired. Brim had seen it before. An agent gets thrown in at the deep end, has myriad experiences facing danger and death, and thrives on the thrill of adrenaline. Then he returns and crashes back to the banality of everyday wartime life. Landing was always hard.

"Please sit down," said Freddie with all the civility he could muster. "I'd offer you tea, but there is none."

"Do you want to go out somewhere?"

"Not really, no. To be honest, I'm all in."

Brim reached into his jacket pocket and pulled out an unopened half bottle of Haig:

"A drink then?"

"Yes, thank you." Freddie's spirits lifted. He stood up and retrieved two faded tumblers from a kitchen cupboard. Brim poured them both a generous measure. They raised their glasses in toast. Awkward silence prevailed. Freddie was clearly in no mood for jovial loquacity. Brim broke the ice.

"I didn't have a proper opportunity to thank you, Freddie, the other evening and to acknowledge just what you have achieved. It was a bloody good show. The Prime Minister wants to thank you personally, too."

"Is he here then? Outside in a cab? You should have brought him up for a whisky."

"You know what I mean, I think."

"Do I?" he sipped his drink. A definite edge.

"Yes."

"To join you all at Number Ten would have been, what, unprecedented?" put in Freddie.

"Something like that, Freddie, yes," said Brim, a little embarrassed.

Freddie downed his whisky and poured another, irritated at his exclusion. There would have been no debriefing without his efforts. The whisky placated his anger. He shut his eyes and savoured the sensation.

"What's the verdict then, Brim? Are you allowed to tell me, or is that privileged too?" he asked.

Despite his tone, Freddie knew it wasn't Brim's doing. It was standard protocol; the professor would likely have preferred Freddie at the meeting. Freddie craved to vent his feeling of exclusion and now sat back, pleased to have let off steam. He also knew when to stop.

Brim nodded as if reading his mind; Freddie noticed he had

an uncanny ability to do this: Were all spymasters mind-readers, or was Brim exceptional?

Brim flipped open his silver cigarette case and lit a Senior Service.

"The King says no budging any members of the Royal family from Windsor. He reckons they are safe there. Safer than the Palace, at least."

"I see. Anything else?"

"The PM agrees to a strike against U-302. When she surfaces, provided any passengers and cargo are disembarked and detained, she will be destroyed. Not before."

"I see. And what if she doesn't?"

"Doesn't what? I don't follow, old sport." Brim said, mystified.

"Surface."

Brim frowned; a notion possibly unconsidered, looked at his watch and spat out some lose strands of tobacco.

"Today is the 30th. My guess is she will surface later tonight, in darkness. We have a big team of watchers – with telescopes and high-powered binoculars – scanning the Norfolk coastline and all ears are on the radio, covering likely frequencies. We can't miss them, Freddie. ... as soon as they're off that sub, our agents will grab them. A Corvette will sink the U-boat. Job done."

Freddie was unconvinced; Brim was saying less than he really knew: "That U-Boat's Kapitän will be wary: even surfacing in the dark he's a sitting duck while dropping off any personnel and equipment. He'll know he's being tracked."

Brim huffed: "Well, it's a chance we'll have to take, isn't it? It could all be a ruse, and it wouldn't be the first." He thought for a moment. "The Germans can also be very stupid. Thanks to you and Alistair we have secured this intelligence. Now we're acting on it."

"Yes."

Brim could not tell Freddie the whole truth. Despite what had first been agreed, the Navy now had instructions to force the U-Boat to surrender, using whatever means they wanted. British Intelligence, MI6, MI5 desperately needed to know why the Germans would risk such folly with the U-Boat. More importantly, they reasoned there could be new Enigma coding machine on board. If so, it could prove invaluable to Bletchley Park. And the Admiralty. Brim felt sorry he could not divulge this Intel to Freddie, who had done so much.

He stubbed out his unfinished cigarette onto a tin ashtray:

"Is something wrong, Freddie? You seem preoccupied. I thought you'd be delighted we take it all seriously."

Freddie looked through the curtains again at passers-by below: mothers in headscarves pushing prams, serviceman lugging their worldly goods in haversacks on their backs.

There was something wrong.

"Herr Seiler died while I was away. He came with me from Zermatt to Basle and then up to Illkirch-Graffenstaden. I believe you know that."

Brim finished his whisky and topped them both up: "What happened?"

"I don't know. I made my radio signal from the Hotel Dollenberg in Illkirch – your cypher to Lochar – and when I returned to his room, he was dead ...

I found him sitting up in his bed. Heart I should guess. Or liver. He loved his booze. But it was a shock, I can tell you. And no one to, well, share it with."

"Bad show, Freddie. I knew you were close."

"Alistair wasn't happy when I told him, didn't approve of me leaving him there in the room."

"You had no choice. You were on a mission. Strictly speaking, Herr Seiler shouldn't have come with you in the first place."

Freddie nodded: "No. But I'm glad he did."

He looked out of the window again. It was getting even darker. Or was it the dirty window? The black-out made this section of Baker Street look gloomy; shops with sparse stock and a grocer's store declaring, "We take ration coupons". He thought of his travels; the opulence and colour of Baden; the sheer magnificence of the mountains; the sounds and smells of France, Switzerland, Germany and Spain. It all seemed unreal.

"How was Alistair?" asked Brim, his face cast in shadow.

"Bloody furious he wasn't coming back."

"That was never an option, Freddie."

"He believed it was, didn't he?"

"I know. But there we are, old sport. Duplicity sometimes has to be my business. So tell me, what will you do next?"

"Next?" A trace of concern wavered in his voice. Was he being fired? Was that why he wasn't invited into Number Ten?

"You deserve a holiday. The Canaris/Abwehr business is over. Mission accomplished. Unless you have another theory?"

"What about Alistair?" he asked.

"Oh, he'll remain in Baden. It's probably too dangerous for him to go back to Potsdam, although that's where his radio transmitter is."

"He has mine at the Lochar's house."

Brim stood up and tried to rally his protégé:

"True. Now, come on. What about some dinner? You can fill me in with all the other details of your mission. My treat – well, HM Government's treat – somewhere fancy in the West End? Or that place we went to before in Pall Mall: Dégustation. Anywhere you like."

"If it's all the same to you, Brim, I'd rather just stay here. Sit it out until midnight. See what happens up in Cromer – the SOE crew are on the wire. I might just go to a pub and get a pint and a pie. I know a half-decent place on Marylebone Road."

"If you're sure."

"I am, thank you. I'll come to the office in the morning."

"Do that," said Brim in his familiar way and turned to walk away. "Tell me, Freddie. Are you telling me everything? Did anything happen when you were away? You are not yourself. I understand what it's like coming home after all you've been through. The people you've met."

Freddie pondered this notion – 'coming home' - Where was home? He didn't have one. Not without Herr Seiler and Chalet Monte Rosa. He laughed it off dismissively:

"Good Lord, no. What else could there be? The whisky makes me maudlin. I'm not used to it. A luxury. Thank you."

Brim stood up and made sure the creases of his trousers were straight. He left the dowdy room and Freddie heard him trot down the wooden staircase and onto the street. He'd left the remnants of the half bottle of Haig. Freddie poured himself the rest of it. He sipped some whisky and closed his eyes. His recalled that magical evening in the garden of 27 Schwartzmattstrasse.

Astrid.

The soft warm grass. The musky scent of her body. The look in her eyes.

"I need you, Freddie," Astrid had said softly. He would never forget it.

He gulped the rest of the whisky down until it burnt. Brim was right, he wasn't himself. Astrid obsessed him.

"Oh Brim," Freddie said quietly to himself in the darkness. "My God, what have I done?"

His chin fell to his chest with a sharp jolt. How he wished Astrid were his girl. He felt the salty tears roll down. He just could not stop himself.

He should have felt guilt, but he did not. He felt love.

Jupiter

Potsdam, Berlin, Germany

SOME 600 MILES EAST OF BAKER STREET, Alistair clambered up the short, wooden ladder through the hinged hatch-door and began to inhale the distinctive, all-pervading smell of preserved wood. He almost tumbled into the cramped attic of his house in Potsdam.

He heard the clock chime in the downstairs hall. It was midnight the 31st August 1943. He felt restless, pre-occupied and recognised he could be in danger. The Potsdam house had not been broken into or searched; of that he was sure. He'd checked everywhere: doors, windows, bolts and locks. There was nothing suspicious. Even the fine, single threads of Astrid's hair he'd taken from her brush and invisibly taped across closed doorways and cupboards remained unbroken.

Manfred and Ingrid had pleaded with him not to return to Berlin, but he knew he had to. Every instinct he possessed told him he was right. Astrid had remained in Baden with them; this was a journey he had to make alone. He slipped on his headset and turned the radio dial. He needed speed, and rapidly tapped out the identification signal; vital to ensure the sole recipient knew he was genuine.

J – U – P - I – T –E – R

A few seconds later, the radio operator at Biggin Hill replied.

P – R – O –C –E – E – D

Military communication in England was on alert around the clock, but Alistair was aware his message would only be relevant to one expert, one highly trained Wren. He drew a breath and tapped out the encrypted message.

CODE RED ALERT – ANY NEWS ON MOTHER'S CONDITION? STOP.

"Mother" related to the key matter in hand – between sender and receiver, and "condition" to severity of the situation.

A few moments later came the reply he had been dreading. Yet, in a way, it was not unexpected.

N – E – G – A –T – I –V –E.

"Damn," he cursed. The U-Boat had not surfaced; no team of highly trained commandos had tried to sneak ashore, with or without cargo.

Worse still: there was no evidence of the sleeper spies in London he had warned Brim and British Intelligence about. And yet he knew what Canaris had told him was true. He had no reason to lie. And it was Rommel who'd said sleeper spies in London ... at the Berghof back in June, not Canaris.

Alistair threw off the headset; his decision was made. He knew he was right.

Decoy

1st September 1943. Alexanderplatz, Berlin, Germany

THE NEXT MORNING ALISTAIR made his way to Alexanderplatz. He'd had a restless night at the house in Potsdam. No Astrid and little food in the larder. But he did find a bottle of schnapps and two bottles of beer outside in the shed. Astrid's secret wine cellar.

He then walked west towards Unter den Linden, the elegant tree-lined boulevard of grand houses which ran from where he stood, right to the Tiergarten in the heart of Berlin.

Walking cleared his head. It gave him time to think, devise a plan, and check he was not being followed. He started in the Mitte district, had coffee and a frankfurter in Hackescher Markt, then crossed Friedrichstrasse to Pariser Platz. Definitely no tail. Inwardly, he sighed with relief.

In the weeks Alistair had been away from Berlin many buildings had been ruined or obliterated; some streets he barely recognised. Allied bombing had wreaked havoc on the Humboldt

University buildings and the library. Whole sides of buildings had been ripped open and were exposed to daylight, their insides still curiously intact. He saw parents carrying ragged, malnourished children and bombed-out families pushing stacked handcarts. He felt sure that it would get worse and wondered what it would be like in a years' time.

Alistair shrugged these thoughts away. He had a job to do. A task he had invested many years of training for. He wore a dark-blue, double-breasted suit, white shirt and black tie. He had no idea why he'd selected it. The mirror in Potsdam told him he looked smart; that was enough. He recalled his first visit to the magnificent house on Unter den Linden when chauffeuring Canaris in the beautiful black Mercedes. He strolled along the street taking utmost care to watch everything. As he strode cautiously, he remembered the drive back from Tempelhof Airport:

"What number, Herr Admiral?"
"Over there, by those two trees, pull in."

*

Alistair found the two linden trees – limes – and the solid, imposing neo-Gothic house once again. The street door was open. Inside, he found the familiar, wide, sweeping staircase rising from the marble-tiled hallway to the galleried first-floor landing and the Admiral's apartment.

But why was the front door open? he wondered. Quietly, he mounted the stairs two at a time, every nerve alert to possible danger.

Alistair knocked sharply on the apartment door, stood back, stretched his hands and waited. No response.

He waited for ten seconds.

"Herr Admiral!" He then called out firmly, "It is I. Alistair Valentine. I need to speak with you urgently."

The right-hand side of the large pair of wood-panelled doors opened cautiously – just a fraction – and Maria Franco peered out, clearly petrified. She shook her head almost imperceptibly in warning and mouthed the word "run".

Too late.

The door snapped back, nearly knocking her over, to reveal a tall, fair-haired man in SS uniform. He had a livid scar on his left cheek, dark-blue eyes, black and red swastika armbands and a 7.65mm Luger pointed at Alistair. The man he had seen before.

"So!" he said loudly, turning his head to call over his shoulder to Canaris in a chair behind him, "Your errant chauffeur has returned. This will save me a journey to Potsdam."

Krebbs's conceit was his undoing; he hadn't expected Alistair. As Krebbs said the word "Potsdam", Alistair pounced.

He grabbed Maria's arm and hurled her out through the open door onto the hall landing. She fell to her knees, eyes wild with fear.

Krebbs jerked his arm out to follow Maria's fall. He couldn't compute what was happening. Alistair gripped his forearm like a vice. He then grabbed the handle of the door and smashed it shut. Krebbs's ulna and radius were trapped, shattered in the woodwork and his limp fingers at last squeezed the trigger. A wayward round spat out into the stairwell and ricocheted loudly in the emptiness.

Krebbs screamed in pain. Alistair kicked the door open, still retaining his grip on the limp forearm. He then snapped his tightly balled fist straight into Krebbs's Adam's apple. The action was so fast and powerful it crushed both cartilage and windpipe. As Krebbs swivelled, the back of his head crashed into the doorframe, breaking his skull. He collapsed onto his knees. It took just seconds for him to die. He gurgled blood and frothy saliva, and fell flat on his face, the crunching sound of his nose breaking as it smashed down onto the cold marble floor.

Maria screamed.

Alistair dragged the lifeless body into the lobby of the apartment and swiftly shut the door. Inside he saw Canaris was sitting bolt upright on a dining room chair. Immobile. Blood running from the corner of his mouth. His left eye was bruised and weeping. He looked astounded by what he'd just seen.

"Thank you." Canaris muttered. Then, regaining some composure: "I thought we'd said goodbye, Herr Valentine?"

"Who was he?" asked Alistair, ignoring the question.

"Sturmbannführer Otto Krebbs," Canaris looked away, "assault unit leader in the SS. I mentioned him."

"Yes. Any more of them?" Alistair panted.

"Not unless there's an SS staff car outside or nearby. Black Mercedes, you know the type."

"There wasn't. I walked here; didn't see anything suspicious. No obvious followers."

Maria came back into the hallway still shocked, Alistair

beckoned her over:

"I need your help." Alistair's tone was firm. This was a side of Alistair seldom seen: an instinctive, trained killer, fast and professional. He had been driven by his two old demons: risk and danger. More often than not, they saved him.

Maria did as she was asked, still trembling and couldn't take her eyes off the body on the floor. The puddle of bloody saliva.

Alistair looked at her and the Admiral. They both knew what had to be done.

"Get the uniform off him," Alistair said, "please?"

"You mean undress him?" She whispered.

"That's what I mean, yes."

Hesitantly, she bent down onto her knees, her eyes avoiding the dead man's contorted face, smashed throat and cracked skull. Slowly she started to undo the silver buttons of the black tunic.

"Leave the shirt and tie; they're a bit of a mess. I won't need them."

"Yes," her voice quivered.

"He works for Himmler then, does he?"

The Admiral nodded.

Alistair only then noticed Canaris was tightly tied to the dining room chair with a sturdy length of curtain cord. He walked over and started to untie him.

"What happened?"

"He came over here about an hour ago, asking questions about the Schwarze Kapelle. He wanted names. Krebbs asked about the murder in Salzburg. Who was the new chauffeur with impeccable credentials? 'A traitor in the Abwehr was the only explanation', he said. I hope they have not harmed your friend Monika. Her father is an admiral, a good friend of mine. Then, you appeared, thank God."

"What did you tell him?" asked Alistair, glancing quickly at Maria and Krebbs.

"As little as I could. As far as I was aware, I had been assigned a replacement chauffeur because of illness. I said I knew nothing of a murder."

"Good. What's going on, Admiral?"

"My team has uncovered a hoax," said Canaris. "I had a call before Krebbs appeared. The U-Boat landing at Cromer was a decoy. Himmler and Doenitz lied at the Presidium meeting at the Berghof. The U-Boat patrolling the North Sea is no threat. The cylinders on-board her are empty. Her Kăpitan doesn't know that ..." Canaris was breathing heavily ...

"They have a crew of innocuous fishermen in northern France who are moving by sea to Jersey and then to England."

"The U-Boat is a decoy," said Alistair. "That makes sense. What else?"

"The boat will carry the cylinders of Tabun. The ones destined for Windsor Castle. As far as I know the aerial attack with the ten Heinkels remains the same."

Alistair sighed with realisation: "I see. Then what?"

Canaris looked confused: "What do you mean?"

"How will this crew get the cylinders into Britain, if not at the coast at Cromer?" Alistair's voice was raised with impatience. He untied the final tight knot in the curtain cord:

"Thank you; that feels better ... by some kind of vessel to the south coast of England. It is destined for a large harbour – one of the biggest ..."

"Poole?"

"Yes, Poole, that's it. Then to Windsor. I do not know how. By road, I imagine."

"When?"

"Soon, I don't know when exactly. That's all the detail I have. There is no one I can ask for the moment."

Alistair glanced over at the body, almost undressed. Maria had stripped him to his underwear, but left the shirt as instructed; it was soaked in blood and saliva. The SS uniform had all the bloody matter swiftly wiped off with soap and water; it remained faintly visible but not obvious. Maria then neatly folded the uniform over a chair.

Alistair started to take off his own jacket and trousers: "You may want to look away, Señorita."

Maria didn't want to.

"What are you doing?" The Admiral smiled, he knew, of course. In moments, Alistair was dressed in Krebbs's SS uniform; his white shirt and black tie more or less matched the ruined ones. He riffled through the dead man's pockets and fished out his ID card.

"So, I'm 27 years old and live in Berlin. I wonder if I'm married or not? It doesn't say. No matter. Let's hope the boots fit."

Alistair quickly re-dressed the body in his own clothes: "Pity, I was rather fond of this suit."

He put Krebbs's ID card in his pocket.

"You'll never get away with this." Canaris looked bewildered.

"Well, I'll just have to try, won't I?"

"Then I will come with you."

Maria's hand shot up to her mouth in protest: "Wilhelm, no!"

Canaris stood up from the chair: "If you think you can just walk into Tempelhof or Tegel wearing an SS Uniform – and – what?"

"Steal an aircraft? Yes. Why not? I must get word to the British. Any radio signal is certain to be intercepted. It's far too risky. This has to be face-to-face, everything I know."

"Ah," Canaris smiled, "Professor Brimblecombe."

Alistair flinched: "Yes, exactly." He narrowed his eyes and conceded, "I have to get word to Brimblecombe in particular."

"It's suicide! My God! Don't you realise – if the German army don't shoot you down over German airspace, the British will over theirs."

They both knew the obstacles: the coastline fortified with British and American troops: tanks, anti-aircraft guns, soldiers. Impenetrable, that was the point. Alistair stood still; all he knew was he had to escape.

Maria stood and looked at them both.

"What if Sturmbannführer Krebbs was escorting me back to Spain and you were seeing us off from the airport? That would be credible, wouldn't it?"

"Can you fly a German warplane, Herr Krebbs?" asked Canaris, entering into the spirit of the charade.

"Unlike my brother, I can't fly any plane, never wanted to. But

I'll find a way. I'll have to."

"I see," said Canaris, mulling over his words. He frowned, his mind a whirl of possibilities.

Alistair checked the lobby. It seemed nobody in the building had responded to the single pistol shot. He dragged the re-dressed body of Krebbs out of the apartment and threw it over the balustrade of the gallery landing. It landed with a heavy thump on the marble floor below. Maria followed him out and looked down, further shocked at the sight of violence.

"Well, he can't stay up here can he? He makes the place look untidy."

She shook her head in complete disbelief at his nonchalance: "No, I know, but ..."

Canaris came out onto the landing and joined them. He was suddenly animated.

"I have an answer. Come! I will telephone for transport to Berlin-Gatow airfield. The Kommandant – Oberst Heinz Funk - is a friend and a key member of the Schwarze Kapelle. If anyone can get you out of Berlin, it's him; or one of his pilots."

"Thank you, Herr Admiral, you are brave," said Alistair.

"And so are you." Canaris turned and went to make the call.

Alistair sighed: "Somewhere for Krebbs? Is there a coal cellar?"

Maria nodded and pointed down: "Under the staircase is a door."

"Give me a few minutes," said Alistair. "Maria, can you wipe up as much blood as you can from the lobby, please?"

He trotted down the stairs, found the door and started to move the body. In the dark cellar with a hefty shovel, he skilfully covered the body in a deep layer of finest anthracite at the back of the coal heap, taking great care to wipe clean his boots and Krebbs's uniform as soon as he'd finished.

As he returned to the main hall Maria and Canaris joined him.

"I have made the call. Everything is fixed," said Canaris.

Alistair nodded: "Thank you. I am sure everything will be alright."

"We'll see, won't we?" said the Admiral, his expression grim, "I hope you are right."

Channel

The English Channel.

"TRY AND KEEP HER STEADY, DIETER," said Captain Richard Lambert; he was clearly in charge of the Clarissa and everybody knew it. Dieter Scheiderbauer, helmsman and navigator merely grunted something in German as he stood in the wheelhouse; one hand on the wheel and one on the stack of naval charts. The sturdy trawler was making five knots with fore and mizzen sails filled and taut, heading north-east on a course from St. Helier to Poole. Conditions were calm, late morning sun high and hot, the light south-westerly astern and helpful. They were fifty nautical miles from the English coast. The three French fishermen sweated hard on the otter beam nets as they hauled in a small, shining, writhing mass of cod, haddock, whiting, pilchard, a few mackerel, with a couple of lively tope mixed in. A successful catch, a blissful scene, a normal day. But this was no normal day and no normal vessel.

Clarissa's Red Ensign fluttered innocently in the light sea breeze. Lambert had his eyes pressed to the lens of a pair of powerful Zeiss binoculars as he scanned the horizon – 360 degrees – back and forth.

"Strange," he muttered loud enough to be heard by Scheiderbauer.

"What is?"

"There! On the horizon. Corvettes ... destroyers."

"For us?" asked Scheiderbauer.

Lambert shook his head: "Not us."

"Where do you suppose they have come from?" Scheiderbauer asked in German. His lack of English was a concern to Lambert. If for some reason they were boarded by Coastguards, Lambert would have to cover. They had rehearsed such a scenario many times over the last year, but it still remained a problem. There was nothing they could do about it. The French fisherman gabbled away all day in their strange colloquial accent and were almost invisible, such was their authenticity.

"Who knows?" said Lambert, "Southampton? Portsmouth? Any of the naval bases from that direction."

Lambert scanned the horizon again, all points of the compass.

"Damn! There is something following us now. Another vessel. Fast."

"Who?" demanded Scheiderbauer, immensely concerned, "You said it would be clear."

"I-I can't see ..."

Suddenly the radio crackled into life and Lambert could hear the words – 'Come in please.' and a hiss of static – 'Come in please.' - the latter more emphatic, more dramatic.

Lambert ran back from where he'd been standing, grabbed

the microphone and affected his best English accent: “Hello.”

“This is the British Coastguard. Please identify yourself.”

“We are the fishing vessel ‘Clarissa’ from Grimsby, now based at Fleetwood. I am Captain Lambert. May I help? Is there a problem?”

“Cut your engine and await our signal to board.”

“Wilco. Out.” Lambert sounded calm and jolly, but he wasn’t. His heart thumped.

Lambert walked amidships to where the fishermen had just reset the nets.

“Just in time,” he thought.

Scheiderbauer looked around, sensing that something was not right. Lambert clamped his eyes back to the binoculars and, sure enough, a mile or so away, was an old wooden Coastguard boat chugging towards them, billowing smoke.

Lambert looked to his east: “Kill the engine, Dieter. Try and get a bearing. What’s the time?”

“Midday, just after.”

Lambert went below to the cabin and collected a handgun, checked it was loaded. He looked at the wooden crates containing the gas cylinders and sighed. They couldn’t afford to fail now, not after all this time, all this charade and effort. He would kill the Coastguards – all of them – if he had to. It was a chance he had to take. He tucked the revolver loosely into his waistband in case he needed it and went back up on deck. The fishermen continued to gut some of their catch: blood, bones and entrails swirled around in the sea water. Lambert picked up the binoculars again and stared east through the powerful lens.

"There's a flotilla of them. What's going on?" Lambert said in German and French, pointing. They all looked in the same direction, except for Scheiderbauer who was more concerned with his charts in the wheelhouse.

Within a short time, the Coastguard was alongside them. One of their crew hurled a couple of lines across at the Clarissa; one was caught by Lambert, the other by one of the fishermen and they were secured fore and aft. The two vessels bobbed up and down on their buoys.

The skipper of the Coastguard called out: "Please identify yourself."

"Lambert. We spoke on the wireless...at least, I assume we did!"

"Ah yes. Where are you headed?" asked the skipper.

"Back to port. Hamworthy, Poole."

"You're a long way out, aren't you?"

"Yes! We've been out as far as we dare, you know, trying to find the best catch. Needs to be deep! Listen, old man," Lambert said, "what the devil's going on?" Lambert pointed over at the approaching flotilla, which seemed to be changing course.

"Not sure," the skipper cupped his eyes and looked up.

All of a sudden, a couple of Mosquitoes – low level RAF reconnaissance aircraft – flew overhead and then circled off back towards the south coast of England. The noise was loud as their engines screamed and then it fell silent. The sun sparkled on the deep blue sea and the two boats rocked; the swell of the sea was starting to suddenly rise.

The skipper of the Coastguard walked to his foredeck.

"How much have you caught?" he called out, "you're quite low in the water."

"Oh, a few tons," said Lambert, "the fishermen can't hear you with those bobble hats," he continued cheerily, "cod, plaice, you know, the usual for this depth."

"You must have a big hold?" the skipper speculated and pointed at the Clarissa amidships to where he thought the hold might be.

"Yes, we have a seawater floatation tank. Macfisheries insist the catch is kept as fresh as possible. You know how they are. Don't blame them!"

Careful, don't over explain, he thought to himself. He thought of his trainer in Ingelheim, a stout lady in her forties: Don't try and compete with the locals. Their knowledge is greater than yours can ever be. Take it easy. Don't go into detail about anything you can't back up: roads, railways, football teams. Anything.

All this time Scheiderbauer had said nothing, just listening to the exchange and carefully studying his charts. The skipper walked forward to his own wheelhouse, so he was dead level with Scheiderbauer.

"Best let you get back home then." He glanced towards the invisible coast; the sea was getting choppier.

"Yes," Scheiderbauer said with a cheery grin, pretending he understood.

"I believe there might be a military exercise this afternoon. Start up and get back as soon as you can. We'll wait in case your engine fails."

"Yes," Scheiderbauer said, again.

But Lambert was quickly there to rescue him: "military exercise?" he asked, intrigued.

The skipper put his finger to his lips: "Mum's the word, mm?"

He picked up his tackle and signalled for the Clarissa to untie.

"Did you want to come aboard, sir?" asked Lambert, "to check we are seaworthy? All our papers are correct and up to date. I have my – "

"No, you're fine. Throw the lines! Quick!"

Just as Lambert did so, the skipper noticed the grip of the handgun poking out of the sailor's pocket. Now, why would he possess what looks like a Luger pistol? Or am I mistaken?

Lambert smiled. Mum's the word. What could this possibly mean? He had never heard this expression.

"Wait," shouted the skipper, "why are you carrying a weapon?"

Lambert stumbled, caught, his mind raced. The sea was becoming more and more turbulent, the last thing he needed was a nosey Coastguard. He hesitated.

"Well?" shouted the skipper.

Lambert felt for the weapon: "We are all instructed to. I'm – I'm with the Home Guards in Hamworthy. I even take it to bed! My wife Betty hates it. Says it might go off." He laughed and made a huge joke of it all; he might have overdone it.

"All right," said the skipper, nodding his head. But he was perplexed at the use of the plural – Guards – didn't everyone know it was Guard? He made a mental note to call it in to the authorities in Poole. And he would double check the design of a 7.65mm Luger. Particularly the grip.

The two boats parted company and the skipper shouted out: "Back to port, Captain Lambert. Unless you want to get blown out of the water," but his tone was anything but jovial.

"Yes," said Scheiderbauer, a final time, his plastic smile wearing dangerously thin.

There was the toot of a foghorn – a single flat note – and the Coastguard turned and chugged back towards the flotilla.

'That was close' thought Lambert. "Start the engine," shouted Lambert in German to Dieter. What's the time?"

"Twelve-sixteen," called the other man. Lambert went to the wheelhouse and grabbed the chart as Dieter struggled to turn the engine over. He looked out across at the Coastguard's boat and could see the skipper looking at them through his binoculars. Lambert had a bilious feeling in the pit of his stomach: "Start, damn you, start."

Finally, she caught, and the engine fired up. But the sea was still extremely turbulent.

Scheiderbauer swore: "Now we are off-course as well. This current."

He glanced up at the sun, took the dividers, made a calculation and plotted a course.

"But we have plenty of time, I think."

Lambert came into the wheelhouse and tapped Dieter on the shoulder: "You did well."

Bus

Dorset, England

SOUTH OF BLANDFORD FORUM, near Corfe Mullen, an old Dennis school bus was parked in a lay-by. Its passengers – children in their late teens - unable to have been evacuated and not suitable for conscription, were enthralled at this ancient area. It had strange names – Wimborne Minster and Canford Bottom – and unusual, unexplained stone monuments.

The children had special needs and requirements and they all sat beside the bus on woollen travel rugs having their first ever picnic. They were a noisy but happy group, and they all enjoyed their cheese and tomato sandwiches, washed down with freshly made lemonade.

They were being looked after by a charming couple who ran a hotel in Kensington. Harald Wolf, the driver, didn't say much because he had to concentrate on driving, they were told. And map reading was not his forte. He was a short, thickset man with a pock- marked face and always seemed to wear a trilby hat, no matter the weather.

But his wife Gertrud was quite the opposite: a lively person who more than made up for her husband's miserable demeanour. She was in her mid-thirties, with blond hair in the Victory Roll style and beautiful sky-blue eyes. Her narrow face and high cheekbones gave her a Scandinavian appearance. People often commented on what a strange partnership they were. The Beauty and the Beast was an expression which had been associated with them more than once. She showed them where they were on the RAC map.

"And soon, we'll be able to see the sea!" Gertrud said cheerfully, "How about that?"

"Then where?" A voice shouted out; a shrill East London accent. Poor boy had never been out of Hackney and had certainly never seen a sheep or a cow. Until today. Until the Wolfs had had the kindness and time to take them.

"Poole. And do you know? Poole has one of the biggest natural harbours... in the..."

"In the world, Miss!" They all shouted out, happy to be young, proud to be English.

And who would have guessed Harald and Gertrud Wolf were originally from Munich? And although they had owned the George Hotel in Kensington since the mid- thirties, they had been recruited and trained as German spies in England. Abwehr spies under orders from Admiral Canaris: Schlafende Spione in London.

Both their fathers had been killed in World War One by the

British and that had fuelled their desire to help the German cause. In their own way, they had been swept up by the tide of Fascist fervour in Britain. They had met Giles Walcott, an Irish Republican, at a BUF rally in 1937 in London. Since then, Walcott had looked after them financially and philosophically. He painted them a dream and they believed it. Harald and Gertrud had no idea they were really working for Heinrich Himmler.

Gertrud called out to the children enthusiastically: "Come on then! Back on the bus! Poole Harbour beckons us! ... Then we will take you to your hostel and drop you off. Just think of it, a week of freedom! Plenty of fresh food! And no air raid shelters!"

Her blue eyes sparkled with enthusiasm.

Nothing, it seemed, could go wrong. They were the kindest people in the world.

Escape

Berlin-Gatow Airfield, Germany

KOMMANDANT OBERST HEINZ FUNK moved animatedly outside the Gatow Academy – Luftskriegsakademie – talking enthusiastically to Canaris while hopping from foot to foot. Funk was an immense man, a foot taller than the Admiral, pristine in full uniform.

Berlin-Gatow airfield was Funk's baby. He cherished the grass runways, the prefab buildings, the cluster of hangars. The site was deserted, barring control-tower staff. The air cadets were on manoeuvres.

Inside the Academy building, Alistair was half dressed. He prepared to put on his flight suit, draped on a chair. Krebbs's uniform lay in a heap on the floor. It had served its purpose on their journey from Unter den Linden to Gatow. The young soldier driving the black Mercedes staff car did not dare speak to his three special passengers or question their destination.

Maria Franco watched Alistair carefully: "I thought the whole idea was I would come with you? It was my suggestion."

"If we were stopped, Maria; and we weren't," Alistair said and looked at her.

She was wearing another low-cut, close-fitting summer dress. It complemented her: she was slim, shapely, with high cheekbones, full lips and captivating brown eyes; unquestionably beautiful.

"Besides," she said, "I am a burden to Wilhelm, can't you see that?"

"No. It really isn't my business, Maria." His tone was firm.

Maria stepped towards him, her eyes pleading. Again, he glimpsed her breasts, full and suntanned. A hint of a smile crossed her face.

"Why can't you see, Alistair?" She delicately traced his lips and chin with her index finger. "Why can't you? I want to come with you."

"I'm married for a start; and certainly not going to Spain."

She came even closer: "But your wife is in ... Austria? At a music festival?"

"I know."

She tried to kiss him, pressing her body against his underwear and wrapping her bare arms around his waist.

"Please, Alistair." Those big eyes pleaded; she pursed her lips. "Please."

"It's just not practical, Maria." He was starting to shuffle; he had to get out of this.

"Don't you find me attractive? Desirable?"

He sighed with impatience: "Maria, listen. I have to fly out of a Luftwaffe-controlled airfield, probably in a stolen German plane. Whether or not I find you desirable is irrelevant. Do you understand?" His voice was raised.

She looked down like a scolded child: "Yes."

Funk and Canaris strode in with another man, all seemingly oblivious of the situation.

"Alistair!" announced Canaris, "This is your pilot, Flt. Müller."

Müller was a short, dark-haired man, with a few days' stubble on his grease-stained face. He nodded without expression, looked at Alistair, still half-dressed, then Maria.

"I'm not evacuating a couple." He spoke good English but with a heavy accent.

"They're not a couple," said Canaris indignantly, "she's with me, a family friend."

Müller wanted to say – it doesn't look like it from here – but decided against it, given present company. Instead:

"Your flight suit is there." He pointed at the chair. "I hope it fits."

Canaris looked at Maria, then at Alistair, trying to read the situation. She turned to Canaris:

"I – I was asking if I could go with him, Wilhelm."

"It's not up to him," interjected Müller, returning to German," I am the pilot. This flight is incredibly dangerous. I have enough problems." The little pilot stomped out of the building to his aircraft.

"Come, Maria, leave Herr Valentine to dress," said Canaris diplomatically.

Alistair heard twin engines being gunned outside as he

walked towards Funk: "You'll be flying in this 1935 Heinkel HE111, an early prototype. She's a long-range bomber," Funk said proudly, "so solid. So German. Beautiful, yes?"

"Strange colour?" Alistair remarked, looking up at the large aircraft a bit doubtfully, as he approached Funk.

"Grey primer," Funk lowered his voice, "built in secret."

Alistair was amused because Funk was a showman. But what he said was true. Germany had not been allowed to have a military air force under the terms of Versailles; many aircraft had been built covertly, under the guise of Lufthansa. This implied passenger or cargo flights. This early example, still awaiting a topcoat of paint bore the livery of Lufthansa on its tail. Despite obviously having been 'mothballed' for eight years, Alistair was impressed, and Funk could see it: "The power plant is the two Junkers V12s. No Reich markings to betray her ... or you. I can see, maybe you are thinking, she is too old?"

"Not at all. Is she armed?"

Funk walked towards the glass nose: "One 20mm MG cannon here in the front and a 7.92mm machine gun in the rear, both loaded. Full tank; flying range 1950 km."

Alistair looked at Canaris: "We should go."

"You board from underneath, where the hatch is," said Funk finally, "I will secure."

"Good luck again." said Canaris.

He turned and started to leave. Maria stood silently and watched Alistair board the aircraft, her expression gloomy. At the top of the perimeter road, two Wehrmacht diesel trucks hammered along the gravel, spraying dust as their tyres skidded, trying to find traction on the loose surface.

"Come, my dear," said Canaris, taking hold of Maria's arm, "we may need to get you back to Spain quicker than I had anticipated."

*

Within a few minutes, Müller had powered the aircraft down the short runway. The Heinkel climbed effortlessly up into the afternoon sky, leaving Berlin-Gatow airfield looking like a postage stamp below. The climb was steep and fast, the old plane rattled as she reached her cruise speed of 435 km/h.

The cockpit interior was dark and had only a few dimly lit dials. It was so cramped and narrow Alistair wondered how five crew would manage for hours on end.

"Why are you doing this?" Alistair called on the internal radio, "I mean, I'm glad you are, but I'm half English and you are, well, a German."

Müller waited a moment and breathed deeply: "My parents were arrested – taken – to Sachsenhausen concentration camp. I escaped, but only by jumping from a moving train. I was nearly killed. But luck was with me that day."

"I'm sorry," said Alistair.

"Actually, my parents were only half Jewish. What does that make me? A quarter? I don't know. They were Russian immigrants, but it was enough. They weren't Aryan."

The cockpit fell silent. Outside it was dusk, the sun now over the horizon. He thought of his brother Freddie and wondered: where he was and what he was doing at this moment?

The hiss of the radio broke his thoughts: "I've set a course – dead reckoning – west to Amsterdam, over the Elbe, to the North Sea. It's all manual flying. Where do you want to go exactly? Nobody told me; just that it was an emergency evac."

Alistair had a chart on his lap.

"As soon as we are clear of the Dutch coast, I need to make a MAYDAY signal to London. You do have a Morse transmitter?"

"Yes, but we can use radio."

"Too risky. I need to make an emergency, coded transmission that will be intercepted by the British; an encrypted code that the Germans will not understand; at least they won't work it out for a while. Then it will be too late. I hope."

"I understand, but this is very risky."

"I know and I am eternally grateful. You'll be famous for this."

Müller jiggled the control stick and dipped the pedals. Alistair looked over his shoulder. The Heinkel juddered and lost a bit of altitude, then levelled out, her air speed good. He looked out of the window at the orange and red horizon.

"You fly this aircraft well. How many hours have you flown her?"

"None. She's been in storage for eight years," he said straight-faced.

"Great," thought Alistair, "I'm 15,000 feet above Nazi Germany, in a filched Luftwaffe aircraft, with a Jewish comedian."

He couldn't help but laugh and thought: What will Freddie say when I tell him about this?

And suddenly, he couldn't wait to see him again.

Mayday

The Admiralty Citadel, London, England.

THE ADMIRALTY CITADEL WAS BATHED IN GLORIOUS soft afternoon sunlight and the air was changing, just perceptively, from summer towards autumn. Pedestrians around Piccadilly could discern a very slight drop in temperature at street level as they went about their normal lives. Thirty feet below them in the Submarine Tracking Room, the atmosphere was a hive of frenetic activity as usual. The clatter of typewriters and encryption machines filled the cramped space, and the sound of hushed chatter was relentless and tense.

Commander Ian Fleming was standing beside the North Atlantic Plotting Table with Brim – their minds focused – when Freddie Valentine limped into the room accompanied by a Royal Marine. Fleming's expression was unusually blank. Thomas Trout looked up, surprised to see a civilian in such hallowed quarters.

"Sir!" shouted the Marine and snapped to attention.

"It's all right, Sergeant," said Brim, "he's one of us. How was your evening?"

The Marine turned and walked away, having spun a hundred and eighty degrees with military precision.

"Disappointing, much like yours I should imagine, Brim."

Brim merely grunted in agreement.

"No dice then?" asked Freddie to the two men. He had to raise his voice to be heard.

Fleming looked at Brim.

"No, but we've just taken the most extraordinary call from the skipper of a UK Coastguard patrol boat."

Freddie looked confused and focused closely on the two men: "Really? You mean the North Sea? The intercepted message?"

"No", said Fleming, "couldn't be further away. South coast; Dorset."

"Dorset?" Freddie was incredulous.

"It seems they had a – how did he put it? – 'bizarre encounter' with a fishing vessel out in the Channel earlier on today, around midday, in fact. She's called the Clarissa and checks out fine. But the Coastguard skipper, Ray Porter, spoke to her Captain, who he said, was exceptionally well spoken. He tried to make conversation with other members of the crew, while they were alongside – the navigator-cum-helmsman and three fishermen."

"And?"

"Well, this is the peculiar thing. They ignored him."

"But is this significant?" persisted Freddie, looking at Brim, confused.

"It wouldn't have been except for three separate things. The Clarissa was sitting very low in the water and yet there didn't appear to be many fish around. And not the normal flocks of gulls hovering above, which you would normally associate with a big catch. There were some, but not many."

Freddie almost laughed: "Hardly conclusive though…and?"

"When Porter returned to Poole, he contacted several of the fish wholesalers including the one that Captain Richard Lambert mentioned by name, Mac Fisheries, and they'd never heard of Lambert or the Clarissa."

"Hmm, you said three?"

"Oh yes. The Captain of this Clarissa had a revolver poking out of the waistband of his trousers. Porter later identified it as a 7.65mm Luger. He had noticed it when Lambert bent over to untie his line. When he challenged Lambert, he told him he was a member of the Home Guards. Guards, plural. Said it just did not ring true. And although many sea crew are armed, why a Luger? Why have it just tucked in like that? Seemed odd."

"Why indeed?" said Brim. "Quite a detective then, our Mr. Porter. Interesting."

"Sir! Sir!" A young Wren from Comms came running into the room, her eyes shining, "Signals, sir! The radio operator at Biggin Hill has just received a Mayday."

The three of them turned, sensing a breakthrough. She clutched hold of the message and continued:

"The sender's identification signal is: 'Jupiter.'"

Fleming, Brim and Freddie were astounded.

She continued: "When the radio officer asked him to 'Proceed', the response was: 'Code Red Alert … Mother is flying home ... in an unmarked Heinkel HE111 ... Stop ... Her condition is Poole ... Mr. Cromer is dead ... Stop.'"

Freddie was aghast: "Cromer is dead, of course. A trick. Thank you, by the way for relaying the message with such passion and enthusiasm. Goodness only knows we need some good news. Well done, Miss."

The young Wren blushed, nodded at Freddie wistfully and turned to leave.

Fleming lit one of his Morland cigarettes: "Yes, Cromer was a trick, a decoy, but the target is now obviously Poole. This is crucial intelligence, from Jupiter. Clarissa must be part of it."

Brim said to Freddie: "Are you thinking what I'm thinking?"

Freddie looked at Ian Fleming: "I never know what you are thinking, Brim!"

Brim pursed his lips and smiled: "If Alistair's managed – somehow – to second a German aircraft she's ...."

"Most probably armed?" replied Freddie.

Fleming grinned broadly and exhaled a cloud of blue smoke. He knew exactly what Brim was thinking. But could it possibly work?

Brim banged the edge of the table: "Listen please everybody. We have received some vital new intelligence ..."

The room fell silent, save for the sound of the fans. He continued: "Contact all Comms: Biggin Hill. Bletchley. Army. Navy. Airforce ...

"Advise them to hold fire on an approaching Heinkel. Most probably via Holland but originating from Germany. A Heinkel.

Yes, you did hear that correctly ...

... she is unmarked and friendly ... a British agent is evacuating from deep cover ... that's it ... use emergency frequencies. Thank you." He could barely contain his emotion.

The room burst back into its frenzy of activity.

Brim turned to Commander Fleming: "Ian, contact the PM and Cyril Downing. Put them fully in the picture. What's the nearest airport to Poole? Come on, Freddie. Let's go now."

"Will do," said Fleming.

Freddie smiled: "So we were right all along; right idea, wrong place. The U-Boat was a bloody red herring. After all that. Cunning bastards!"

"Correct," said Fleming. "The sleeper spies were never going to Cromer, but to Poole. That's why we couldn't find them."

"Yes, and I'll bet my bottom dollar they are in a bus of some kind," said Brim. "Bus or a coach. We'll just have to find it......." Brim called out to the station Commander: "Bill, contact RAF Northolt. We'll need a plane to Dorset, fastest you can requisition. And ask them to locate the nearest airfield to Poole. Christ! We'll put down in a bloody cow field if we have to!"

"Sir!" shouted Bill, his voice full of enthusiasm.

Freddie was beaming with pride: "Alistair, how on earth did you manage to nick a bloody German aircraft?"

Suddenly he couldn't wait to see his older brother, and everyone could see it too especially Brim. Triumph was near, but it would not be easy.

It never is.

Harbour

Poole Harbour, Dorset, England.

POOLE HARBOUR IS ONE of the largest and most beautiful harbours in the world. Its entrance is a narrow aperture between Studland Beach in the west and the Sandbanks peninsula to the east. It was nightfall and the FV Clarissa – now under sail – was just eight nautical miles offshore. Captain Richard Lambert had received specific instructions from Erich Spengler about how and where they would make contact with their rendezvous at 10pm. But not who they were or what they looked like. He assumed it would be some sort of onshore signal that would not cause undue suspicion.

Lambert stood rigidly on the foredeck with his Zeiss binoculars and scanned the British coast. He smoked a cigarette anxiously. He could see no evidence of the Home Guard and the odd pill boxes on the coast seemed unoccupied. Nothing to really worry about. He checked the Red Ensign for what seemed like the millionth time. He knew this was the most perilous and unpredictable moment of his life. Exposed, out at sea, they were sitting ducks. And he'd never felt more vulnerable.

He thought about their encounter with the Coastguard skipper earlier. That had been a close call. But had they got away with it? Was Dieter Scheiderbauer obviously not an English speaker? Were the three French fishermen convincing in their apparent silence?

Slowly they crept forward.

He swept his glasses from west to east. Studland Bay – Sandbanks – Poole Bay and up to Flag Head and Canford Cliffs. He knew from Luftwaffe aerial reconnaissance photographs that there were anti-aircraft guns and Artillery at Hengistbury Head in the very next bay east of Bournemouth. But that was way out of range from here, judging by his charts and maps.

Scheiderbauer was perched on his stool in the wheelhouse, his normal position. The radio receiver was on and he was scanning the medium wave and short-wave frequencies, blasts of classical music and the occasional weather forecasts, the odd rasp of music hall laughter.

Lambert thought about the Artillery again, armed with their Short Magazine Lee Enfields or SML's for short. They fired a .303-inch calibre with a maximum range of 2,000 yards. There would be Bren guns, anti-tank and two-inch mortars. He threw his cigarette into the sea and shuddered.

Despite his anxiety, the coast was clear, or so it seemed. The mouth of the harbour was six nautical miles away now; and way beyond that Brownsea Island. They were making about six knots and still in open sea...

Suddenly, the Clarissa began to jolt and shudder, there was a scraping noise. Lambert called out to Scheiderbauer and asked him what the matter was. He was struggling with the wheel while the three fishermen gathered the sails.

"The water must be very shallow – our prop is fixed – I think we might be running aground; unless we've snagged a net or something."

"Damn!" shouted Lambert. The British coast was so near, success so close.

Sandbanks. Of course, but they were nowhere near Poole Harbour yet.

*

A few miles away on the Banks Road, the old Dennis bus was parked at the most perfect vantage point. Gertrud and Harald had dropped their noisy passengers off at the hostel.

The couple now had a clear view of the English Channel on one side and Poole Harbour on the other. Bright moonlight sparkled on the harbour and countless yachts and boats bobbed up and down in the huge expanse. The bus was decked out with red, white and blue flags.

"I think I can see them, but they are a long way off," said Gertrud Wolf to her husband. He was hoisting a banner onto the roof of the bus:

THE GEORGE HOTEL. KENSINGTON

SUMMER CAMP 1943

The signal.

Gertrud too had powerful British binoculars around her neck. The Wolfs were very keen bird watchers as the books in the bus attested to – 'Birdlife in Dorset' – being one of the well-used and well-stained examples.

"What are they doing?" said Harald, looking at his wristwatch. "It's ten o'clock and they are not moving."

Gertrud frowned: "Yes, but they are nowhere near the harbour entrance yet. We need to load those cylinders and get out of here and on the road to Walcott's place."

"But how do we get to them? Can they possibly have run aground? Surely not. They can't be that stupid, can they?"

Harald climbed down from the bus and crawled under the back of it. He unscrewed two panels in the chassis and recovered two handguns:

"Here, take this, just in case." He handed one of the handguns to Gertrud. "We don't know who the captain of the Clarissa is or anything about his crew. They could be anyone. Just what Walcott has told us. They may be armed; it's as well to be cautious."

She took the weapon, checked it was loaded, put on the safety and tucked it into the back of her skirt: "True. God, I am nervous."

"Me too. Come, let's drive down to the harbour. At least we'll be nearer."

"Ja," she said, and bit her lip, annoyed at having uttered a German word.

It was her first mistake.

Attack

The South Coast of England

COMMANDER IAN FLEMING had just said 'goodbye' to Brim and Freddie Valentine. They were headed out to RAF Northolt in an Army Jeep, where a Percival Proctor aircraft was waiting to fly them down to Dorset.

Fleming clutched a microphone and pressed transmit: "Come in Biggin Hill. This is Citadel, over."

There was the intense crackle and pop of static which was being broadcast simultaneously through the loudspeaker in the Submarine Tracking Room. They were all tuned to the same frequency.

"Receiving, Citadel, over," said a distant voice.

"Good. Contact: Jupiter. Find out where he is. His nearest position, that is. Scrambled Morse like he used. No radio contact until he crosses the RAF-designated outer marker line at Dover / Blériot-Plage. We need him to hug the British coast at Dover – Dungeness – to Hastings and Bexhill; before he carries on. Understand? Over."

"Wilco. Over," replied the voice at Biggin Hill.

"Then set a course due west. He knows the destination because it is the one he told us. Over."

"Will do, Citadel. Over and out." The recipient was brief, but she understood the instruction.

Cyril Downing came into the room and acknowledged the various staff: uniformed Wrens and Naval officers, all with their shirt sleeves rolled up and jackets off. Despite the palpable tension in the room, he was upbeat:

"This is quite extraordinary, Commander Fleming; Valentine hijacking a German war plane. Whatever next?"

"Yes, it is, sir; although how he did it, is the million-dollar question," said Fleming with a smile of admiration. "Let's just hope he makes it back from the continent alive."

"Yes, and able to complete phase two." Downing raised his eyebrows. "I say. Any chance of a cup of tea?"

*

This particular south coast artillery dugout was cold, dark and draughty, the sandbags damp from a recent downpour. The seven-man watch were dressed in camouflage, their faces blacked out. They were tired, bored and hungry.

"God, I could murder a bacon sarnie," said one of the men.

"Yeah. And a nice hot brew. Plenty of sugar," said another, smoking a cigarette, which he cupped in his hand to conceal the glow.

"Your sister's muffins would be a treat, Terry!"

"Both of them, dripping butter," chirped another mischievous voice, "lovely!"

"Oy. That's my sister you're talking about," said Terry enjoying the friendly banter.

"Well, thing is, he doesn't fancy your brother, Terry," said 'the cigarette', "not his type. Too tall."

"My arse is damp from sitting on these bleeding sandbags, soaked right through! Never mind her muffins!" said another jovial voice.

They were camped out less than a hundred miles southwest of the Admiralty Citadel, at Hengistbury Head, a protrusion of elevated coastline midway between Bournemouth and Milford-on-Sea. From here, this watch of specially trained Artillery could clearly see the Isle of Wight to their left, and the Needles, poking out of the sea like pre-historic monsters.

The men's charge was a QF 3.7-inch anti-aircraft gun, affectionately nicknamed 'Betty', although nobody knew why. She weighed 20, 541 pounds, was 16 feet 3 inches in length, with a projecting barrel of 15 feet 5 inches. The carriage included the recoil system, laying arrangements, fuse setting and loading machinery. Betty was ready and lethal. It was Sergeant David Broadbent, an Oxford man, six-foot four, who first heard the alien noise. He had an acute sense of hearing and told the men to 'shush' and 'douse the fags'.

"Hm, it's a twin engine. Listen a jiffy," he said with a deep, well- educated voice.

"One of ours? That's a bit strange," a voice joked, loaded with nerves.

"Must be," said Broadbent. "The Jerries wouldn't send one lone wolf out, would they? I mean, why?"

His tone was firm but reasoned. He put a set of Army issue binoculars or 'bins' up to his eyes and scanned the night sky: "Can't see a damned thing, but it's definitely getting closer...the weapon is loaded and ready, Corporal?"

"Yes, sir" replied a rough Bristolian accent, "I checked it myself."

Broadbent lowered his bins and looked at the men: "Good."

Five hundred feet up in the air, the grey Heinkel, like a wily shark, was almost at stall speed, shaking and buffeting. Alistair clutched the radio mike and listened carefully.

Back at the Admiralty Citadel, Commander Fleming was shouting through the headset:

"She's called the FV Clarissa. She's currently run aground about five miles outside Poole Harbour. The Coastguard have just notified us. We know nothing more at present."

"Understood, Citadel," said Alistair, bouncing around in his seat. "Attack?"

"Your shout, Jupiter. She's well offshore. So, shoot on sight and get the hell out. From what you've said she must be carrying the gas cylinders. Out."

"About twenty-one miles out, losing height. I can't fly her any slower," said Müller, "or she will stall."

Below, Sergeant Broadbent was issuing instructions: "Prepare for engagement, men. Elevate the barrel, check breach assembly.

Our rate of fire is twenty rounds per minute. Don't waste it. We're lined up, so await my command."

He put the bins back to his eyes and spoke almost to himself: "Pitch black out there; she's noisy, near and closing. A twin engine V12. What the hell?"

The men were tense, rubbing their palms, swallowing deeply, each desperate for nicotine.

"I don't believe it...it's a fucking Heinkel...I'm sure of it...line up...line up...wait for it."

Behind them on the seat in the Jeep, a field radio squawked: "Sergeant Broadbent! Come in! Urgent! Come in!"

But it was unheard, with the sound of the engine noise and the shouts of terror and excitement from the gun crew.

"Fire!" shouted Broadbent. "Let them have it!"

The mighty gun rattled off a dozen rounds – TAT – TAT – TAT – TAT.

The recoil was violent and unforgiving, as was the smell of cordite. The acidic taste of gunpowder filled the air like a smoky poison.

A thousand feet up in the air, Alistair shouted at Müller indignantly: "They're bloody shooting at us!"

"Can you blame them?" Müller shouted back. "We're flying a German bomber! Scheisse!"

Streaks of tracer from other ground artillery just missed them, searing through the night sky like fireworks. On the ground, Alistair could see the fuses exploding and the plumes of blue smoke.

"Nine point nine miles, until target, at this speed," called Müller. "Not long."

"I can see Sandbanks," shouted Alistair. He crawled down the narrow gangway to the glass nose and grabbed a hold of the cannon, switched off the safety, looked through the sights and stared. The Heinkel dropped down to two hundred feet; a predator, ready for the kill. The plane was rocking now; roaring, powering forwards, ready for attack.

Alistair yelled: "That's her! That's bloody her!" He closed his left eye and focused.

"One chance Valentine," Müller screamed back, "make it count."

Alistair lined up through the sights, aligned the cross hairs, squeezed the trigger gently, and then saw the image, horrified:

"Wait a minute," he screamed out, "she's being towed by four tugboats. Coastguards. Shit! English Coastguards!"

The engine screamed and whistled in protest as she dived, she wanted to go in for the kill.

At Admiralty Citadel: "Abort mission. Abort!" shouted Fleming, "We can't risk civilians. No!"

Fleming knew that the Clarissa was too near the coastline now and the explosive fallout would be colossal, given the combination of the cylinders and the Heinkel's lethal cannon. And he could not possibly risk the Coastguards' lives.

"Out," snarled Alistair, as Müller pulled the plane sharply out of the dive. He screamed: "Fuck! Fuck! Fuck!"

The engines roared in response and they were pressed back into their seats. A deep breath.

Alistair shouted in frustration at Müller: "How accurate is the machine gun in the tail?"

"As good as any. What are you thinking?" he replied warily.

"Go in again, low, I'll try and take out the wheelhouse. Kill the crew at least."

"Whatever you say, Valentine, but don't forget we're a sitting duck."

"Just do it." shouted Alistair back. Now he was really in his element: risk and danger. This had to count. One more try. He crawled back on his hands and knees to the rear of the plane; the freezing cold airframe pressed hard against his limbs...

Müller took the aircraft back up to 1,000 feet and flew a circular clockwise route: Verwood, Fordingbridge, the New Forest, Petersfield; then finally west to Horndean and Southampton. In just under ten slow minutes she was flying above the Solent and heading west again, just on stall speed. The old grey shark powered on.

"Watch those damn gunners!" yelled Alistair. In the excitement of attacking the Clarissa, he'd almost forgotten the threat that lurked in the dark below them. The British artillery desperate for a kill. But it was too late.

The big gun at Hengistbury rattled off twenty rounds directly at them. Bullets smashed into the fuselage, the flaps and the wings. Fragments of metal and twisted wires flew behind them. Alistair was flat on his stomach, the gun pressed against him, cold night air blowing in.

"I can't control her, Valentine...I can't!"

"Can you dump the fuel?"

"There isn't much, but I'm already draining her."

"Can you glide it?"

Out of nowhere, a battery of machine gun rounds spattered into the nose, shattering the glass, and the engine finally stalled, emitting clouds of oil-rich smoke and fumes. Too low to parachute. Too low for anything. Shattered fragments of glass flew into the cabin, stinging and puncturing Müller's face like a pub dartboard.

Silence, but for the spinning of the props and tunnel of wind blowing through the open nose of the plane.

"What can we do?" Alistair screamed. He turned and started to crawl forward.

"Pray," said Müller. He was spitting blood and shards of glass, his tongue and lips bleeding. He struggled with the controls, a hundred feet off the ground now, then fifty. Branches of trees smashed into the undercarriage as the ground loomed right in front of them. Finally, she crash-landed and came to a screaming, ear-shattering halt in a freshly ploughed field. Alistair froze, closed his eyes and waited for an explosion...

"Dear God!" Müller screamed.

Alistair was behind Müller's seat now, the fuselage twisted at a bizarre angle. Müller's breaths were fast; he was choking: "Are you alright?" But Müller's head slumped forward and there was no response.

"We have to get out. Have to," Alistair shouted again. "Müller? Are you alright?" He shook his shoulder, but it was useless. He was dead. Alistair struggled forwards towards the nose of the plane, the palms of his hands pressing down onto glass, fragments of components and wire. Then he noticed sparks flying from the engine bay, and the buzzing of electrical activity. The smell of fuel was overpowering...any moment now... she would explode ...

At Hengistbury Head, nineteen miles away from the crash site, Sergeant Broadbent addressed his team triumphantly:

"Fucking Krauts! Teach them to attack our boats in Poole Harbour!"

"Yeah, and disguised. Did you see the Lufthansa tail fin?" said the Bristolian soldier, "Bastards!"

"It was luck a couple of rounds got them, though," said another of the artillerymen, most unwisely.

"Luck?" said Broadbent, "What's luck got to do with it? It was a scattergun and we got them." He lit a cigarette: "When we stand down, I'll buy you all a pint at the NAAFI. You deserve it. But watch out for more enemy aircraft...you never know, she may have been a trailblazer. This could be the start of a fucking aerial invasion!" But he glanced at his watch with an expression of pride anyway. My God! They'd shot one down...

"Somebody grab the field radio and tell the CO we've downed a Heinkel bomber. God knows where it crashed. But I wouldn't want to be in their shoes... bloody Germans!"

"Yeah. What were they thinking?" said Terry, whose sister's buttered muffins were so highly regarded by Broadbent's Regiment. What were they thinking?

Reconnaissance

Dorset, England

IT WAS DARK IN THE CABIN of the Percival Proctor aircraft. Brim and Freddie sat in the rear seats, behind the pilot. There was a dim glow from the assorted dials on the instrument panel, but a fine moonlight illuminated their tiny space like some ghoulish theatre of shadows. The Proctor was a British radio trainer and communications aircraft, used primarily by the RAF and Fleet Air Arm, and ideal for the sort of low-level reconnaissance Brim had in mind.

The PO (Pilot Officer) was a quiet academic named Peter Tite. He was aware that his passengers were on some sort of a covert mission. Brim and Freddie said little as they looked out of the rear side windows. A pilot on missions such as this never asks questions; information about 'purpose' is gradually revealed. And tonight, would be no exception. It was Brim who eventually broke the nervous silence:

"You knew, didn't you, Freddie?"

"I had an inkling, yes," he replied, reading Brim's devious

mind.

"At the Baker Street safe house, you didn't want to go out."

"What and celebrate? There wasn't anything to celebrate. No. I just wasn't in the mood."

"I bet you polished the Haig off!" Brim huffed. He wanted more from Freddie. But he wasn't going to get it, even with his skills. And to be honest, he wasn't really in the mood either.

"Look, I know you're worried about Alistair, but the ..."

Suddenly the wireless came alive and the pilot switched to loudspeaker.

"Come in Foxtrot, over," said control at RAF Northolt.

"Foxtrot, responding. What's up?"

Brim and Freddie both instinctively lent forward, as if such an action might make their hearing abilities more acute.

"Secure scrambler. Royal Signals at Blandford Camp has reported a downed aircraft near to the base. Called in by a local farmer. Said it was 'grey and definitely not British'. No fires, no signs of life."

"Was the canopy open?" called Freddie.

The pilot repeated the question.

"I have no information," said control at Northolt.

"Did you get that?" said Tite, quickly glancing over his shoulder to check his companions understood there was no information.

Control continued: "There's an airfield with three grass runways, not far from them or the crash site. The place is called Pimperne Camp. 50.52 North/02.09 West. Grid reference is ST 893080. It's used by the AVRO 504K's. Signals are sending men there to meet you."

"Understood," said Tite, clearly a man of few words; or more aptly, discretion.

Brim unfolded and refolded an RAF Ordnance Map to the relevant grid reference: "Yes, look here – Pimperne – just north of Blandford; between Stourpaine in the west and Tarrant Launceston in the east. But where's the crash site?"

Tite repeated the question.

"Somewhere in that grid reference square to the east of Blandford."

"Understood," he said.

"Another thing, maybe relevant?"

"Go ahead."

"At Poole. The US Army – 266th and 551st FA Battalion reported an enemy aircraft about to attack a British fishing vessel approaching the harbour, four nautical miles out. She did what appeared to be the reconnaissance first, then went around again in a huge 360-degree turn. But not before an anti-aircraft regiment stationed on Hengistbury Head put twenty rounds in her. Obviously the same one."

Brim cut in: "The crew of the plane are not hostile. Repeat: not hostile. The crew of the fishing vessel most certainly are. This is a National Security issue. Complete secrecy. Over."

And Brim, of course, was quite right. He knew the consequences of indecision. The last thing he wanted was any other service involved and particularly not the US Army. It was vital that none of these recent events were betrayed to the local police, Home Guard or the general public. And particularly not the media: newspapers and the BBC. It was well known that German Intelligence listen to BBC broadcasts around the clock. It must remain secret.

Canaris must not be compromised in any way. Brim would have to co-ordinate this exercise with Royal Signals. And them alone. If Hitler discovered that Canaris had not only helped Alistair escape from Germany in a Luftwaffe aircraft, but had also divulged to him secret Reich information...they would kill him. DAS SCHLOSS was Himmler's project.

The radio crackled: "Received and understood. What's your ETA at the Pimperne Airfield?"

Tite immediately changed his course and heading, set the trim: "Hard to say. At this speed, half an hour. We'll need runway flares."

"Signals are on the case. Over and out." There was a whoosh and hiss of static once again.

"Does that all make sense, gentlemen?" Tite enquired, "I mean, I didn't think we were going on holiday, but when my CO said: The PM's Office and the Admiralty are involved, well, I did not know what to think.

"It makes perfect sense," said Freddie, his voice dry and croaky. He wondered if he was going down with a cold; but no, he'd had this feeling before. It was called nerves and all he could think of was Alistair.

And Astrid.

What the hell was going to happen next? Surely Alistair would survive the crash. But what if he didn't? What next? He loosened his collar and strained to look out of the window; the blackout below revealed no secrets. And all he could do now was wait and hope. Freddie looked at Brim. He had closed his eyes in search of a few moments' peace; but Freddie could tell by Brim's furrowed brow that he too was thinking about Alistair and the downed Heinkel.

And the only question that really mattered now was: had he made it back to England alive?

Schlafende Spione

Sandbanks, Poole Harbour, Dorset, England.

CAPTAIN RICHARD LAMBERT waved the tugboat men off and thanked them in his best English. He sounded the part. And he looked it. The Coastguard had towed the Clarissa from the open channel into a shallow depth between South Haven Point on the port side of the harbour entrance and Sandbanks on the starboard side. Running aground, because of the weight of their cargo and a low tide had cost them time and unnecessary exposure. Lambert was anxious and concerned. But at least now she was moored on the quayside. It was one o'clock in the morning and no sign of a signal.

Harald Wolf had watched the entire rescue operation, concealed out of sight, just a half mile inland. He smirked at their stupidity; his pock-marked face creased into a grin. The Captain of that vessel would pay for this time delay, he thought to himself. No matter who he might be.

The old Dennis bus was still decked out with the red, white

and blue flags. She still sported the holiday banner, a necessary piece of their cover. He drove slowly down to the quayside, where Lambert and his crew stood on the deck of the waiting vessel. There was a brief wave of acknowledgment between the two men, then the bus pulled up alongside the Clarissa. Wolf got out of the bus and climbed aboard. There were no handshakes, no smiles and no greetings. They conversed in quiet German.

"Where the hell did that Heinkel come from?" said Lambert angrily as if it were the other man's fault. "An HE111 – very early Luftwaffe. One of ours, for Christ's sake."

"I don't know or care." said Wolf. "You are late. Just get your men to unload the crates onto my bus so we can get going. We have a long journey." His attitude bordered on aggressive.

Lambert went up close to Wolf: "We are late because we ran aground. We didn't anticipate the weight of the vessel and the sandbanks. Or the low tide."

"Anticipation is what separates the foolish from the wise." Wolf laughed with disdain and turned to walk away.

Lambert grabbed him by the back of his jacket with such force that he literally spun around:

"I didn't plan this; I am following orders. So should you. Is that clear?"

Wolf shrugged; it was the wrong gesture to a man like Lambert.

"I said is that clear?" Lambert repeated. He wasn't going to have a year of his life demeaned by a civilian sleeper spy. He had done all the work, after all. Training hard on English waters, risking his life every day of the week for a year.

“Yes, it is clear. I apologise.” Wolf picked up his hat, sensing that Lambert was not a man to pick a quarrel with. And this was not the time or place for an altercation; they had a job to do.

Lambert issued instructions to Scheiderbauer and the three fishermen. Using the on-board winch, they lifted the four wooden crates from the vessel onto the harbourside. The rear emergency door of the bus was open; all the seats had been removed, exposing the reinforced floor of the bodywork. A series of rollers – rotating metal cylinders – had been added, to make loading easier and quicker.

Nobody noticed Gertrud, because she had hidden herself just inside the front passenger entrance. She was holding one of the handguns, just in case. Her job was to watch and wait and she didn’t trust anyone. They too had waited a long time for this moment; and she didn’t like the look of Lambert. He looked dangerous and had treated her husband like an insolent schoolboy.

It took the men twenty minutes to lift the crates from the harbourside and load them through rear door. The rollers certainly made it easier. Thick leather straps with solid-steel brackets had been welded into the interior. Wolf had thought out every detail - even blacking out the windows of the bus as well.

Once loaded, the three-metre-long crates were strapped closely together and tightly secured. Wolf produced a large sheet of sacking material and covered the crates completely, just in case they were stopped. The three fishermen and Scheiderbauer re-boarded the Clarissa, sweating and breathing heavily from their exertions. Lambert followed after them, nonchalantly. He went into the wheelhouse and turned to Wolf:

"I have some English money for you," he said unexpectedly, "two hundred pounds, for petrol and hotel expenses."

Wolf was instantly wary; this was not expected: What was Lambert doing? Walcott had given them plenty of money for the mission.

Lambert bent down to retrieve the money. In that split second, Wolf nodded to Gertrud, still concealed by the bus. It was a trick, it had to be. She was ready. From her concealed spot, she pointed her handgun through an open gap in one of the passenger windows and aimed carefully at the wheelhouse. When Lambert stood up, he was holding his 7.65mm Luger by the barrel, as if to offer it. In his other hand was a roll of bank notes, bound with an elastic band. Wolf quickly shook his head at Gertrud and she lowered her weapon, her expression confused.

Lambert looked mystified: "Thought you might need this; but I see you have a weapon." He replaced the Luger on a chart shelf beneath the wheel.

"For a moment I thought you were going to shoot us," said Wolf, half joking.

Lambert shook his head: "No. Why would I? I suggest you take the money and go." Scheiderbauer and the three fishermen watched the proceedings slightly concerned as Lambert got off the Clarissa and dropped down to the harbourside.

"I'll see you in St. Helier, Dieter. As planned." He waved to his colleague and the crew with a bright smile. Wolf untied the moorings and took the money from Lambert:

"Yes, thank you. English currency is always useful."

In the wheelhouse of the Clarissa, Scheiderbauer started the engines as she started to float out into the harbour. Lambert watched the fishing vessel. Gertrud watched him. He had a look of the English aristocrat, dressed in a padded wax jacket and corduroy trousers. The flat cap completed the picture of an upper-class gentleman on his way to a fishing trip. Or a hunt. She smiled at him:

"Not accompanying your shipmates, Captain?" asked Gertrud, with a distinct edge.

"No." Lambert didn't want to engage in conversation at a time like this. He glanced at his watch.

"Oh, I see" she said warily, knowing she was being dismissed.

"Come," Wolf said to Gertrud in English. "We don't have much time. It will be sunrise soon."

"Ich weiβ genau, wie spät es ist, Harald."

"I know exactly what the time is, Harald," she replied, spiked with venom, just a little too loudly. And she used the name Harald in its Germanic form. And this was her second mistake.

*

In the darkness, just thirty feet away, an old tramp who had been asleep in a telephone box, awoke from his drunken slumber. There wasn't a soul around; the town was asleep in the early hours of the morning.

He thought he'd been dreaming. But he hadn't. He'd heard a German sentence, although he didn't know what it meant. The voice of a woman.

Later he would remember one solitary word of that sentence – Harald – and exactly how it had sounded: guttural; distracted and irritated. And that single name would have a significance nobody could have possibly predicted. He struggled to his feet, picked up the receiver and dialled 9 – 9 – 9. He squinted through the glass, but there really wasn't much to see.

*

Richard Lambert watched Harald and Gertrud board the bus and drive away. She gave him a little wave that was quite unexpected and a smile which seemed to say: You've abandoned your crew, but why? You cannot fool me, whoever you are.

He turned from the harbourside, pulled up the collar of his jacket, thrust his hands into his pockets and strolled away. By the time Scheiderbauer and crew finally got the Clarissa out of Poole harbour and into open sea, Lambert would be well on his way to the bus station.

The next part of the plan was in place. Lambert pictured Erich Spengler sitting in his office in Wilhelmshaven, possibly wondering if the cylinder transfer had gone smoothly. As he boarded the bus for Windsor, he imagined his stack of Swiss francs in a Zürich bank vault and smiled to himself: What on earth shall I spend it all on?

Chase

Pimperne Airfield, Dorset, England.

THE TINY RUNWAY AT PIMPERNE was lit on either side with flares as the nifty little Percival Proctor approached and touched down. It braked sharply and skidded on the moist grass. Freddie could see two Army vehicles and a group of soldiers dressed in battle fatigues. The moment the aircraft came to a halt the flares were extinguished. It was quick and methodical. These men were professionals. In front, Tite took off his goggles and stretched: "I say, are we in cider country?" he asked hopefully. The soldiers, except for one, ran over – at the double – to meet them. Tite got out first, followed by Brim. Then Freddie unbuckled his belt ready to do the same.

"Can I give you a hand, Freddie old boy?" a remarkably familiar voice asked.

Freddie was shocked as Alistair climbed up onto the wing and helped him out of the aircraft. They joined the others. One of the soldiers stepped forward and presented himself: "Major Forbes Powerstock," the man saluted and then thrust out his hand,

"Royal Signals, Blandford Camp."

"Brimblecombe," said Brim formally, "Foreign Office."

"Valentine," said Freddie, smiling broadly at Alistair, "the same!"

Powerstock chuckled in amusement: "Yes, of course."

Alistair held out his hand: "Freddie! I can't tell you how good it is to see you!"

"You too Alistair," he said with a croaky voice, "you too." The two of them embraced. And this time, for the first time in years, they really meant it. It was as if their association with espionage had produced in them a unifying bond; a sense of purpose and meaning.

"What happened?"

"We were shot down, but I can't blame them," said Alistair, "anti-aircraft gun. Only doing their job, I admit. But it was my fault really, given my mode of transport..." He quickly and quietly filled him in on the details Freddie didn't already know. Except Maria; that was a story for another day.

"And your pilot?" asked Freddie.

"Dead, I'm afraid. Shard of flying glass. Bloody fluke. He was a decent bloke too. But he drained the tank, got us down. Crash landed at, where was it now?"

"Hammett's Farm. A local farmer found you lying near the wreckage," said Powerstock. "You owe him your life, you know. You're a lucky man."

"Yes, I do. And I must somehow repay him."

"Is crashing aircraft a family tradition? At least this one was German," said Brim. "How are you, Alistair?" The two men shook hands, smiling at Brim's comment.

"I'm really not quite sure. One minute I'm at Berlin-Gatow. And now I'm at an airfield in Dorset. The whole thing is a whirl."

"You get around," said Powerstock.

"Sir!" a soldier called from one of the Army vehicles; he was clutching the receiver of a field radio.

Powerstock dashed over, listened to a message and returned.

"That's interesting. It seems an eyewitness in Poole - a local tramp – called the Police. He claimed he heard German voices and saw two people – a man and a woman driving away fast in a bus decked out with bunting. Police have arrested four men trying to escape from the harbour in a fishing vessel."

"Did they say what the name of the vessel was?" asked Brim quietly.

Powerstock raised his eyebrows and frowned: "I think he said Clarissa. Would that be right? And I believe the name 'Harald' was mentioned. The driver of the bus."

Alistair said: "Harald is the Germanic Norse version of Harold, as the English know it. Our driver is therefore a German. No question."

Brim looked at the two brothers: "Right. If they're driving from Poole to London, there's only one road and that's via Ringwood. They've got at least an hour's start on us by road. We'll have to get going."

"But not by air, surely?" asked Freddie, glancing up at the Percival Proctor.

Tite, who had been leaning quietly against the aircraft, probably considering a large glass of cider, looked up, startled:

"You, you mean in this one, do you?"

"I can't see another one......can you?" Brim glanced around theatrically.

"But she's low on fuel," Tite protested feebly.

"This is an airfield," said Powerstock quickly, "and there is a fuel depot."

Brim clapped his hands together: "Major Powerstock, I'd like you to join us on this recce. I'm sure you know the entire area very well."

Powerstock visibly stiffened: "I'd be honoured, sir," he tapped his side-arm, "and equipped."

"Good," said Brim, feeling progress. "Let's fuel and go. You alright with that, Tite?"

"Yes, yes of course." His evening wasn't going to end up as he'd hoped, with several pints of scrumpy.

"Oh, one thing, sir," said Powerstock, "what about the Police in Poole?"

Brim fixed him with one of his serious stares: "As I said before, this is a National Security issue. Our coastline was attacked by an enemy aircraft and the artillery at Hengistbury Head shot it down. I don't want any of the real story going public. Is that quite clear?"

Brim didn't want Admiral Canaris compromised in any way; that was his rationale. And that meant no Police, no newspapers and certainly no BBC. He knew the Germans monitor the Oversea service.

"Yes, sir, clear. And the crew of the Clarissa? One German national and three French fishermen. None of them, apparently speak English."

"Put them on ice, Major," said Brim.

*

Brim was frustrated. By the time the Percival Proctor had been fuelled and was airborne again, the bus was parked, hidden in an outbuilding many miles away in the grounds of Needle's Eye House.

Needle's Eye

Needle's Eye House, Weybridge, England.

GILES WALCOTT STEPPED OUT of the front door of his elegant Regency mansion – Needle's Eye House - and wandered over to meet Harald and Gertrud Wolf in one of the outbuildings. He cut an impressive figure, a good-looking man and quite the country gent.

In many ways Walcott resembled the late Otto Krebbs in Berlin, but without the livid scar. He was tall, blue-eyed, well-built, with the look of a Norwegian or Swedish. His blond hair, parted in the middle, was swept back with hair oil and gave him the image of a Hollywood matinee idol. He was an amateur aviator, who also raced cars and rode horses. Walcott had had a passionate affair with Erich Spengler's daughter Rosa, while she was studying at Trinity, Dublin. Spengler had financed 75% of Needle's Eye, in the hope that one day they would marry. Walcott was the son Spengler never had; a man who would soon meet another woman who would take his breath away ...

In one of the large outbuildings the old Dennis bus was

parked. Beside it was a dark green horsebox, a Rover 12 HP Saloon and a 1938 Bentley with a tow bar. Walcott approached the doorway and noticed the rear emergency door of the bus was open. The four crates lay there looking innocent, their journey almost complete.

"Any problems?" asked Walcott, oozing charm. "You are much later than I expected." He spoke in fluent German; shook Harald by the hand and kissed Gertrud on each cheek. How beautiful she looks, he thought to himself.

Harald shook his head: "Lambert was late arriving in Poole. The Clarissa ran aground and had to be rescued by the Coastguard. I didn't like the look of him."

"Nor I," said Gertrud, remembering the tall figure of Richard Lambert in his green wax jacket and superior expression. They had decided not to mention the crashed Heinkel and what looked like an attack on the Clarissa. At this point, Walcott didn't need to know.

"No matter. You are here. And so are these cylinders. Well done, both of you. Germany is proud of you." Walcott mustered as much sincerity as he could.

The three of them walked over to the house. Walcott explained there would be a drinks party later, followed by a formal dinner. The front door of the house opened.

"Ah, you haven't met my wife Joselyn, have you?" He had switched to English and asked them to do the same, for the moment.

Gertrud answered for both of them: "We didn't even know you were married. You have never mentioned a wife in all the times we met in London."

"Oh." Walcott feigned surprise. "No German, remember. She'll know soon enough, by then it will be too late to matter."

Joselyn had a sensuous, wide mouth, full lips, and dimpled cheeks when she smiled; which she did often. Her face, though not classically beautiful, was alluring, an exquisitely crafted work of art. She had deep-blue eyes, jet-black hair and an hourglass figure she had inherited from her late mother, an Italian beauty from Portofino.

Walcott had been captivated by Joselyn the moment they first met and had pursued her relentlessly with flowers and champagne. When that had not worked, a blue sapphire secured their first date. She had deliberately played hard to get. And she had a very good reason. But there was more to Joselyn than met the eye. She was an American for a start, from Massachusetts. And it seemed there wasn't anything she couldn't do, from playing tennis to sailing and more. But none of this mattered to Walcott. She was a 'trophy' wife, a decoration who had the admiration of his male friends and the envy of the women at their country club. Walcott relished the image he presented: a gentleman with the trappings of wealth: a valuable Surrey mansion and a wife many men would kill for.

"Pleased to meet you both," said Joselyn, her blue eyes sparkling with charm. They walked into a spacious hallway, where Albert Collins, the butler, greeted them. "You'll want to freshen up, I guess," said Joselyn. "Albert will show you to your room. Drinks at seven. Then dinner."

Harald almost bowed and said: "Delighted, Mrs Walcott." He

was fawning over her and could not have sounded more English. They turned and followed Collins up the wide, carpeted staircase. Gertrud could at once see her husband was enchanted by this American beauty and it clearly annoyed her.

"Who are they, Giles?" Joselyn asked, a moment later, taking his arm for appearances sake.

"Business. You'll know more later." He disconnected himself rudely from his wife and walked away to the privacy of his study.

He closed the door firmly and turned the key. Walcott too had secrets. To all intents and purposes, he looked English and he spoke English faultlessly. But he was Irish, a devoted Republican and committed fascist. In the early 1930s, after a visit to Mussolini in Italy, Walcott's conversion to fascism was confirmed and cemented. He had plenty of motive to be very anti-English.

*

Drinks were served in the conservatory, a delightful extension which overlooked manicured lawns and extensive gardens. A greenhouse dominated a corner of the view, lush with vegetation and fruit.

The Wolfs wore evening dress, as did Walcott and Joselyn. They were joined by the acerbic Cynthia Fuller, very obviously a key figure in whatever business was going on. She was a chameleon: dangerous and manipulative. Whereas Joselyn acted the role of provincial and spoilt, Cynthia was well travelled, vituperative and cunning.

Cynthia – or 'Cyn' – as Walcott insisted on calling her, had somehow managed to wheedle her way into the Royal Mews in

Windsor. How she had done it exactly, nobody knew or questioned. And certainly, Joselyn had no idea why she was there or what role she played in her husband's life. Yet. She and Walcott seemed to be very much in their own world, with frequent eye contact and an undercurrent of mutual understanding. This was not missed by the sharp-eyed Joselyn, but she chose to ignore it. Joselyn had, several times, asked Walcott what the occasion was 'in aid of' and each time he simply restated 'business' in a dismissive way. It irritated her, but she could not show it. Joselyn would have to bide her time. But then again, she was used to that.

By 7.30, the drinks party was in full swing. The Wolfs however chose to keep themselves to themselves, despite Cynthia questioning them about the fate of the Clarissa and her crew. She had persisted to the point of annoyance:

"She was going back to Jersey," Harald had tried to explain. "This is not our business. Getting here was our business."

Albert Collins came into the conservatory and announced that dinner was about to be served and would they all care to follow him into the dining room, please? Joselyn noticed that Walcott was drinking more than usual, a sure sign of nerves. Walcott ignored his wife's admonishing glance and wandered over to one of the large windows that faced the driveway.

"I don't know what's happened to Mr. Devlin," Walcott said suddenly. He glanced at his watch and then warily at Cynthia. "We'll have to go on with dinner without him. Mind you, he's had to travel a long way." He seemed to be almost speaking to himself.

Cynthia flinched, a flash of anger: "Who is Devlin?"

"An associate," replied Walcott.

"Why don't I know about him?"

"You didn't need to know about him," said Walcott. "You all will later."

Cynthia felt bitter about this latest exclusion from Walcott's plan. But she covered it well. She was dressed in a black-silk, off-the-shoulder gown, as if she were attending a "roaring twenties" party. Her hair was styled, her jewellery elaborate and expensive. It was as if she was trying to outdo the beautiful hostess and their guest from 'the hotel' in London: Gertrud too looked chic.

Cynthia drank Walcott's expensive Burgundy and smoked voraciously between courses, prompting Joselyn to open the dining room windows wider to make a point. Cynthia thrived on conflict. It was her way.

The meal, served by two girls from the village, in their teens, was faultless: smoked fish as a starter, roast lamb for main course and apple strudel for dessert. There was a large chunk of cheddar cheese surrounded by grapes picked from the estate's greenhouse. At one point Walcott said:

"Everything on the table has been sourced from Needle's Eye. Except for the lamb, of course. We had to send out for that."

"Delicious," said Harald.

Gertrud sipped her Chablis with reserve. She was clearly uncomfortable with the way the evening was progressing and concerned about this man Devlin. Why hadn't they been told?

A tap on the dining room door. It was Collins: "Will you take coffee in here or outside, sir?"

"Here," said Walcott. "We're waiting for someone."

"Ah yes," said Cynthia, helping herself to another generous glass of Burgundy, "the mysterious Mr. Devlin. Do you know who he is, Joselyn? You are the hostess."

Joselyn suddenly looked very uneasy: "No. Giles's business is his concern."

"Very well," said Collins quickly and withdrew, sensing trouble.

"How very agreeable of you, Joselyn. Are all Americans so delightfully unselfish? Or is Giles here so lucky to have such a wife as you?"

Walcott seized control: "That's enough, Cyn. And I think you have drunk enough too. Spare some for Mr. Devlin. You have a big day tomorrow. We all have."

Joselyn suddenly shot out of her seat. "Excuse me ... Giles, I wish you'd tell me what the hell is going on?" She stormed out of the room. The two young waitresses, who were standing by a serving trolley, looked shocked.

Walcott ignored the situation and lowered his voice: "Harald, listen. I want you and Gertrud to go to Windsor early tomorrow. Take the Rover that's parked in the barn where you left the bus, the keys are in it. Meet me later at the racecourse. Oh, and I have booked you a double room at a hotel in the centre of town opposite the castle. In the name of Harris."

"Why?" asked Gertrud. "Why do we have to go before the cylinders arrive?"

Cynthia poured herself another glass of wine, amused at

Gertrud's displeasure.

"Have a look around. Spend some time there. Check the level of security, police presence, MI5 ... we have time ... the three escape cars are already parked on Castle Hill in Windsor. You'll see them: an Alvis, a Talbot and a thirty-one Lagonda. All fast. But the Alvis needs fuel, a job for tomorrow."

"All right," said Harald cautiously. "This is not a problem, Walcott."

Walcott seized the moment, sensing negativity: "Look, the British security services have no idea where the cylinders are – even if they know they exist – which I doubt. You lost them, a good job. The bus is now out of the picture, relax. Thanks to Cyn the Royal Mews horsebox will take the load from now."

Harald nodded at this praise: "Thank you. Can we speak German now your wife has left the party?"

Walcott smiled: "No."

Outside, hidden behind the dining room door, Joselyn heard the words: security, police presence, MI5 ... cylinders ... and can we speak German now your wife has left the party?

No.

Joselyn needed to find out what was going on around that table. She returned to the dining room as if she had just nipped out to pay a call of nature and smiled demurely at Walcott.

"Ah, there you are, darling," he said attentively. "We were worried about what had happened to you."

"Were we?" said Cynthia. She lit a cigarette as Joselyn sat back down next to Walcott. Her timing was designed to irritate her hostess.

There was a discreet knock on the door, Collins opened it cautiously: “There is a gentleman to see you, sir. Said you were expecting him. I wasn’t aware of another guest and there isn’t a room prepared.”

“That’s all right. He won’t be staying. Show him in, will you?” said Walcott abruptly. The dining room door opened, and the missing guest walked in. The Wolfs, Cynthia and Joselyn were taken aback by the sight of their visitor. Walcott stood:

“Michael! There you are. Good evening. We were getting worried about you.”

Cynthia huffed: she wasn’t worried about anyone. Not now.

“It doesn’t look like it,” said Devlin with a snarl.

Devlin

Needle's Eye House, Weybridge, England

MICHAEL DEVLIN WAS A DOUR, humourless individual: short with the wiry build of a featherweight. He had a misshapen, broken nose and a mop of straw-coloured hair. He looked tired, gave the assembled party a half smile, revealing chipped yellow teeth:

"Sorry I'm so late. I won't bore you with the details, but it's taken three days." He addressed his excuse to the host, then turned to the others and smiled grimly.

"You've missed the food," said Walcott light heartedly, "although I'm sure ... sorry, everyone, this is Michael Devlin."

"I'm not hungry," said Devlin, "but I could well use a drink, then I'll say my piece."

He sat next to Cynthia and immediately filled a glass to the brim with Chablis. He downed it in one go. "I'm sure you have plenty more, Giles, you with your cellar and all." He smiled and lit a hand-rolled cigarette.

"Surely," said Walcott and promptly re-filled Devlin's glass.

This time he only drank half of it and scanned the table with bloodshot eyes.

"Can we lose the women? It's not their business."

Walcott suddenly looked anxious. Cynthia folded her arms, her brow furrowed in anger.

"I'm not going anywhere. I'm the most important member of the organisation," Cynthia announced. She was perfectly serious: she had acquired a Royal Horsebox and Humber car to tow it.

"And neither am I," said Gertrud, "I am also important." She spoke in rapid German, hoping Devlin would not understand. Instead, he replied in equally rapid German with no trace of an Irish accent.

"Just the ones who matter then." He pulled on his cigarette and sank the rest of his wine. "Ah you must be the Wolfs."

In that split second, on hearing the German, Joselyn understood the situation. Suddenly all her training with British Intelligence paid off. She knew the truth, or part of it. Brim's instinct had been right: there was more to Walcott than the BUF. She had to remain deadpan to save her life.

"Joselyn, do you mind, my darling?" Walcott said. "As I mentioned earlier, just business."

But she was already on her feet. Devlin stretched across the table and helped himself to a lump of cheddar with his hands and a generous glass of Burgundy.

"Yes, go off and play your tennis," said Devlin spitefully, "or whatever it is you do."

"Right," said Walcott, "what news from Rosslare?"

"If that's what you want, Giles, yes," said Joselyn humbly and left the room quietly. Cynthia smirked once again, as the dining room door closed very softly.

Michael Devlin sat back in his chair and closed his eyes, savouring the expensive wine and composing his words:

"Since the Norman invasion, Britain has sought to conquer, dominate and inflict their rules upon us, the Irish. Why?"

He looked at Walcott; the others looked confused. He continued.

"For seven centuries, we have tried to liberate ourselves from British oppression; well, now it will be different. Now we will." He swigged more wine.

Gertrud looked shocked: "Walcott, this is new. We didn't know the Irish were a part of this."

Walcott smiled: "Oh yes."

Cynthia looked scared: "Giles. What's going on here? Who is this man?"

Devlin ignored Cynthia but stared at Harald and Gertrud.

"You don't know the half of it." Devlin switched back to German: "Fuck Himmler! This is where we get our revenge against the Brits. Isn't that right, Giles? For your Ma and Pa too." Devlin's eyes shone, manic. "The Brits won't know what's hit them."

"Revenge for what, Giles? What is this all about?" fired Gertrud, her blue eyes flashing with anger.

"Freeing Ireland. The cause." Devlin's voice was raised to make the point.

Harald shook his head and looked at Walcott: "But this is surely about German victory over Britain?"

"The hell it is," snarled Devlin. "It's about liberating Ireland from England; the monarchy; the politicians; the lot of them."

"Giles!" shrieked Cynthia. "What is this? Who is this ghastly creature? Get rid of him."

"Shut the fuck up, whoever you are," Devlin said. "The moment the cylinders explode – 12.15 – tomorrow, all hell will break lose around Windsor. It will create pandemonium. Panic, confusion and most of all, distraction ..."

He looked around the table. Harald and Gertrud were spellbound, shocked. And so was Cynthia; she had been misled by Walcott.

"At 12.15 I will send a signal from Southampton to a Luftwaffe airbase in the north of France. This will start a series of targeted airstrikes on London and the south of England, and the payload will be lethal ..."

The Wolfs and Cynthia couldn't hide their shock; Walcott merely smiled, relishing the revenge for the murder of his dear parents all those years ago. Devlin continued.

"So, Giles, that's the news from Rosslare," said Devlin with a twisted smile. "Does anybody around this table have a problem with that?" He fixed his eyes on each of them; they shook their heads, paralysed with fear. No, was the consensus.

"Good," said Devlin. "Now you can feed me. I'm suddenly fucking starving."

Joselyn

Needle's Eye House, Weybridge, England.

'TIN-POT FASCISTS AND CHOCOLATE DICTATORS' Brim had called them. Cowards, all of them. Keep an eye on Walcott and his BUF cronies. Stay close. We want to know all about him. And, she had certainly done that.

She ran up the sweeping staircase towards her bedroom in tears. But tears of anger, not sorrow. She had overheard most of the conversation and certainly Devlin's vicious diatribe. Collins was an unforeseen ally; he'd left the door to the dining room open just enough.

Who the hell was Michael Devlin and how could he know Giles? What was the connection? All she knew was, she had to act: Southampton was his destination.

She switched on the light in the panelled bathroom, feeling livid, yet simultaneously animated and full of drive. She removed her make-up with warm water.

Giles had deceived her. She had expected as much. He had lied about his past, his family, his political ambition, and his radical treachery against Britain. She had known he was a fascist with the BUF, but this was cold-blooded mass-murder, treachery beyond belief. Just who were these people? Gertrud and Harald Wolf; German spies in London? Their English was so perfect, she would never have spotted. But Devlin, she thought, is the real monster.

Devlin. She gritted her teeth because she couldn't afford more ire, not now. He was a ticking time bomb. He had to be stopped. She had to stop him: it was her job. She soaked a flannel and washed off any trace of perfume; the scent could betray her. As she went about her ablutions, she was subconsciously planning and preparing.

Joselyn redressed in a pair of tight-fitting, black riding trousers and a black cashmere sweater. She retrieved a pair of leather gloves, some money and her passport from her bottom drawer. She looked around the bedroom, considered putting a couple of spare pillows under the blanket on her side of the bed. But to what end? How much time would it buy her? Ten seconds. No, with any luck she would be miles away by then. In any case, Giles would be chin-wagging with Cynthia until the early hours, plotting and scheming ... or something else.

She flicked off the lights and crept down the sweeping staircase, clutching the balustrade for support. She must not make a sound. Just as she touched the very last step, a side door started to open. She froze in fear, couldn't run...

Collins.

Her index finger shot up to her lips in a 'sh' gesture. If Collins felt any surprise at either her appearance or timing, he gave no sign. He merely closed the door and came over to greet her, his footsteps soft and cautious. He was on his guard.

He spoke in a low voice, looking around: "Is everything all right, ma'am?"

She did not have to lie, and she couldn't afford to waste time, so she looked him in the eye and confided: "Is Devlin still here?"

Collin's eyes widened as if in exasperation: "As large as life; yes, unfortunately."

"Good. Which car did he arrive in?"

Once again, if Collins thought anything odd about the question, he remained stoic and composed: "The shooting brake, ma'am. End of the drive. Parked hurriedly."

Joselyn breathed a sigh of relief; her unforeseen ally had remained informative and discreet. Suddenly, she raised herself up onto tiptoes and pecked him on the cheek: "Thank you," she whispered in his ear.

Collins's face remained impassive: "The scullery door is the least obvious, ma'am, if you are planning to do what I think you are."

She nodded, turned and vanished without another word.

Once outside, she could just about discern three voices: Giles, Cynthia, and Devlin. She stood very still in the driveway and tried to listen. At least she knew where they all were.

The car was carelessly parked, with the two nearside wheels dug deeply into the recently mown lawn. Devlin had obviously braked sharply and skidded to a halt. She cautiously tried the driver's door handle.

It was locked. She looked inside; on the back seat was a suitcase, new and expensive.

Suddenly the front door of the house swung open and Walcott stepped out, looking around; he was followed by Devlin and Cynthia. So, she had been right. The trio were in deep, animated conversation. The Wolfs must have turned in, sick of the whole turn of events with Devlin and the Irish angle.

The passenger door was locked too. Devlin suddenly broke away from the others – waved goodnight noisily – and started to walk towards her and the car. Despite the amount of drink, he must have consumed, he was remarkably steady. She started to panic now; he was getting nearer.

Joselyn tried the shooting brake's rear door handle; it was unlocked. She opened the door just enough and crawled inside. It was pitch black, so she cautiously felt her way around in her gloved hands: a coil of rope, spare tyre and a large tin can. Nothing soft to rest on. She clicked the tailgate shut behind her. She caught her breath and listened: Devlin's footsteps, dangerously close. He was singing some Gaelic song, slurred and repetitive. But suddenly, it all went quiet. She felt the front wing of the car sink and heard a gush of water. My God, she thought to herself: the dirty slob is relieving himself on my drive! Despite the situation, she had to suppress an amused chuckle: my former drive.

Quickly, she felt for the spare tyre and unscrewed the valve. There was a sudden hiss of escaping air. It wasn't a pillow, but it would have to do. She only prayed that the duration of Devlin's micturition outlasted the tyre's deflation.

Powerstock

The Percival Proctor/Airborne.

THE PERCIVAL PROCTOR had made two 360-degree reconnaissance missions, anti-clockwise over the whole of east Dorset and the Hampshire borders. Finally, they turned west directly over the A30. They had seen two buses, neither of which fitted the bill. The second recce was at just over 500 feet and very turbulent. Tite buzzed on the intercom:

"Gentlemen, we have to make a decision now: back to Pimperne or on to Northolt. The fuel gauge is registering half a tank, and where we are now is equidistant."

Brim, Alistair, Freddie and Major Powerstock had their Army-issue field glasses pressed to their eyes; they felt as if they had scanned the whole of England. Without success. It was Brim who spoke first:

"We have to admit the sleeper spies and no doubt their accomplices have evaded us, but it was a chance we had to take... We might have found them...

They must have had additional assistance from someone

within those hundreds of square miles down there..." He glanced out of the cabin window. "We have no choice but to return to Northolt, do we."

They all knew that the target of the enemy's ambition was Windsor Castle. Brim would need to speak with the PM and Sir Cyril Downing as soon as they touched down at Northolt.

Powerstock looked across at Brim, not really part of the team, but very much wanting to be:

"And what about me, sir, I am still officially assigned to Royal Signals, although they are happy you have temporarily commandeered me."

"Yes," said Brim, "I'd like you to remain with us, Major Powerstock and possibly take charge of the tactical side of operations at Windsor. We don't know what to expect. We'll need a good man like you, experienced, and your knowledge of COMMS will be a bonus."

"Sir!" said Powerstock. He couldn't hide his pride.

"To Northolt then, Tite, all agreed." Brim sounded confident and upbeat.

Tite altered course for RAF Northolt and pulled the stick to gain altitude, tapping the fuel gauge as if it might lend them a few extra air miles: "Forty minutes."

"When we find them," said Alistair after a while, "we'll possess one element they could never have anticipated... an unexpected ace up our sleeves."

He looked at Freddie, who nodded. Oh yes, he understood. The spirit of Herr Seiler was right with them in that cabin, egging them on. The gambler, the bluffer.

"Do we?" Brim looked at Alistair and then Freddie, who were now both expressionless.

"Two," put in Freddie. "If you think about it."

Alistair merely nodded. Brim pursed his lips but said nothing. He was a gambler too and he knew when to stay silent.

Revelations

Windsor, Berkshire, England.

"HERR SEILER USED TO SAY: 'Early morning is when a town reveals its innermost secrets'," said Alistair, as they strolled together on the cobblestones. He had a somewhat mischievous, unreadable look on his face.

"'And so do its ladies.'" Freddie reminded him.

"'Yes. Because they are wearing no make-up!'" Alistair was giving a very plausible impersonation of their late dear friend; it was more of an affectionate homage than anything else; and when spoken in the Schweizerdeutsch dialect made it sound all the more touching. They had walked all around the town of Windsor, getting a general feel for the place and its maze of narrow streets. It was 5.30am and deserted. They walked in silence for a while, then Alistair spoke quietly. He had something on his mind:

"I'm sorry about how I was at the Lochars, Freddie, I really didn't mean it. You had no choice but to leave Herr Seiler there in that hotel. I realise that now I have had time to think about it. It must have been very difficult for you."

Freddie nodded as Alistair continued.

"And, if it's any consolation, I would have done the same thing. Also, I should have accepted your apology – you know concerning our mother's letter –and so on. It was wrong of me."

"That's alright, Alistair," Freddie said solemnly.

"And about Astrid..."

"Yes," said Freddie warily. This was the moment he'd been absolutely dreading, but instead his brother became uncharacteristically self-conscious:

"I have something to confide in you, which I feel I must. It's, er, very personal."

"Go on." Freddie was startled but intrigued.

"You see, the thing is, I've lost my libido."

Freddie was incredulous: "Since when?"

Alistair mulled the question over as they walked. They didn't look at one another as he replied, slowly and thoughtfully.

"I can tell you exactly when, Freddie. It was soon after Mother died." Alistair swallowed. It had been a difficult but necessary admission.

"I see." Freddie understood.

"I became a bit unbalanced; that's the truth of it."

"You – you disappeared – if that's what you mean by unbalanced," said Freddie.

"She was my rudder, Freddie. That's one of the reasons I reacted the way I did that night at Waterloo. After she died, I had to get out. Sorry." Alistair sniffed; trying to hold his emotions in check.

"Where did you go?"

"Cape Town. After the funeral I flew to London...booked a ticket on the Union Castle line sailing from Southampton...and went..."

"I see. Herr Seiler and I were worried sick. But strangely, wisely, he had an inkling you might disappear for a while. It seems we were all affected differently, in grief."

"Leaving was my way of coping with that grief. Distance, I suppose."

"Yes," Freddie agreed. He wouldn't have minded leaving himself at the time. But couldn't.

They strolled on. Freddie said: "Have you sought any help? You know, medical advice?"

"I saw Dr. Lionel Goldschmidt, Head of Urology at Somerset Hospital, Cape Town. He examined me – I won't go into detail – and concluded, 'my condition' as he put it, was 'psychological'. There was nothing physically wrong with me and I'd recover, in time."

"I'm glad you told me, Alistair. That can't have been easy."

"No. I'm glad too."

"Everything will be fine." Freddie paused. "Another Herr Seiler maxim: 'things are meant to be, the way they are meant to be'."

"Yes. He meant destiny?"

Freddie nodded: "I really think he is right. This business we are involved in with Brim brought us together. What were the chances of that?"

"With Brim, who knows?" The two brothers laughed and

continued a while in companionable silence, then the million-dollar question:

"And what about Astrid; you know I have to ask. What was the nature of your, well, relationship with her?"

"Let's just say that ours was a partnership of convenience. I am extremely fond of her, Freddie, as a good friend and accomplice; but I never needed her in that way. Not as you did that night in Baden." Alistair shot him a sideways glance to gauge reaction.

Freddie stopped walking: "So you knew, then?"

Alistair took his arm: "It was I who suggested it, Freddie."

"What?"

"You see, for reasons I cannot reveal, she is desperate for a child. I know the reason for her feelings, but I cannot betray her trust. Not now."

"I see."

"And we are not legally married. The 'marital status' was to sanction our living together in Potsdam, for the lease of the house and other domestic bills. All the paperwork is fake, organised by Manfred, Nexus and a dear lady called Monika who was captured and murdered by the SS."

"It's all starting to make sense now."

"Good. Because I told Astrid you'd make the perfect husband and give her the child she desperately needs."

"I'm not sure I understand."

"Oh, but you will, Freddie, you will. I promise."

Red Lion

Red Lion Hotel, Windsor, England

BRIM, FREDDIE AND ALISTAIR were staying in an old, thatched establishment called The Red Lion Inn near the foot of the castle. They had arrived the night before and Brim had asked Major Powerstock to report to Baker Street, to co-ordinate COMMS with Hugh Dalton, while they were driven from RAF Northolt to Windsor. It was so typical of Brim's strategic planning. They had enjoyed a very agreeable supper at the rustically beamed inn; but Brim had retired to bed early to 'leave them to it'; plus, he did not relish another five o'clock start. Brim's real motive was of course to leave the two brothers alone to talk and reacquaint. Brim had no idea whatsoever, that they had already reacquainted, in the most honest of ways.

*

By 6.30am they had reached Royal Windsor Racecourse, where they looked around the stables and stands and then started back towards the centre of Windsor.

“Breakfast?” suggested Alistair.

“Yes, but it won’t be Bauernfrühstück!” Freddie joked, deliberately mentioning Ingrid’s traditional farmer’s breakfast in Baden. Happy days indeed, he thought, recalling for a moment that delightful evening with Astrid.

The dining room was thick with tobacco smoke and packed with a mixture of civilians and soldiers from the Victoria Barracks just behind Sheet Street, home to the 1st Battalion Guards, the oldest regiment in the British Army. The atmosphere was loud with the banter of soldiers who were temporarily home on leave. Even at this hour of the day there was laughter, singing and merriment: Roll out the barrel, we’ll have a barrel of fun ...

They found Brim in reception, telephone receiver pressed against his right ear, his shoulder clamping it against his head, while the other ear was plugged with his thumb.

He greeted the two brothers with a smile and then mouthed the word: ‘Powerstock’. They both stepped nearer and tried to listen.

“What’s that? I can hardly hear you. Ruddy din in here. Like a bloody cattle market. Speak up, man!” He grinned at them both.

“Might be something, sir,” roared Powerstock, “or maybe nothing. A hotel manageress in Kensington has reported a missing couple – the proprietors – and their old bus.”

“What?” The message was repeated louder, and Brim angled the receiver so they could share.

“It seems they took a group of unfortunate war children down to Poole on a holiday. Dropped them off at a Youth Hostel in a place called Hamworthy and haven’t been heard from since.”

"Poole, you say?" Brim called out the three words to involve Alistair and Freddie more in his conversation.

"Yes."

"Who were the couple?"

"A Mr. and Mrs. Wolf. Charming couple. Been there for donkey's years. Do charity work – hence the holiday. Members of the local Conservative Club. An ugly brute and a beautiful wife, apparently. Probably nothing."

Brim pursed his lips, sensing a possible clue: "But it's all we have. Dig deeper if you can. We need to know exactly who they are. Age. Place of birth. As much as you can find out."

"Got it, and I know just the man for this." Powerstock said.

Brim could picture Powerstock jotting notes down in a cramped little office in the Baker Street complex.

"Who was it reported to?" asked Brim.

"The Police Station in Kensington."

"Good. But keep it contained. Get your man to speak to the hotel manageress and try and get a photograph of them. Wedding. Family shot. No matter how old it is."

"Yes, sir."

"We're all here. Rooms 9, 7 and 4."

The line went dead.

"Mr. and Mrs. Wolf," he said out loud. "Who are you really? And where the hell are you now?"

"Anything, Brim?" asked Alistair.

"Maybe." he said. "Come on. Let's get some tea and toast, if you can stand the noise in there. I'll fill you in on what Powerstock had to say. He may just have something."

Thoroughbred

Royal Windsor Racecourse, Windsor, England

ALISTAIR AND FREDDIE approached Royal Windsor Racecourse. There was some activity there this time. A Humber was parked and beside it, a dark green horsebox with a Royal Coat of Arms. It had words painted in gold on its sides:

ROYAL MEWS WINDSOR CASTLE

A man was exercising a horse, leading it by the reins around a fenced-off area by the stands. Its breaths were fast in the early morning mist. A man and a woman were sitting in a Rover 12 HP Saloon. The man was wearing a trilby hat and studying a local road map with great care. The woman, with blond plaited hair was watching the exercise regime without interest. She looked bored.

Alistair and Freddie wandered over to the perimeter fence and shortly after, the groom with his trusty steed walked past and stopped. He was well over six feet in height, well-built, with the look of a Norwegian. A good-looking fellow in his late thirties. His jacket bore a familiar motif: Royal Mews Windsor Castle.

"You're up early!" The blue-eyed groom joked; was there a hint of Southern Ireland in those few words? Particularly the word early. Alistair's acute ear picked it up immediately, but he needed more.

"And so are you," replied Alistair, returning his smile politely.

"Indeed, I am," said the groom. "We like all the horses exercised and fed before breakfast. Best time of the day," he said, inhaling the country air. "Work up an appetite."

"Are you practising for an event?" Freddie asked him, stroking the horse's face.

"No. This is one of the Windsor Greys from the Royal Mews. One of eight actually."

"I see."

"Thoroughbred. Are you interested in the horses then?" The groom enquired politely.

"Only casually."

"They take their name from when they were kept here at Windsor in Victorian times and drew carriages for the Queen."

"Fascinating," said Alistair. He studied the groom discreetly: he could have been an American film star with his looks and charm.

"They are being transferred from Hampton Court Palace." The groom lowered his voice. "Security reasons, I believe. We exercise them here and Windsor Great Park. Safer than London."

The horse snorted loudly and nodded its head as if agreeing. The groom grabbed hold of the reins. Freddie noticed he was wearing a collar and tie under his jacket, but he couldn't identify the motif embroidered below the knot.

"Good boy, Prince......must get on now...plenty to do!" He raised his hat politely and wandered off, the horse behind him, his head lowered.

"Breakfast then?" asked Alistair.

"Yes, I'm famished, although I don't think much of those powdered eggs."

"No," Alistair agreed, "Ingrid would be horrified.

They walked past the Rover Saloon occupied by the silent couple. Freddie doffed his borrowed cap, but they ignored him.

"What do you reckon on that groom? Irish?" asked Alistair.

"Yes; south-east area I would say. Why?"

"I'm not sure really. He looked too affluent to be exercising a horse at this hour. I don't know, you'd think he'd have a stable boy to do that."

"I know what you mean."

"Anyway, I wonder if Major Powerstock has any news from Baker Street." Alistair pondered as they started to walk back in the direction of Windsor.

"Yes, I wonder." A few moments passed. "I'm glad you told me what you did, Alistair."

"You had to know, Freddie. About Astrid."

"I can't wait to see her, you know."

Alistair put his arm around his brother: "No Freddie, I bet you can't."

*

They found Brim in the hotel dining room once again, sitting chatting with an older man who looked as though he was an insurance salesman for the Prudential. He was dressed in a dark grey lounge suit, collar and tie. He was over 60, balding, with gnarled, arthritic hands and a sallow, unhealthy complexion.

"Ah! Good morning, gentlemen! The wanderers have returned!" said Brim in his usual jocular fashion. "This is Detective Inspector Brian Cummins from Scotland Yard."

"Retired." said Cummins miserably. "Pensioned-off early because of ill health." He raised his hands painfully as if to demonstrate his predicament. "But my brain still works."

"DI Cummins is a friend of Major Powerstock," Brim began to explain, until Cummins stopped him politely.

"We're related by marriage as it were," confirmed Cummins in a strong West Midlands accent. "Forbes is my wife's cousin from Dorset......Blandford Forum, to be precise."

"Come and join us then," said Brim, keen to get started with whatever it was. He was fond of springing surprises. The two brothers sat down

at the table and a waiter took their breakfast order.

"Now, DI Cummins has some news," continued Brim, "do you not?"

"Well, the thing is, I don't actually have any news as such, but that, in itself is significant, if you get my meaning?"

"Go on," urged Freddie, intrigued.

"I went to the George Hotel in Kensington, as instructed by

Forbes – 'under the radar, off the record' – as he tactfully put it. I spoke to the manageress who had reported the missing couple to the Police. Beryl Thomas, charming lady from Brighton."

"And the missing bus?" prompted Alistair.

"Remains missing," said Cummins glumly. "You see, the manager of the Youth Hostel in Hamworthy has another group arriving from Birmingham. When the Wolfs disappeared, he called the local Police in Poole who then contacted the police station in Kensington. The two stories married up and the children, well adolescents, need to be collected by someone else, presumably organised by the Wolfs."

"So, what about them?" persisted Alistair. "The Wolfs. Where are they?"

The waiter arrived with a pot of tea, cups and saucers and some unappetising cold toast. There were no powdered eggs and certainly no bacon.

"Beryl, Mrs Thomas that is, said I could look around. I sort of implied......well, told her that the Dorset Police believed they'd been murdered."

"Good God!" exclaimed Brim. "You didn't tell me that on the telephone!"

"Sometimes, Professor Brimblecombe, you have to grab the bull by the horns. And lie! Or at least to exaggerate in order to get what you want. In any case, the Police aren't really interested in a missing bus and a couple of hoteliers. They have enough on their hands with the war effort. Even some looting, but don't get me started."

Alistair poured the tea and buttered some toast, if indeed it was butter. It looked more like candle wax and they all waited. DI Cummins wasn't the speediest of story-tellers.

"She accompanied me of course to their private quarters on the top floor of the hotel, a dingy Victorian edifice on Cromwell Road. Forbes Powerstock had asked me to try and find photographs, identification, documents, ration cards, petrol coupons, letters, mementos and so on."

"And?" asked Brim.

"Nothing. No personal effects whatever. It's as if the Wolfs didn't exist."

"They didn't exist," Brim lowered his voice, "not in their assumed role as hoteliers. They are German spies masquerading as regular English citizens. That much I can tell you in total confidence, because of who you are and your connection with Powerstock." He pursed his lips and regarded the two brothers, aware of the magnitude of what he had revealed. But there was a reason: he wanted more.

Cummins nodded slowly in comprehension: "Good job I'm thorough then, I'll have earnt my ten quid!"

"Meaning?"

"In my Police experience, there are three places most people choose to conceal papers, other than a safe. First, inside picture frames, and in this case, there were three of them in the entire flat. Amateur water colours"

"Go on," said Brim.

"Second, under the proverbial creaky floorboard. I found nothing; I mean, I didn't rip the place apart, but you can normally tell if a board has been unscrewed and then replaced."

"And the third?" asked Freddie.

"Somewhere in the plumbing is a favourite. Sealed containers in water tanks, water closet cisterns, you name it. I checked the loft, garden shed, an outside WC and the garage in a nearby Mews where they parked the illusive bus. No trace of anything."

"No," said Brim, "and that's because they weren't planning to return."

"What were they planning?" asked Cummins.

"That I am afraid I cannot say. I've probably told you enough already, but there we are."

DI Cummins stood up painfully: "Well if you don't require me any further, I'll get back to London. It's the wife's birthday."

"My driver will take you back to Hammersmith," suggested Brim.

"It's alright, Professor," said Cummins dolefully, "there is a bus at ten. I can buy her a present in town. And a card."

They shook hands and Cummins left without another word.

"We're back to square one," said Alistair in a whisper "after all that. A bloody dead end."

"What about the crewmen from the Clarissa?" asked Freddie. He could clearly see that his brother was seething with frustration.

Brim sighed and looked out of the window at the castle: "The Police in Poole are still holding them indefinitely, as war criminals. They're waiting for translators. But my guess is that only the Captain knew anything. And he's vanished. We must locate the Wolfs. They drove the bus."

"We tried. We failed," Alistair snapped angrily.

"And the old tramp who dialled 9 9 9?"

"He can't remember much apart from the name Harald, according to Powerstock," said Brim. "No, we only have one option and that is to remain here and wait. We can't let them know we're onto them – whoever they are - wherever they are or whatever they plan. We have no option."

"Are you going to deploy any military presence here?" asked Alistair.

Brim shook his head decisively: "No. As I said, we cannot risk exposure. We need INTEL and Powerstock is doing all he can. Everyone is."

*

Back at Royal Windsor racecourse, the atmosphere in the Wolfs' Rover was tense. They spoke in German, a sure sign that their nerves were fraught.

They both failed to notice a man in a dark green wax jacket. He was sweeping the racecourse and stables with a pair of high-powered Leica binoculars. A tout perhaps, certainly a man with an interest in all things equestrian.

"I want to go back to the hotel and have some tea. I might buy a book," said Gertrud irritably, "and try and have a doze." She yawned: "There is nothing we can do until later when the official entourage arrives."

"Alright. We have already scouted around Windsor town twice, so I'm sure Walcott won't mind." Harald's tone was agitated. Gertrud got out of the car and left him to his road maps; she couldn't wait to get away.

Giles Walcott, the groom, was feeding the horse and making a fuss of him. Gertrud wandered over and switched back to English: “Who were those two men you were talking to earlier?”

“Oh, I don’t know, Gertrud. Walkers. Brothers I reckon, similar in appearance and what, about 18 months apart in age.” Walcott replied casually.

“Walkers? At that time of the morning? And not at war?” said Gertrud suspiciously. “All the men of their age are away, surely?”

“Who knows? Why, they could be on leave. One of them had a limp, he could have been wounded. Who cares? Is something wrong Gertrud, you seem tense?”

Gertrud’s voice trembled: “Devlin is what’s wrong, Giles.”

Walcott continued to make a fuss of the horse, his tone blasé: “Oh?”

“He is a monster.”

Walcott said: “No, just enthusiastic.” He tried to laugh it off; it didn’t work. Gertrud was irked and tired:

“Giles, please listen to me.” Gertrud’s voice was raised now. “When we first met you – at those BUF meetings – your intentions were to support fascism. You were a political idealist.”

“I still am.”

But Gertrud was firm: “No. This isn’t about Mosley and his toy soldiers. This is mass-murder.” There was a rising urgency in her tone now: “And I am scared. We both are.”

He was about to reply, but she cut him off: “It’s sickening,” she said. “You enrolled us as sleeper spies. You told us this was a simple kidnapping. To use the Princesses as a publicity coup for Goebbels. Those were your exact words. Remember?”

"Yes, of course I remember," he said hesitantly, "and I ..."

She snapped again: "Devlin is a psychopath."

"No." Walcott was worried; he couldn't afford to lose them. Not now, not at this late stage.

Gertrud looked Walcott in the eye: "Harald and I can't be part of mass-murder, Giles."

"Oh? And what do you think you Germans are doing all over Europe?" barked Walcott.

Gertrud was startled; she and Harald were out of touch with reality. Walcott attempted the charm tactic and smiled. He gently took her arm: "I – I can see how you must feel about Devlin, Gertrud. But this is about the war, not the warrior. The resolution of the long conflict with England is all that matters. Look, why don't we take you both to South America, when this is all over?"

Gertrud looked at him, surprised: "South America?" This was new, she thought to herself.

"Yes," he said softly and looked her in the eyes. She returned his gaze with suspicion:

"What about Devlin?"

"Forget Devlin. Joselyn and I have a place in Argentina. You can come and stay with us. The weather is idyllic, you'll love it." Walcott dare not confess that Joselyn had left him last night with no explanation; taken all her savings and passport with her.

She gave him a faint smile that implied hope: "Maybe."

"Gertrud, our mission will mean the end of the war. Germany will be victorious. That's what we all want, isn't it? That's what you both spent years waiting for as sleepers, isn't it? You and

Harald?"

"Yes," admitted Gertrud.

"There will always be casualties, Gertrud," Walcott reasoned, "in any conflict. Now there is a future, for both of you. A safe haven. What do you think?"

She bit her lip: "I will speak to Harald."

"Do that," said Walcott in his soft persuasive lilt: "Soon it will all be over. You'll be free."

She nodded and turned to walk away, back towards Harald.

Walcott dared not risk a smile: "By the way, Harald will need to put some extra fuel in the tank of the Alvis, as I said last night. There's a full jerrycan in the garage. Don't let him forget."

"Alright, he won't forget," Gertrud said quietly. "Now, I'm going back to the hotel."

"Yes, have a rest. It will do you good," Walcott said, breathing a sigh of relief. He thought: Thank God she hasn't asked me any questions about Joselyn. Where the hell has that stupid bitch got to?

*

Wax Jacket replaced the lens protectors of his binoculars and folded them away. He had seen all he needed to see. At least the sleepers made it from Poole; and so had the cylinders.

Das Schloss

Castle Hill, Windsor, England.

ALISTAIR AND FREDDIE had made several circuits of the town and were going back down to meet Brim at the Red Lion for lunch. Alistair noticed again three impressive cars on Castle Hill and wondered who they belonged to: an Alvis, a Talbot and beautiful Lagonda. He was about to mention it to Freddie when they saw the Rover from earlier at the racecourse: the silent couple. The car drew up just down from the Priory Bookshop on Castle Hill and the blond woman alighted, her face flushed with anger. The Rover then pulled away with such speed that it almost collided with a horse-drawn milk cart. The horse reared up in fear and the milkman swore in anger. The couple had obviously had words, whoever they were.

Alistair watched, intrigued. The blond woman looked to her left and right as if she was wary of either being watched or followed – a curious instinctive action – and proceeded to walk up the hill. She walked with a graceful economy which suggested physical fitness and power. She was not young, but that did not matter. It was her looks and the way she moved that made her appear so attractive. Twenty seconds later, she opened the door of the bookshop and walked in.

"I'll see you in a few minutes, Freddie," said Alistair. "I'll meet you in the hotel's lounge bar. I'll have a gin and tonic, if you're buying, that is. A double would fit the bill."

Good luck, thought Freddie, she looks an arrogant bitch, if ever there was one. He caught his breath and walked off with his characteristic limp, while Alistair crossed the hill to the bookshop and pretended to look into the bookshop window, casually playing for time.

A moment later the shop door opened, and the woman walked out, her head down, counting change and carrying a brown paper bag.

Alistair turned from the window and caught her eye: "Oh. Hello again, Miss." he said in a familiar tone and flashed her his most captivating smile. "Have you bought something exciting?"

He glanced at the bag and feigned an interest. She looked momentarily puzzled, her eyes flickered, but he could see that she recognized him and was trying her best to disguise it. Her eyes were sky-blue and held a certain nervous energy; her expression implied she was preoccupied. Worried, even. But then there was the very briefest of smiles which punctuated her face. She was beguiling to look at.

He briefly considered her features: of Scandinavian heritage, perhaps, with those high cheekbones and beautiful blond hair.

"I saw you earlier," he said quickly, "at the racecourse. My brother and I went out for an early morning walk...he has to keep his legs exercised." He lowered his voice. "Doctor's orders. Climbing accident, daft so-and-so." He stepped nearer to her; her perfume was familiar, from before the war. French or Swiss. He could not remember, but the memory was there.

"Oh, yes," she said hesitantly. Their eyes met.

"That was a beautiful horse!" He raised his eyebrows and grinned broadly, trying desperately to engage her in conversation.

"Yes, yes, it is." Her face was a blank now. There was no mention of the horse's gender, breed, nothing. No interest. Or enthusiasm.

"Toodle pip then. Must dash." He turned quickly away and left her standing there alone, clutching her bag of books, wondering what exactly had just happened.

Alistair walked towards the Red Lion Inn, his mind consumed with the scent of a woman and the shape of her face. Perfection. But it wasn't just her face; the way she moved contained power and rhythm, and he felt a sense of intrigue about her that he could not explain.

*

Alistair walked into the lounge bar of the Red Lion to find Brim and Freddie supping half pints of ale at the bar and noticed an untouched gin and tonic waiting for him.

"Everything alright?" asked Freddie. He could sense Alistair's mood.

"Yes. At least, I think so." He picked up his glass, took a generous mouthful and frowned. There was something about the attractive woman in the bookshop, their encounter, which niggled him and, for a few moments, he couldn't work out what it was. Brim and Freddie said nothing and left him to his thoughts.

What was it? thought Alistair:

'Yes, yes, it is.'

Four arbitrary yet significant words. He could hear the exact sound of her voice in his mind and played the words over and over. It wasn't her accent; she didn't have one; or the way she said it. It was what she said. If she were an employee of the Royal Mews, which she looked as though she might be, wouldn't she have said: Yes, he is.

And maybe have been a bit more effusive. Or was his mind racing? Why was she there so early in the morning? What was she doing there? It was deserted on the racecourse save for the groom and the lone horse.

And who was the man in the Rover with her? The man in the trilby hat?

What was it Powerstock had told Brim on the phone: Mr. and Mrs. Wolf ...been there for donkey's years...an ugly brute and a beautiful wife. His mind raced; he certainly was an ugly sod, the poor bugger, and she was certainly a beautiful woman. Could these possibly be the people they were all searching for? The sleeper spies. Or was he going to make a fool of himself? He decided:

"Brim, can we find out from someone in Windsor Castle who knows about a transfer of horses from Hampton Court Palace to here 'for security'? An equerry or senior member of the Royal Household? Royal Mews?"

Brim puffed out his cheeks, a tad confused, but nodded: "I don't see why not, old sport. I can make a telephone call to the PM's office or Cyril Downing. One of them can find out, I am sure. Why, something up?"

"I think there is, yes."

Brim finished his drink and walked towards the telephone at Reception. Any request from either of the Valentine brothers was always taken seriously, no matter how apparently odd.

"Come on, Freddie, let's go up to my room," said Alistair. "We need to be ready. I think this is it."

*

Joselyn felt cramped and stiff in the back of the shooting brake but dared not move for fear of being heard by Devlin. If he caught her, he would kill her there and then. It was dark outside and totally deserted. They had been on the road for at least an hour and travelling at around 40mph; he was being cautious, not wanting to draw attention to himself. There were blackout shades on the headlights.

The inside of the car smelt of petrol and worn leather, and although she had rested her head on the deflated tyre, she felt vaguely nauseous.

Where were they? She had no point of reference whatsoever. She lay, curled into a ball. All the signposts had been removed to confuse any German paratroopers who might be lurking around lost in the countryside.

She tried to picture the map of England which was pinned up

in her father's office at Grosvenor Square. An old pre-war road map which had been folded and unfolded so many times that it was fragile with age.

Weybridge to Southampton. Which route would Devlin take? The quickest? The quietest?

She squeezed her eyes tightly shut and tried to concentrate, imagining she was actually looking at the map, tracing her finger along the crinkled paper:

Woking – Aldershot – Winchester, maybe? South-west. But how long? How far? Would Devlin stop? He obviously had sufficient fuel and most of the garages were closed anyway because of petrol rationing. And the hour. And he certainly wouldn't be needing the toilet, that was for sure.

What was her plan when they arrived in Southampton? She had no idea, no choice but to respond. Watch him and react accordingly.

What was in the suitcase on the back seat, a few inches away from her? What was Devlin planning to do once he had sent a signal to the Luftwaffe in northern France? Where could he run to? So many questions. But there was one thing Devlin could not have anticipated. Or Walcott...

And that was her.

When she opened her eyes, she realised she had fallen asleep and outside, it was now dawn. She glanced at her watch. Could she sneak a quick peak out through the back window? No, the car was slowing down. They had arrived.

*

Back in Windsor, by the castle, the equestrian cortege had started to arrive: a procession of eight official looking Humber cars, each towing green horseboxes with gold lettering painted on their sides:

ROYAL MEWS WINDSOR CASTLE

Brim had spoken to the PM's office, who had put him in touch with the Royal Mews. Yes, there was a transfer scheduled and yes it was genuine. No question. Then Alistair noticed the last car in the procession was being driven by the groom from earlier and the man with the trilby hat. They must be part of the Royal Household, unless ...

Alistair, Freddie and Brim stood outside the bookshop on Castle Hill and watched the procession with a group of other onlookers.

"Brim. How many cars and horseboxes were expected?" asked Alistair.

"Cyril didn't say," Brim replied.

"We need to find out. Now. Quickly."

Brim darted back to the Red Lion.

Alistair noticed the same three cars were parked on Castle Hill just across from them: the Alvis, the Talbot and the Lagonda. All of them quick and powerful. Perfect for a fast getaway.

Out of the corner of his eye Alistair could see the blond woman walking towards the Alvis with a jerrycan, presumably filled with petrol, face like thunder. Somebody is in a hurry, he thought casually.

Alistair nudged Freddie: "Be ready."

"Yes," he said under his breath, pulling something from inside his jacket pocket.

Alistair scanned in all directions, looking over his shoulder for Brim. The group of watchers was starting to grow.

Among the crowd a man wearing a green wax jacket melted in; his right hand was thrust deep into his pocket. He too was scanning the crowd.

The Castle gate was open, and the eight Humber cars and horseboxes slowly mounted the entrance ramp and drove into the Courtyard. Castle staff guided them in, one by one.

Alistair watched the blond woman arrive at the Alvis, unscrew the petrol cap, and lift the jerrycan. It was a rusty and looked heavy and unstable. Carefully she tilted the nozzle into the aperture of the fuel tank. It was unsteady. Alistair considered offering to help her, decided against it. Suddenly, something happened, and a gush of petrol slopped out over her skirt, stockings and shoes, soaking her in fuel. She threw the jerrycan down in temper; her clothes ruined. Petrol glugged out onto the pavement ... she was flustered and angry ... not knowing what to do:

"Verdammter Mist!" she shouted impulsively. She thought it was contained, but it was loud enough for both brothers to hear and understand. And so did Wax Jacket; he saw her and he heard her as clear as day ...

Her third mistake.

Brim came bounding through the crowd, pushing people out of the way and panting: "Seven! There are seven!"

That was enough. That was a cue. Alistair and Freddie dashed across the street and stood in front of her. She attempted to run.

"Halt," shouted Alistair. She froze on the spot, shocked. One German word.

Freddie produced Alistair's 'Stephan Beck' Abwehr ID card and pushed it in the woman's face. He spoke in rapid German: "I am Beck."

Alistair produced another ID card:

Sturmbannführer Otto Krebbs. SS.

The crowd moved closer. Brim un-holstered his gun. Wax Jacket watched in disbelief. The look on her face was sheer horror. Her beautiful blue eyes shone with fear.

Harald Wolf got out of the eighth Humber, the last of the procession, waiting to enter the Courtyard. He was holding a weapon, just too far away to see what was happening with Alistair, Freddie and his wife. He started to walk towards the unfolding drama. He was wearing his trilby hat.

Freddie continued in German: "Haven't you heard? Hitler is dead. Somebody assassinated him." He sounded very plausible.

The crowd moved closer as one, mystified at hearing German – that alien enemy language – being spoken on the streets of their town.

Wolf approached: "What's going on?"

"We came to recover you – but our Heinkel was shot down by the British – you saw it happen," said 'Stephan Beck' firmly. "Remember now, Harald?" Freddie was still very convincing.

Alistair smiled: "Of course, you must be Gertrud Wolf?"

She didn't respond, still shocked and confused. The crowd were aghast; there was the sound of police whistles. Brim came nearer to the encounter. Nobody noticed Cynthia Fuller get out of the eighth Humber and nobody noticed the handgun which was clenched in her hand. She paced purposely forward.

"It's over," shouted Gertrud. "Can't you see?"

Alistair and Freddie watched the two women.

"No, it isn't." Cynthia flicked the safety catch but was prevented from using the gun by a policeman, who tackled her down to the cobbles with a thud.

Cynthia snarled with anger and frustration as the PC put her in a painful arm lock and looked around at his fellow officers for assistance. Wax Jacket realised there was nothing he could do; to act now would be fatal. He turned.

*

In Southampton, Joselyn had waited as Devlin parked outside the White Lion Hotel in the High Street. She couldn't stay there in the back of the car; she'd have to get out, because when he returned, he would see her. That much was obvious.

Devlin got out of the car and walked towards the entrance of the hotel. He paused and looked back at the car. He'd left the engine running; he shook his head and dashed in.

Now! Joselyn turned the catch of the shooting break door and pushed it open as much as she dared. It was incredibly heavy, and she was so stiff; but at last, it opened.

She climbed out awkwardly and looked around: the odd sailor in uniform, a few early morning workers. The air smelt of the sea. Of course, they must be near the sea. Southampton port. She closed the door with a soft clunk and ran across the street to hide in a shop entrance and waited. She glanced at her watch: 10am exactly.

A few moments later, Devlin emerged from the hotel, leaned in through the open window and switched the engine off; put the keys in his trouser pocket.

He opened the rear door and grabbed a hold of the suitcase. From her concealed spot in the shop doorway. Joselyn thought: My God. Is he checking in?

If so, she had no choice but to wait. She was incredibly hungry, thirsty and needed the loo. Devlin turned and went back into the hotel.

*

In Windsor, Brim fired his gun into the air to warn the crowd who were on the verge of mass panic: "Get back everyone, British Intelligence."

Two policemen arrived on the scene, unarmed, and ran towards the centre of the growing conflict.

Alistair ran and executed a flying rugby tackle which brought Harald down with a smash of teeth and nose on cobblestones. He yelled. His trilby hat flew off and his gun skittered across the cobbles.

"Secure both of those women," shouted Brim, scanning the crowd. Cynthia and Gertrud were both being cuffed by police now. Wax Jacket was moving quickly away; Gertrud saw him and there was a moment of recognition. The wheelhouse. Poole. He froze in his tracks. She was about to speak, her eyes wild, a senior police Officer restrained her:

"In the van, you," he snapped and grabbed Cynthia roughly, "and you."

Wax Jacket ran for his life ...

The first seven legitimate vehicles and horseboxes carried on moving forward before slowly grinding to a halt, their drivers confused about what was going on. The procession was half in and half out of the Castle Courtyard.

The 'Needle's Eye horsebox' remained at the end, separate. The passenger door opened, and Giles Walcott dropped to the ground in his phoney Royal Mews jacket. Alistair, Freddie, and Brim watched the fair-haired man. Their eyes met.

Alistair: "The groom from the racecourse. We were right, Freddie."

One of the policemen said: "We thought you two were bloody Germans!"

Freddie suddenly bent down and grabbed Harald's weapon and fired up high and carefully into the side of Walcott's horsebox. The round pinged into the metal.

"You'll kill the horses," yelled Walcott, trying to get sympathy.

But Freddie remained cool: "But there are no horses, are there. Not in your horsebox."

He limped over, his weapon raised: "Are there?" He shouted: "Move towards me slowly, try anything and I'll kill you."

Giles Walcott did as he was bid. From the look on Freddie's face, Walcott could tell he was serious.

Brim approached Walcott: "I know exactly who you are, Walcott."

"Well, lucky you," Walcott said. He did not disguise his Irish accent this time.

"You're a traitor, Walcott," said Brim, "and we know it."

Hearing the word traitor, the crowd moved in, both fascinated and amazed at the spectacle unfolding in front of them. What was a traitor doing in Windsor?

Alistair and Freddie walked over to Walcott's horsebox and opened the rear door. Inside four sinister looking military grade cylinders – like missiles - were strapped down on wooden chocks. There was a tangle of wires, detonators and high explosives. And four timers, armed.

Walcott stood transfixed: his and Spengler's plan in pieces now because of these people. He was waiting for a chance to pounce.

"So, Walcott," said Alistair calmly, "what do you believe is in these cylinders?"

Two more policemen grabbed Walcott's arms: "How the hell should I know?" He spat the words out.

Suddenly, Walcott broke free of their grip and walked angrily up to Alistair, eyes wild. He produced a small-calibre handgun and fired it at Alistair. The round went wide.

Alistair moved towards him like lightening. The others just

watched – Brim, Freddie, the two policemen. Walcott could see that look on Alistair's face. The mark of a killer.

He delivered a colossal roundhouse kick – Mawashi-geri - to Walcott's left kidney. It knocked the wind out of him; he dropped the gun. Alistair then snapped his tightly balled fist straight into Walcott's Adam's apple. His lethal calling card ...

The action was so fast and powerful it crushed both cartilage and windpipe. Walcott's dying body dropped to the cobblestones, gurgling blood and frothy saliva. It was over. Walcott died the same way as Otto Krebbs had done in Berlin ...

Fifteen seconds of agony.

The crowd were speechless as they watched Walcott die; the spectacle was brutal and efficient.

"My God," said Brim, shocked. He had never seen his protégé in combat before. He recalled Captain William Fairburn's summary report from Sgian Dhu:

'Valentine (Alistair.) 100%:
outstanding, but dangerous.'

Freddie sensed Brim's alarm: "Now you know why we never fought, even as children, Brim. But I've never seen anything like that before."

Brim pursed his lips, the way he did: "Nor I."

Alistair walked coolly over to Cynthia and Gertrud who were sitting in the back of the police van in handcuffs. He spoke calmly:

"I happen to know exactly what's in these cylinders. Do you?"

The two women were speechless, staring out of the van, shocked at Walcott's sudden, violent death. Alistair continued as if nothing had happened:

"A harmless anaesthetic gas or some such nonsense. Is that Walcott told you? Is that what you seriously believed when you drove them up from Poole Harbour?" Alistair's tone was chilling. "And yes, British security services knew all about you sleeper spies, Gertrud. Have done for some time."

Cynthia and Gertrud were clearly frightened; Gertrud enthralled by him, nonetheless.

"A little present from your friend Himmler? Alistair pointed at Walcott's dead body: "What did Himmler promise Walcott – eh? What lies? A free Ireland? Sanctuary in South America? Away from Europe?"

Gertrud lowered her head, remembering just that promise.

"I'll tell you what's in these cylinders. Pressurised Tabun Gas with a highly explosive warhead. We'd have all have been killed – including you - everyone within a ten-mile radius ... I doubt Walcott knew the truth. Himmler certainly did. He intended for you all to die. How does that feel?"

Alistair walked away from the police van towards Walcott's horsebox. Freddie, Brim and three Royal Guardsmen joined him.

"Come on, Freddie. Help me work out how to disarm these timers without killing us all."

"Was this part of your training at Sgian Dhu, Alistair?" Freddie asked.

But it was Brim who replied: "Yes, it was, Freddie. Rather fortunate I would say."

None of them noticed Cynthia check her watch. A twist of a smile.

*

Joselyn had waited across the road from the White Lion Hotel for an hour. Devlin must have been sleeping. When he emerged, he looked fresh and relaxed. He turned right out of the door and made towards the Port of Southampton. He was walking fast, empty handed and continually looking over his shoulder. The shooting brake was still parked outside.

Joselyn kept fifty feet behind him as she knew she had to: lurking in shop doorways, using trees, telephone boxes, anything she could find for cover. Finally, they arrived at Marine Road, a dismal row of detached two-storey Victorian houses, and Devlin approached number 19 and let himself in with a key. A quick glance over his shoulder.

Joselyn looked at her watch: it was 11.45am. She had barely half an hour before the 12.15 pm deadline in Windsor. Behind Marine Road she quickly discovered a back alley, a narrow weed-ridden unmade path with old prams, discarded bicycles and scrap furniture.

She walked quietly along the path, clutching her shoulder bag, counting the houses. Number 19 was as shabby as the rest of them. She let herself in through a low garden gate and waited.

12.05 pm: It was quiet. She looked up at an upstairs window. A net curtain. Was there a silhouette behind? She would have to be careful. She scaled the garden wall of the neighbouring house and found herself near the roof of number 19. If Devlin was at the back, she would have to attempt an assault from the front. She crept along adjoining wall from back to front and looked down onto the street. A few doors along was a window cleaner's van, the odd car, a few children. Nobody saw her. She climbed down a drainpipe and dropped to the ground at the front of the house.

12.08 pm: She tried the front door. Locked. The windows were all closed and looked secured. There was nothing she could do now...except to ring the doorbell.

*

Outside Walcott's fake horsebox, Major Powerstock was busy working the Army COMMS telephone contacting the bomb disposal unit (BDU) at Andover. He was also in touch with Royal Signals at Blandford Camp, his base. Two armed Majors from the Victoria Barracks, Windsor were at attention keeping watch. The rear doors of the police van were open, and everyone could see the two women handcuffed to a rail: Gertrud and Cynthia.

Brim had gone into the Royal Mews office to contact the PM on the King's private telephone. A secure line direct to Churchill at Number Ten.

Alistair and Freddie were inside the horsebox examining the four Nazi cylinders.

"Any luck in there?" called Powerstock. "BDU are on their way. Be here soon as."

Alistair replied: "The timer is set for 12.15. But it looks as though it has to be activated manually. There is no time delay facility. Not that I can see, anyway."

Freddie added: "Harald's job presumably. He'd never have

known then. It would have exploded immediately."

Alistair continued: "I'm not an expert. But I would say this warhead is charged with high explosive, to be detonated by the manual timer. The cylinder's activation nozzle is released when the warhead explodes. Instant discharge. God, it would have been catastrophic."

The two brothers stepped down from the horsebox; Alistair first, he then helped Freddie with the awkward manoeuvre. Brim had just returned from the King's telephone: "Number Ten and MI5 are fully in the picture. The PM will put His Majesty and the Queen fully in the picture. Ironically, they are out at the moment. At the Palace." He glanced at Alistair, then at the horsebox as if for explanation.

"These are not conventional bombs, Brim. Far from it. The timing mechanisms are sophisticated, but simple. The blast would have propelled toxic chemical nerve gas into the air at an alarming rate. Lethal to anyone who came into contact with it. Hard to say over what area."

Brim: "Major Powerstock, be sure the BDU are aware of all these facts. These cylinders will have to be destroyed somewhere safe. Anything else, Alistair?"

"Admiral Canaris told me Erich Spengler is behind this plan. He probably manufactured these weapons and IG Farben the Tabun."

"I see," said Brim. "Spengler and Farben were at the original Nazi fund raising meeting in Bavaria in 1933. It all makes sense. They are working in cahoots with Himmler. And that also means with Hitler."

Alistair said: "DAS SCHLOSS, the meeting at the Berghof that day. So, Admiral Canaris didn't let us down, did he? My God, Canaris saved the day."

Brim put his arms around both brothers: "No, gentlemen. It was you two who saved the day. The Admiral helped...let's just pray someone else is alright."

Alistair and Freddie did not compute the last few words because the police officers who had cuffed Gertrud and Cynthia came over:

"The two women are still stowed in the meat wagon, sir; what shall we do with them?"

"Take them to the secure Army facility at Twickenham, armed escort right to the door. And check there's no tail, you never know. We'll get statements later." Brim said with exasperation.

Alistair, Freddie, and Brim strolled slowly back towards the police van. Gertrud looked directly at Alistair. Her blue eyes sparkled with a malevolence that was chilling and this time they were unreadable.

"Come on, let's get back to the Red Lion," said Brim. "We need a drink. Oh! Major Powerstock."

"Yes, Professor Brimblecombe."

"Handle those cylinders like eggs, if you can remember what they look like."

Southampton

19 Marine Road, Southampton, England

JOSELYN STOOD DEFIANTLY with her shoulder bag strap looped over her shoulder and her hands concealed behind her back. She waited for thirty seconds or so – at the ready – and then the front door suddenly burst open violently. Devlin stood there with a rifle, its breech broken and draped over his left inner elbow as if he were attending a country shoot. And yet he didn't seem that surprised to see her. Had he noticed her in the garden climbing the wall and knew it was too risky to shoot her in broad daylight? He smiled at her with a dirty sneer:

"You haven't come here to play tennis now, have you?"

Joselyn ignored the comment and tried to ignore his leering expression:

"Do you have a licence for that firearm, Mr. Devlin?" She sounded serious, official in tone and manner. And it was the way she pronounced licence like something out of the Wild West.

Now a flicker of concern passed over his face – what was this? He looked quickly out onto the street for any form of support that she might have brought with her. It was empty.

The smile vanished.

She took her hands from behind her back and with a swift two-handed grip produced a Browning Hi-Power pistol and aimed it directly at Devlin's lower abdomen. Her knees were slightly bent, legs parted in combat stance. Trained. Devlin could see that the safety was off and assumed correctly that the high-capacity 13-round magazine was loaded. Police issue? Military? Security Services? Whoever she was she looked dangerous and he could also see from the expression on her face that she was serious. Like all the others at Needle's Eye, he'd been totally duped.

"Just who are you?" His southern Irish lilt accentuated the words into a poignant question. "You're Walcott's little tart and he's one of us."

For a split second she hesitated, then recomposed: one of us? Of course, he's an Irish Republican terrorist.

"Inside. Drop the weapon or I'll kill you."

He clumsily tried to swipe her with the broken rifle, but the space was confined and awkward, the weapon a hindrance. She darted backwards in readiness and now her pistol was pointing at his face:

"Drop it or die," she snapped loudly.

"Fuck you."

But he did as he was bid, because he had no choice and threw it down noisily as if to make a point. Or was it to distract her? Whichever it was made no difference. She wasn't going to be tricked. And now he knew it.

"Where's the transmitter?"

"Upstairs."

"You go up. I'll follow."

He was seething with fury now, sensing defeat; so close, so very close. But he had no choice. Devlin mounted the steep narrow staircase slowly and Joselyn stayed four steps behind him, in case he threw himself back on her. But he knew instinctively that the pistol would now be pointed directly at his spine and she wouldn't hesitate to pull the trigger. She obviously wasn't the type.

Joselyn knew too that this next part was the most difficult piece of the manoeuvre: a dark narrow space and a sharp turn to the upstairs hallway. Did he have an accomplice? Surely not; they'd have shown themselves by now; acted. She watched his back, his arms, his hands, his footfall, just as she had been trained: Watch every movement, every detail, one hesitation and you shoot to kill. No exception.

"Where is it?"

"Spare room, back," he replied sharply.

"Go in and stop. Face forward. Don't turn."

In front of them, on a chest of drawers in a bay window sat a radio transmitter, a set of headphones and a Morse code pad. She quickly looked around the room for booby traps. Nothing obvious, no trip wires. She waited and listened, taking in every detail: an unmade single bed, stool, table lamp. It smelt foul: damp, stale tobacco, the sheets redolent of yesterday's sex.

She glanced at her watch, raised her pistol to his head: "Rip out the cables, throw them down."

"If I don't – "

12.11pm: "You die instantly. Simple."

"You wouldn't dare, Yankee fucking whore."

12.12pm: Devlin made that one false move, whatever it was. A twitch. A final distraction. A movement. She wasn't sure exactly, but she reacted...

Joselyn squeezed the trigger and the single round passed through Devlin's skull and exited through his face into the window frame. He dropped to his knees in a praying position and fell sideways in slow motion. No sound, no scream; just a final thud.

12.14pm: Joselyn quickly ripped all the cables and wires out of the transmitter and smashed the exposed radio valves with the handgrip of her pistol. She destroyed the Morse pad.

Then she dropped down onto her haunches, the threat destroyed. She couldn't look at the remains of Devlin's head; but there was a clump of blood, brain and bone fragments slipping slowly down the window like fresh afterbirth.

Her second kill. And her last. She knew that now.

She felt sick and tired. She knew she had to exit the kill zone quickly and get on her way as fast as possible. She desperately fumbled and fished the car keys out of Devlin's damp trouser pocket. He had obviously wet his pants at some stage during their conflict. But there was no ID or wallet. She dashed to the filthy bathroom to swill her hands and the keys and dried them on a net curtain. Her breathing was falling fast now. But she knew she had to stay calm, focused. She put her pistol back into her shoulder bag and walked, light-headed and nauseous, down the narrow dark stairs and out onto the street and sucked in the sea air. Her heart was pounding; but she had survived. Another brush with death, but she was alright.

In her mind she planned her escape route; the keys were in her pocket and safe. Joselyn knew what do and she would do it; she turned and headed for Devlin's hotel without another thought.

Except her survival.

Spengler

Wilhelmshaven, Germany.

RICHARD LAMBERT, erstwhile captain of the Clarissa, was exhausted. Weary from war, weary from a naval mission he had spent more than a year training for. And weary from travel, a convoluted trek from Windsor to Wilhelmshaven.

He had been instructed to return to Germany and to report back to Spengler. He had no choice. But his prime motivation was a stack of Swiss francs. That is what Spengler had promised him. The trouble was that his mission had not been entirely successful.

Spengler, his daughter Rosa and he were now sitting in the port offices of Spengler GmbH in Wilhelmshaven. Spengler's opening words were a shock:

"You're alive, so the Windsor cylinders can't have detonated. And there was nothing on the BBC either."

"Thankfully alive, yes." Lambert sat and regarded father and daughter with apprehension. His vague attempt at levity fell short.

Spengler narrowed his eyes: "What happened in Windsor,

Captain Lambert?"

So, no first names, no niceties, official. And no refreshment. Lambert was starving and thirsty. On the last leg of his journey from England, he had dreamt about Bratwurst, Sauerkraut, foaming beer and German bread. To no avail.

"The unexpected, is all I can imagine, Herr Spengler."

"Meaning?" Spengler asked impatiently.

Lambert was suddenly fearful: "My job was to deliver the cylinders to Poole."

"Yes. Yes. Yes. Which you did."

"Sir, I – "

"I understood your orders were to then leave Poole – after delivery – go to Windsor and observe the sleeper spies and make sure they fulfilled their obligation to me."

"Yes."

"So, my question, once again, is what happened in Windsor?"

Lambert looked at Rosa, as if for some moral support. There was none. He forced himself to recall exactly the chain of events before he turned and ran from the frenetic scene. The truth was he was frightened, but dared not admit it.

Verdammter Mist! Gertrud's third mistake when she had slopped petrol all over herself and given the game away. Two critical words he had heard. Lambert was not inclined to inform on that beautiful German woman.

Whoever she was.

"Two men appeared from nowhere. One shouted 'Halt' and produced an ID card; said his name was 'Beck.' The other said he was 'Otto Krebbs SS.' One of them said: 'The war is over. Hitler is dead.'"

Spengler shot out of his chair; at first angry, then confused: "All this was said in German?"

"Yes."

"On the streets of Windsor?"

"Yes."

"But why? Who the hell were these people?"

"I-I don't know."

"British Intelligence? MI5? MI6?"

"I don't know."

"You don't know. You were there. What else? Think, damn you."

Spengler unholstered a 7.65mm Luger and placed it on the desk, the muzzle facing Lambert. He dared not move.

"One of the men said they had come to recover them, but were shot down, I assume by the British Army. There was Artillery on that stretch of the English coast. We heard their guns."

Spengler sat back in his chair: "How did this happen? How?" The last word was suddenly shouted with such venom Lambert flinched, afraid to speak.

"I-I don't know, sir." The words came out as a whisper.

"Did they kill Walcott? These men?"

Lambert noticed a trace of sorrow pass over Rosa Spengler's face, just determinable. So far, she had said nothing. He could visualise Walcott's body drop to the cobblestones. The man had killed him with two incredible blows. Spengler was watching him like a hawk.

"Something else, Captain?"

"No, sir."

Spengler picked up the Luger: "Harald and Gertrud Wolf, the London sleepers?"

Lambert considered the phrasing of his reply: "Arrested, Herr Spengler."

"By whom?"

"Police, sir."

"British Intelligence?"

"They were wearing police uniforms, sir. They call them 'bobbies.'"

"I couldn't give a damn what people call them, Lambert. D'you understand?"

"Yes, sir."

Spengler sighed, glanced at Rosa: "And the English woman – the one who got the job at the Royal Household – Cynthia something; I don't recall her surname."

"She was also detained, Herr Spengler." He could see Spengler absorbing the information. More accurately, the failure of whatever was intended. Spengler sighed and rubbed his thick neck with the back of his hand.

"How did the enemy know about our operation in Windsor? DAS SCHLOSS was discussed in secret at the Berghof. Himmler told me exactly who was present. So?"

Spengler stood once again. He suddenly changed to English, surprising both daughter and guest:

"Why did the two men speak in German?"

"I can only imagine it was to trick, confuse Harald and Gertrud Wolf, sir."

Lambert's version of the truth was economical. He was concealing much of what he had seen and heard and was now walking himself into a trap. And Spengler knew it. He paced around, looking occasionally at Rosa. She remained silent. He turned to Lambert.

"I have a passion for Conan Doyle; his observations on human nature remain ..." He looked at Lambert's face ...

"When you have eliminated the impossible, whatever remains, however improbable, must be the truth." He paused ... so that Lambert could absorb the words:

"You are not telling me the whole truth, Lambert. I think one of the sleeper spies betrayed themselves and the British agents – that's obviously who they were - called their bluff. Correct?"

"Yes, Herr Spengler."

"You were so anxious to get back here for your money that you betrayed your mission. Your duty to me. To Germany."

Lambert nodded; his mouth was too dry to get the words out. Spengler watched him; it was as if he could read his mind.

"There is one other person missing from this equation," said Spengler slowly, "and whom you have deliberately omitted. One person not accounted for."

Lambert was confused; not privy to the entire jigsaw picture: "I don't know what you mean, Herr Spengler."

"Joselyn, the American whore Walcott married ..." He broke off as he decided.

"I don't know who she is, sir."

Rosa flinched once more at the sound of Walcott's name. Lambert closed his eyes as he heard the sound of the safety catch release.

"But I'll tell you one thing; we'll find her. And we'll kill her. Just like this."

The blast from the Luger should have surprised Lambert, but it didn't. He was too interested in knowing who Joselyn really was.

Spengler turned to Rosa, who was pale with shock: "If there is one thing we have learned today from Lambert – beside his treachery – is that Joselyn Walcott is our sworn enemy. And she will pay."

"Yes, father," said Rosa. The first words she had spoken since Richard Lambert had walked into the office.

What Rosa Spengler dared not even think about, was that Joselyn was the woman Giles had left her for. They were perfectly content in Dublin when she was studying at Trinity. And along came this beautiful American and he was swept off his feet by her. Chased her incessantly with gifts and flowers. But Joselyn had clearly tricked Walcott into believing who she wasn't: some empty-headed female only interested in tennis and country clubs. There was a lot more to her. Rosa should have been angrier than she was. She had a sneaking admiration for a woman who could fool a man like Giles. And she wondered what she was really like.

"Rosa!" barked Spengler, "You are in another world once again. You have to stop this. It incenses me. Go down to the port and check the manifest. A ship is due. Your friend Langerhans on Solveig."

Whitehall

Whitehall, London, England.

AN EARLY WINTER'S EVENING, in late December. Fine flecks of fresh snow landed delicately on the windscreen of the chauffeur-driven Rolls-Royce Silver Wraith. It slid and crept cautiously from Trafalgar Square towards Whitehall. Dirt-stained piles of hardened snow already lined the avenue – on both sides - right down to Westminster. Brim, Freddie, and Alistair were sitting in the back of the limousine watching the last of the Christmas shoppers trudging home from the sparsely stocked shops.

Brim wound up the dividing screen which separated the rear cabin of the car from the driver. It was now sealed.

"You can't be too careful," said Brim.

"Quite." responded Alistair. The irony noted.

"Bit of news from your friend Gertrud at Trent Park, Alistair."

"Oh?"

Brim was referring to the facility in North London where secret listeners for British Intelligence bugged the conversations of captured Germans. The eavesdropped admissions were both tantalising and frightening. The listeners were German émigrés who had had fled Hitler's regime before the war. Every word was recorded in the 'M' room and notable conversations passed to British Intelligence.

Brim's tone became serious: "Gertrud and Harald Wolf were transferred from the secure Army facility at Twickenham to TP. Keep the buggers under one roof, as the PM wisely put it."

"And?" Alistair asked, intrigued.

Brim pursed his lips: "It seems that some time ago, Walcott revealed to Gertrud that he'd had a serious love affair with the daughter of a wealthy German industrialist. Back in the Thirties."

Freddie sounded amazed: "But how? How can that be? Berlin is a long way from Dublin."

"Exactly. Her name was Rosa. And it happened while she was studying at Trinity."

"Rosa. Do we know her surname, Brim?"

"Spengler."

Alistair repeated the name with incredulity: "That's the name Admiral Canaris warned me about that day in Berlin – Erich Spengler."

"I know," said Brim. "I read your report."

"Is it important now though?" Freddie speculated.

Brim: "Manfred and Nexus believe Spengler was in cahoots with Himmler: the DAS SCHLOSS plot you both uncovered. Possibly supplying weapons; maybe even the Tabun cylinders."

"What can we do now, Brim?" asked Alistair, his tone edged with concern.

"Nothing. But it means one of my agents might be in danger. Somebody I value very highly."

"Which one?" Brim kept the cream of his department compartmentalised for security, and his prudence had proved correct on more than one occasion.

He shook his head once, briefly: "Don't worry now. You'll soon meet her."

The Rolls skidded slightly before turning right into Downing Street. The chauffeur then executed a skilful turning manoeuvre so the car was facing toward Whitehall.

"Hmm, better not keep the PM waiting," said Brim.

"I wonder why Mr. Churchill wants to see us," said Freddie.

"I can't imagine," Brim replied, poker-faced.

"Christmas bonus, perhaps," chirped Alistair. "I could do with some new skis and we're going back to Monte Rosa soon, aren't we, Freddie?"

The Valentines Cup

10 Downing Street, Whitehall, London, England

IT WAS DARK IN THE LITTLE cul-de-sac. A small unlit Christmas tree stood on one side of the front door and a tall policeman on the other. The front door opened, and a dark-suited man walked out and opened the back door of the car for its passengers to get out. He opened a large umbrella and held it over their heads.

"Good evening, Professor," he said courteously.

"And to you, Mr. Collins. Back on duty here now then. Well done in Weybridge. Excellent job."

"Sir."

They walked into a dimly lit hallway. A man was sitting on a leather chesterfield, his features obscured by a black fedora, thick scarf and a naval greatcoat which had its collar turned up. Dustings of snow covered his hat and shoulders, as if he had just walked in. A lady, her back turned to them, was tinkering with decorations on a Christmas tree which stood in a bucket in the corner.

They were escorted by a butler to the door of the PM's study, where he knocked once and admitted the three of them after a loud bark of: 'Come!' from the great man.

Churchill was sitting behind his desk under the glow of a table lamp. He was dressed in a blue polka-dot bow tie, white cotton shirt and a dark lounge suit. In his right hand was an unlit cigar and at his side a crystal tumbler half filled with an amber fluid. The red velvet curtains behind him were tightly drawn against the cold afternoon and the blackout. A log fire crackled in the hearth, casting dancing shadows around the room. The three of them stood there and waited patiently.

"We have distinguished visitors," said Churchill without any pre-amble or introduction, "or maybe you hadn't noticed?" He articulated the words slowly, with a hint of impatience. A rap on the door broke the stillness as the rich baritone voice of the butler made a startling announcement:

"Prime Minister. The King and Queen."

The couple from the front hallway walked in gracefully and the PM stood up.

"Good evening, your Majesties," said Churchill respectfully. "Professor Brimblecombe, of course, you know. But may I present Colonel Alistair Valentine and Group Captain Alfred Valentine."

Brim inclined his head in deference and the two brothers bowed courteously, suitably shocked and amazed. The King was indeed a handsome and well-groomed man. With level blue-grey eyes, swept back fair hair and a high unlined forehead, he smiled broadly. The King held out his hand and greeted them like old friends:

"Now which one of you two had a spot of bother with a Tiger Moth, as Winston was telling us at our weekly lunch yesterday?" He spoke in a clipped tone, with a somewhat nervous sounding hesitancy in its delivery. But his manner was extremely warm and there was a distinct air of camaraderie.

"That was me, Your Majesty," confessed Freddie, with a faint trace of a grin.

"Good show," said the King, "that you survived intact, I mean, more or less at least."

The Queen had remained quiet during this exchange and looked at the flames. She had a petite, dainty figure, a narrow, finely shaped face, dark hair and violet-blue eyes. Her brief, wistful smile when she heard the words more or less suggested the sensitivity and sympathetic nature she was well known for. It also suggested a dry sense of humour, which was rarely shown in public.

The King suddenly became serious: "Before we start, you will be aware that your late father Lt Col Stephen Valentine was awarded the Victoria Cross in 1916."

Alistair and Freddie nodded; this was a subject very close to their hearts.

The King continued: "This is only given in the case of 'bravery or some daring or pre-eminent act of valour or self-sacrifice, or extreme devotion to duty in the presence of the enemy'. I am quoting from memory, but that is more or less the official line."

"Yes, sir," said Alistair, "we believe our dear mother did have the original citation, but over the years it must have been mislaid with time and travel. We've never really had the opportunity to obtain a copy. Although we should have done."

The King permitted himself the briefest of smiles: "Well, you have been rather busy. But when I heard the name 'Valentine' – in connection with yourselves – I became curious. It struck a chord with me."

He took out a piece of paper from his pocket and consulted some handwritten notes: "On the 14th November 1916, the British Military Forces in France made a final push, in appalling conditions, to capture the field fortress of a place called Beaumont Hamel. In the face of the German onslaught, Lt Col Valentine created a tactical diversion which saved the lives of hundreds of British and French soldiers. He was the last one to leave the field of battle and..."

The King put the notes back in his pocket..." And he was killed by the enemy as the others ran. That has come from our Military Records Office, here in London. As I said, I was curious to find out, since I knew I would be meeting you both."

The two brothers bowed their heads in pride.

"Your mother may never have known the finer details of your father's very distinguished military accomplishments and I am sure wouldn't have been able to attend the military funeral in Picardy, in the winter of 1916. The war was still raging of course..."

Alistair and Freddie remained silent; humbled, absorbing the King's words.

"Bravery and courage," continued the King, "obviously runs

rich in the Valentine bloodline."

Suddenly there was another brisk knock on the door, a creak of it opening and the sound of cups and saucers rattling around on a tray.

"Some tea, sir," said a formally dressed young housemaid who must have curtsied a hundred times when she saw the King and Queen. Once she had poured the tea, she retired without another word. She clearly had not anticipated serving the Head of State as well as the PM in one room five days before Christmas.

"Shall we sit down by the fire," suggested Churchill, "and pretend for a while it's not below zero outside?"

"Oh, it's not that bad, Winston!" said the Queen. "We walked here from home – through St. James's Park – across Horse Guards Road and in through the back door. Your butler let us in. He's a hoot! The look on his face when we undid our umbrella!"

"Are you quite serious, Ma'am?" asked Freddie, amazed at what he had just heard.

"Of course. We often walk around incognito as it were. People don't expect to see one in Hyde Park exercising the dogs or even in Piccadilly, do they? And you certainly didn't notice us earlier, now did you? Because, you see, you didn't expect to! And that is the trick, you see?"

"True," admitted Freddie with a grin. Was this real?

Once comfortably seated, it was the Queen who more or less 'took up the reins' as the meeting was to progress. Her tone was now sombre and her words suddenly very heartfelt:

"We were bombed in 1940 at BP. All the windows were blown

out. It was frightful and it will haunt me forever. Our daughters, Princess Elizabeth and Princess Margaret, were very frightened and deeply upset. The noise. We all were. It was simply awful. And although, by the good grace of God, our family was spared, a decision was made to spend most of our time at Windsor Castle. It was deemed safer."

"And thanks to you three, it remained safe," added the King. There was a silence in the room as the significance of his words were absorbed. Alistair swallowed deeply and despite his normal bravado and courage was humbled by such praise and in such hallowed circumstances that all he could manage was:

"Thank you, sir."

"We owe you both immense gratitude." said the King, "You saved the lives of thousands of our men, women and children, so I am told. The fallout would have affected a large part of west London and the Home Counties. The whole thing is quite unthinkable." The King paused and seemed to take a considered breath before continuing:

"Now, we cannot honour you officially, because you work for British Intelligence. And we certainly don't want your identities made public, for National Security reasons. Winston, would you mind, please?"

Churchill picked up his telephone and muttered something into the mouthpiece. He didn't wait for a reply. Moments later there was another knock on the door and the butler and a senior housekeeper walked in carrying a large cardboard box.

"Lift it out, please," asked the King.

The butler needed two hands – and his assistant – to lift out a magnificent gold cup from the box. It must have stood more than two feet in height and glistened in the flickering firelight. The King stood up and walked over to it: "Thank you," he said, and the staff withdrew.

"The first Ascot Meeting was held in 1711, inaugurated by Queen Anne, more than 200 years ago." He paused:

"My dear father, King George V, was presented with this by his mother, Princess Alexandra of Denmark, on February 14th, 1920. It is known as the 'Valentines Cup'. Quite appropriate given your surname and the proximity of Windsor to Royal Ascot where you both showed such courage and resolve."

The two brothers were spellbound.

"It is now a gift from this nation and our family to yours as a token of our enormous appreciation for what you did then and all the time before that. Notice the inscription, if you please."

The King held out his hand and bid them to join him.

Alistair and Freddie stood up and walked over to the King, both struggling to conceal their emotion; a sentiment which did not go unnoticed by the Queen who watched quietly.

THE VALENTINES CUP
FEBRUARY 14th, 1920.
ALISTAIR AND ALFRED VALENTINE
DECEMBER 20th, 1943
HRH KING GEORGE VI

It had been re-inscribed in the same style, as a tribute to them. The two men were so deeply moved that both Churchill and Brim looked at one another in mutual admiration for the two brothers and the enormity of what they had done. Or prevented.

"If only our dear parents were alive to share this moment," said Freddie, in barely a whisper, "and after what you have told us about our father. Thank you, sir."

"They would be rightfully proud," said the King. "But such is the fragility of life. And you both risked yours to save others, just as your father did. We will never forget what you have done for this country." There wasn't one hesitancy or stumble in the King's words; they came straight from his heart.

The Queen patted the couch beside her with a delightful, almost coquettish smile, and said: "Come and sit down, Bertie, your tea is getting cold."

The two brothers looked at the cup and re-read the words and a special moment passed between them. They hugged each other briefly and the King and Queen smiled warmly. Brim and Churchill looked on smiling, as the two men finally put away all of their differences.

"Sorry," said Alistair.

"Don't be silly," said the Queen. "Whatever differences you may have had – and I sense there may have been – no longer matter. And we know a lot about brothers in our family, believe me."

That was it.

The Queen had the last word.

Chalet

Chalet Monte Rosa, Zermatt, Switzerland.

CHRISTMAS EVE and Manfred Lochar opened the front door of the chalet to find a girl with a sensuous, wide mouth, deep-blue eyes, and jet-black hair. She wore a beautifully tailored, long dark coat which was speckled with fresh snowflakes.

"You must be Manfred," she said with a husky, slightly breathless New England accent. "I'm Joselyn Foster. Professor Brimblecombe sent me."

"Ah yes. Please come in. Welcome to Chalet Monte Rosa, Joselyn," he said cheerfully in perfect English. No hint of the hard-nosed spy at Christmas.

"Thank you. Good to be here. Zermatt is quite stunning. Brim told me to take a horse-drawn sleigh from the station. It was pure magic. But very cold."

Manfred showed her into the rustic old chalet and took her single suitcase. Two women were sitting at the dining room table.

"My wife Ingrid and my daughter, Astrid."

Joselyn noticed they were a mirror image of one another.

Astrid, sporting a beautiful engagement ring and a slight maternal bump, came over and greeted her:

"Brim told us about you, Joselyn. Welcome."

"Not too much, I hope. I'm still an Official Secret." Joselyn accentuated her New England accent, to make the point. They both laughed as Manfred took her coat.

Outside the snow was gently falling, but inside the wood burner kept the living area warm and cosy. The chalet smelt of pine, wood polish and old leather, with a hint of ancient cigar smoke. Joselyn absorbed every detail with relish and delight.

Manfred pinched his nose and raised his bushy eyebrows: "Monte Rosa belonged to a dear friend of Alistair and Freddie Valentine, known only as Herr Seiler. He recently passed away."

"I'm sorry," Joselyn said. But she could see his influence was everywhere: on the walls hung old wooden skis and bindings, sepia photographs of long-forgotten ski teams and survivors of the Cresta Run at St. Moritz. There were also hundreds of bottles of wine and cognac, filling shelves from floor to ceiling. "He must have been quite a character."

"Yes, he most certainly was," said Manfred. An understatement, clearly.

"Where are Alistair and Freddie? Brim said they would be here."

"They will be."

"Skiing, of course. Gornergrat-Riffelberg today; challenging," said Astrid. "I couldn't do it, not at the moment." She patted her belly as if to confirm Joselyn's earlier observation. "It's no secret," she said rather mysteriously, "not this time."

"There will be no secrets between any of us when the day is done," said Ingrid in perfect English to reassure their American guest. "We just want you to be happy here. And safe."

There was a flurry of activity outside as two very weather-beaten skiers arrived. While Alistair stacked the skis and poles, Freddie entered the chalet, covered in snow.

"Sorry we're a bit late. Fluhalp down to Blauherd was icy, under ski. And the snow, well! I hope we haven't missed lunch; we're both famished."

"No schnapps at the Matterhorn Bar then?" Astrid said cheekily.

"Heaven forbid," Freddie replied.

Astrid stood from the table, walked over and kissed his cheek: "You're freezing. Take off those wet things and I'll warm you up."

Freddie kissed her back and whispered: "Is that a promise?" Nobody except Ingrid noticed he discreetly caressed her belly, a split second of affection.

Alistair entered the chalet, looking equally damp: "Hello, everyone!" he said with the joyful smile so typical of him. He was a picture of health and vitality. "Eva from the bar said to say Happy New Year!"

Manfred stood and came over to the brothers as they removed their outer clothes:

"Gentlemen, may I present Joselyn Foster."

Joselyn came over to Freddie and Alistair and shook their hands; both brothers were unashamedly impressed. She looked wonderfully chic.

"A colleague of Brim's." Manfred explained.

Freddie turned to his brother, his tone jocular: "Brim doesn't have colleagues, Alistair. She must be a spy."

"Yes, that's it, a deep-cover secret agent!" Alistair agreed. "Whoever you are, welcome to Zermatt."

"It feels like home already." Joselyn gave Alistair a look he would never forget.

Ingrid said: "Look around, Joselyn. Make yourself at home. And Manfred, we need wine. Today is special. I can sense it."

*

Later, after a fine lunch of roast goose and Alpine macaroni Joselyn raised her glass to Ingrid: "My first Swiss Christmas lunch. Thank you, Ingrid."

"You are welcome, Joselyn."

"By the way, I noticed the Valentines Cup, in Herr Seiler's study inscribed, what was it now: December 20th 1943 HRH King George V1. That was only four days ago. I'm intrigued. Was it actually presented to you by the King of England? Why?"

"Yes; it's a long story. Best told by Alistair," said Freddie.

Cognac

Chalet Monte Rosa, Zermatt, Switzerland.

JOSELYN RETURNED TO HER BEDROOM to unpack. She ducked under angular wooden beams and struts to find a chest of drawers, huge wardrobe, and a double bed.

She looked out of the window as dusk fell. Because of the chalet's elevated position, she had a glorious view of the town and the peak of the Matterhorn, bathed in setting sunlight. On top of her clothes in the suitcase was the letter from Brim, delivered to the Baker Street safe house where she had been temporarily billeted. He had given her specific instructions; air and rail tickets and Swiss Francs. He had signed it off: Better security. Happy Christmas.

She heard a soft tap at her door. She opened it to find Alistair standing there – his fair hair swept back and his smile mischievous. He was holding two balloon-shaped cognac glasses and a dusty old bottle.

"What's this, Alistair?" she said softly.

He read the label: "1918. Hermitage. Grand Champagne

Cognac, 25 years old, to mark the end of the Great War."

"You'd better come in. Although I – I'm not quite straight in here yet," she said unconvincingly, pointing at her unopened suitcase.

"It's Christmas." His blue eyes were fixed on hers as she opened the door wider for him to come in. "It doesn't matter."

He wandered into her room and poured Joselyn a discreet measure. At the balcony window, he drew back the curtain: "What do you think of our mountains? That one is famous!"

"Breath-taking, is what I think, Alistair. All of it. I am overwhelmed by your hospitality. Your family are marvellous."

They made themselves comfortable by the wood burner. Suddenly, outside a choir of schoolchildren began singing a Christmas carol in German; gentle Alpine horns accompanied their voices: 'Alle Jahre Wieder.'

Alistair said, "It's always sung at Christmas and Samichlaus Day on the 6th December, when Santa arrives."

Joselyn sipped her drink: "This is spectacular."

Alistair sighed; he wanted to say: and so are you.

She placed her glass on the table and looked him in the eye:

"Will you tell me the story of The Valentines Cup? Freddie said you might, didn't he?" Her soft New England accent was compelling, and Alistair was enthralled by her. He felt life was seeping back into his body for the first time in years.

"Yes. But the problem is where to start."

"At the beginning." Her blue eyes sparkled. "Is usually best."

Alistair composed himself: "Very well ... if you are sure?"

"I am."

"Ten men's shoes crunched across thin ice and snow. It was morning ..."

Der Jagdhund

January 1944. Spengler GmBh, offices, Cuxhaven, Northern Germany

ERICH SPENGLER WAS SITTING in his office overlooking the port. It was New Year's Day, and the boat yard was deserted. In front of him was his right-hand man, Swiss-based lawyer, Peter Braun.

Braun was an impressive-looking character; tall, broad-shouldered, impeccably dressed. In his late fifties, he had sandy-coloured hair, greying only at the temples. He had been listening intently to what Der Jagdhund had had to say for an hour. Every word had been tinged with a touch of menace and blame.

"By the way, Captain Richard Lambert reported back to me," said Spengler. "It was a few months back. I neglected to mention it."

"Oh?"

"Who the hell do we have to blame for the debacle with DAS SCHLOSS?"

"I ..." He stumbled.

"You know exactly who I am talking about, Peter."

"Joselyn."

"Joselyn, yes. And I will tell you what I told Lambert."

Braun waited.

"... We are going to find her and kill her."

"How?"

Spengler paused. "A deadly trap. I do not care how long it takes or how much it costs. I want that woman dead. She destroyed everything."

"Yes." Braun could see Spengler was absolutely serious.

"I trust you still have your contact at the American Embassy in London."

"Yes, Erich. But wartime is ...."

"I know, I know," Spengler said irritably, "but he is still there? Not uprooted and gone back to America?"

"No."

Spengler remained silent for a few moments: "Good. And don't mention a word of this to Rosa. God knows, she might be next."

Spengler stood and twisted his body around painfully towards the window. Braun did not know if he was joking or not. He never did.

THE END

Also by Robert Wallace

The Valentines Series

Valentines Cup

Crimson Wing

Monkeypuzzle

Operation Gunfleet

Standalone novels

One Single Ticket

A gripping Victorian thriller about Brunel.

Clara's Secret

A collection of urban ghost and mystery stories with factual origins.

Screenplays

JAX

Andrew is clearly not the man she thought she knew. The man she married.

Notes from the Author

The Admiral

Admiral Wilhelm Canaris was executed for 'high treason' at Flossenburg Concentration Camp on the 9th April 1945. Ironically and with a tragically cruel twist of timing, the camp was liberated less than ten days later.

But he left one last message:

> *"I die for my Fatherland. I have a clean conscience. I only did my duty for my country when I tried to oppose the criminal folly of Hitler leading Germany to destruction. Look after my wife and daughters."*

After the war, two Spanish diplomats would escort Canaris' widow and his daughters to Switzerland and from there to a new life in Spain as the guests of General Franco. They swore never to talk about the Admiral or the Abwehr during their lifetime.

Among five volumes of Canaris' diaries were listed in detail all of his contacts with the British and his consistent attempts since 1938 to come to an understanding with London.

*

> *"It is the duty of every sophisticated Intelligence service to keep open a channel of communication with the enemy's Intelligence service."*

Quote from an interview between Reinhard Gehlen, Sir Stewart Menzies and Anthony Cave Brown, from the book '*Hitler's spy chief – The Wilhelm Canaris Mystery*' by Richard Bassett, quoted in *The Secret Servant,* p6, London 1988.

Permissions

'The order of the day.' by Eric Vuillard.

Thank you to Pan Macmillan (26.09.19) PLS Clear 15635. For permission to use and quote text in the above book for '20th February 1933, Bavaria, Germany.' This was an extraordinary source of information for a true-life event.

'The M Room – Secret Listeners who bugged the Nazis.' by Helen Fry.

Trent Park referred to by Brim, in Chapter 55 did exist. Secret listeners for British Intelligence during World War Two were very real. From the M Room, they bugged the conversations of over 10,000 POWs, including 59 German Generals. It is perhaps a combination of the ingenuity of Military Intelligence and the naivety of the enemy that such events took place.

ISBN 9781481020084

'Ian Fleming's Commandos'. The story of 30 Assault Unit in WW2 by Nicholas Rankin.

Thank you for allowing me to reference the Special Training Centre Inverailort. The sequences described in 'The Commandos get cracking' was a great source of information and inspiration.

ISBN 9780571250639

Thanks to Nicholas Rankin and Ciara Calvin at Faber

'Richard Hillary – The Definitive Biography of a Battle of

Britain Fighter Pilot and Author of The Last Enemy.' by David Ross.

This superb biography gave me an understanding of the injuries suffered by the brave pilots of the RAF and their recovery. Also, of course, the incredible pioneering work carried out by Sir Archibald McIndoe and his team at the Queen Victoria Hospital, East Grinstead.

ISBN 9781902304458

Thank you to David Ross and Natalie Parker at Grub Street Publishing, London.

'The last days of Hitler.' by Hugh Trevor Roper.

First published in 1947, this account tells the extraordinary story of the last days of the Reich in the Berlin Bunker. It describes who was there, who committed suicide and who escaped. It also describes Himmler in chilling detail.

ISBN 9781447218616

Thank you to Palgrave Macmillan for their permission to reproduce a section of text.

'The Storm of War.' by Andrew Roberts.

Thank you to Andrew Roberts for allowing me to quote from his excellent book. It is an invaluable source of research and was used as background in the missile reference in 'BERGHOF'.

ISBN: 978-0-713-99970-9

Bibliography

'Inside the Third Reich.'

Memoirs by Albert Speer. Published by The Macmillan Company 1970

'Battle of Wits – the complete story of codebreaking in World War Two.'

Stephen Budiansky. Penguin Group 2000.

ISBN 0-670-88492-8

'Enigma – the battle for the code.'

Hugh Sebag-Montefiore. Weidenfeld & Nicholson 2000.

ISBN 0 297 84251 X

'Ian Fleming and SOE's Operation Postmaster.'

Brian Lett. Pen & Sword Military 2012.

ISBN 978 178159 000 3

'The Nazis – the rise and fall of history's most evil empire.'

Paul Roland. Arcturus 2019

ISBN 978-1-78828-483-7

'Valkyrie – the plot to kill Hitler.'

Philipp Von Boeselager. Weidenfeld & Nicolson 2009.

ISBN 978-0-297-85546-7

'Hitler's spy chief – The Wilhelm Canaris Mystery.'

Richard Bassett. Cassell Military Paperbacks. 2005.

ISBN 978-0-3043-6718-4

'Hitler's last days – an eyewitness account.'

Gerhard Boldt. Rowohlt Verlag GmBh 1947

ISBN 0 7221 1735 3

'The secret war of Charles Fraser-Smith – the real Q of WW2.'

Charles Fraser Smith. Michael Joseph Ltd. 1981.

ISBN 978 0 9528408 0 0

'The Debs of Bletchley Park.'

Michael Smith. Aurum Press Ltd. 2015

ISBN 978 1 78131 388 6

'What if? Military historians imagine what might have been.'

Edited by Robert Cowley. Pan Books. 2001.

ISBN 0 330 48724 8

'The heroines of SOE – Britain's secret women in France F Section.'

Squadron Leader Beryl E. Escott. The History Press 2010.

ISBN 978 0 7524 8729 8

'The Secret life of Bletchley Park – the men and women who worked there.'

Sinclair McKay. Aurum Press Ltd. 2010.

ISBN 978 84513 633 8

'Between Silk and Cyanide – a codemaker's war 1941-1945.'

Leo Marks. Harper Collins 2000.

ISBN 0 00 710039 6

'Inside Hitler's Bunker – the last days of the Third Reich.'

Joachim Fest. Pan Books 2005.

ISBN 978-1-4472-1860-9

'Secret Weapons – Death Rays, Doodlebugs and Churchill's Golden Goose.'

Brian J. Ford. Osprey Publishing. 2011.

ISBN 978 1 78096 721 9

'McIndoe's Army – the story of the Guinea Pig Club and its indomitable members.'

Edward Bishop. Grub Street London 2001.

ISBN 1 902304 93 4

'He was my chief – the memoirs of Adolf Hitler's secretary.'

Christa Schroeder (Introduction by Roger Moorhouse.) Langden

Müller 1985.
ISBN 978 1 84832 631 6

'I was Hitler's chauffeur – the memoirs of Erich Kempka.'
Erich Kempka (Introduction by Roger Moorhouse.) Kyrburg, Munich. 1951.
ISBN 978 84832 630 9

'The wisdom of Winston Churchill – words of war and peace.'
Edited by Sean Lamb. Arcturus Publishing Ltd. 2019.
ISBN 978-1-78888-785-4

'The last enemy.'
Richard Hillary. Macmillan and co. 1942.
ISBN 0-7126-7344-X

'Bletchley Park and D-Day.'
David Kenyon. Yale University Press. 2019.
ISBN 978-0-300-24357-4

All these books were marvellous sources of reference. Perhaps the most extraordinary of them was THE ORDER OF THE DAY (Éric Vuillard) mentioned in Permissions. The pivotal meeting on 20th February 1933 in which 24 gentlemen attended a conference to raise money for the Third Reich.

"And there they stand, affectless, like twenty-four calculating machines at the gates of Hell."

Thank You

To my wife Pam for putting up with me during the lengthy process of writing, re-writing and editing this manuscript, and to Marianne, always my first reader.

Thanks also to:

- David Kenyon, Research Historian, Bletchley Park Trust.
- Robert Glasby, Curator, de Havilland Museum, London.
- Peter Murton – Imperial War Museum, Duxford.
- Forbes Wilson – Royal Naval Reserve.
- Richard Bassett – author of 'Hitler's Spy Chief / The Wilhelm Canaris Mystery.'
- The RNLI – Poole, Dorset.
- The Fleet Air Arm Archive.
- Helen Fry – author and historian.

Special thanks to Stuart Amesbury – researcher and great pal.

I am indebted to John Penfold for his enormous amount of hard work: proof-reading and editing. Thank you to Steve Pryer for all of his ideas and initial story contribution.

Len Greenwood for his hours of reading, technical assistance and creating such excellent artwork.

Melvyn and Marianne Plum, Tony Prosser, Andy and Camilla Jefferson, Pascale Penfold, Andy Shaw, Rodney Little (Charlotte, USA.), Steve Turner (Jarnac, France.), Robin Brown (Los Angeles, USA.), Peter Morgan (Sydney, Australia.) Mary

Johnson, John Robertson and Richard Gray (Christchurch, New Zealand.) Anne Scott (Bath.)

David Edwards-May, Inland Waterways, Grenoble, France.

Jean-Michel Zorn, Association pour le Développement et la Promotion du Tourisme Fluvial.

Also, Simone Seiler in Zermatt, – for the name 'Monte Rosa' and, of course, 'Herr Seiler.'

The Frinton Library Reader group for the feedback on the very first draft of VC.

I would also like to thank Sally Brimblecombe for not only being a 'constructive reader', but also for allowing me to use her late husband's name. Nick was a great friend too, but he was never known as 'Brim'; that was purely invented for this novel.

I would also like to commemorate the life and work of my late uncle Harry Wallace. He was a pioneer and inventor of many medical devices and a great friend. On family skiing holidays to Switzerland, we often discussed that Zermatt would be a perfect backdrop for a spy thriller, and I hope I have not let him down in this endeavour.

And finally, to my wonderful sons James and Nibby, who have made me enormously proud. A man could not wish for a finer family. I am blessed with such good fortune.

Robert Wallace, December 2021

Praise for the Author

About *'One Single Ticket'* by Robert Wallace:

"A detective story told at a breathless pace, with a Richard Hannay type hero straight out of a John Buchan thriller, and it goes with a swing"

Professor Angus Buchanan, author of 'Brunel: The Life and Times of Isambard Kingdom Brunel

"The plot is so interesting, and the setting so well done; a delight to get a scenic picture of this special event in history."

Dr. Gabrielle Obrist, Museum of Modern Art, Zürich

Printed in Great Britain
by Amazon

76187622R00214